From Army Bra

An ongoing Voyage on Land and Sea

Copyright © 2020 Paul Whittall

The moral right of Paul Whittall to be identified
as the author of this work has been asserted in
accordance with the Copyright, Designs and
Patents Act of 1988.
All rights reserved.

This is a work based on fact. Names, characters, places,
events and incidents are deliberate.
Any resemblance to actual persons, living or dead,
is purely intentional.

Foreword

Fate….. 'the inevitable agency that predetermines the course of events'. (Collins Reverso Dictionary)

My destiny was to spend my life at sea but there were those who conspired to prevent this from happening. This is the story of a small boy taken far away from that destiny in an attempt to deny it. Despite the best efforts of a British Army Officer, a Mother who believed herself to be the Queen, the disciplined culture of boarding school and an early career in Academe, it was a Fish that came to the rescue and led the way back to the sea.

From Army Brat to Seadog

Introduction……………The Brat

A child does not choose or set out to be an Army Brat. This honorary title is bestowed on all offspring of serving personnel but is especially applicable to those who have lived in a number of different countries as a result of frequent military 'postings'. The word 'Brat' does not necessarily possess the same meaning ascribed to it in civilian life to where it conveys some selfish little creature who deserves to be thrown into the sea or tossed over a cliff in classic Spartan style.

To be introduced by one's military parent as 'The Brat' is to receive a disguised term of endearment tinged with a hint of admiration. The Brat has after all experienced more countries, cultures and languages in his short childhood than many people experience in a complete lifetime. Emerging from baby's initial gurglings, the Brat's first words are 'Sir' or 'M'am' rather than 'Mama' or 'Dada'. This is a useful trait that tends to remain with The Brat throughout life and one which can be strangely unsettling for the person so addressed, especially if younger.

Many Brats end up in boarding schools. Regular postings from place to country and country to culture may give the Service Child a wealth of experience but be lacking in a continuous, settled education which would develop the objective ability to make sense of all this disconnected experience. Thus, after the early years of regularly changing schools and learning to deal with the trauma associated with the temporary position of being the 'new pupil', the Brat often finds himself back in his long forgotten home country in a school deeply suspicious of the intruder and who is further alienated from his new classmates thanks to a deeply ingrained suntan and strange accent.

Kidnapped by a Slinger

My father came from Portland in Dorset, sometimes known as the Isle of Slingers, and infiltrated one of Weymouth's long standing fishing families, kidnapped my mum, married her and the two contrived to produce me. Very shortly after this we left England's fair shores and moved to Lagos and into a country, so Mother told me, full of tenacious room-wrecking monkeys, highly dangerous and unpredictable falling coconuts and intolerable heat being just 200 miles north of the Equator.

Father was in the British Army but my memories of our three year posting to Nigeria, a British Protectorate with six years left after our arrival before its Independence in 1960, are virtually non-existent. I do recall that an extremely large black man had, according to Mother, appointed himself as my bodyguard announcing that he was going to look after me and see I came to no harm. I look at ancient photographs of us together and it would have been a brave man indeed to have confronted him. His name was George and we were, apparently, inseparable with me spending much of the time held up high in his arms to keep me clear of dogs, snakes and scorpions. I vaguely remember having a peddle jeep with an American Star on it and the letters 'M.P.' emblazoned across the bonnet. Early photographs show me and my car wedged down the many potholes that made up the Lagosian dirt track roads and George , roaring with laughter, hauling me back out.

The one vivid memory I have of that time was of my shiny yellow swim suit. And catching my first fish...by hand... at Atican Beach near to the Capital where we lived. I also remember Linda. She was much older than me at nearly 4 years old and liked to swim top-less. Her admiration of my angling skills and my dashing swimwear made me realise that there was something alluring special in this fishing lark.

I have no recollection of the 'intense heat' Mother remembered, nor was I bitten by any of the rabid dogs terrorising everyone in enormous hunting packs, or stung by swarms of malaria carrying mosquitoes, ferocious scorpions or deadly snakes that Mother's over-exaggerating imagination made her so fearful of leaving the safety of her spacious fan cooled flat.

We returned to the UK and the Military base in Donnington, Shropshire, after three largely unremembered years in West Africa. As well as the Spartan military furnishings, our new Married Quarters house contained a simple drum kit and a full size double bass. My Father liked to play jazz and rockabilly mainly that he picked up from American musicians in Lagos...and he enjoyed running. He ran for the Army. He was so good at it that he managed to successfully run away from my Mum when I was four and never came back. Much later in life, I heard he died in his late 40's in a 400 metre Hurdles Race...apparently in mid leap.

A Seafaring Childhood

We returned to Weymouth and what I always look back at as a wonderful fun filled childhood. We, Mother and me, moved in with Grandma and Grandad and my Uncle Vic in a three-storey terrace house with what seemed back then to be very large rooms and which was a short walk from down Boot Hill to the harbour. Many lovers of the sea would have heard of and fished with Vic Pitman aboard his boats *Atlantis* and then the *Valerie Ann*, named after his wife. He was, like so many fishermen around Weymouth Harbour in the 1950's and into the late 1970's, a larger than life character, full of fun, always laughing and extremely knowledgeable about the sea. He also had a wonderful way with words. He would describe the sea and the wind to me in ways that made it all come alive. I knew way back then that my life had to be spent at sea,

Grandad rowed the Weymouth Ferry, the one that visitors to Weymouth would have used to cross over the outer harbour from the Melcome Regis beach side to the Nothe Peninsula on the Weymouth side. My first job, aged five, was with Grandad. We would be up early and wander along the harbour side, past the town-bridge and then the Lifeboat Station towards the Council erected little hut that was for the Weymouth Ferrymen to shelter in. In the summer, Grandad's clinker built wooden rowing boat, called Daisy, was moored there overnight and I was allowed to help bail it out and clean it ready for the day's work. There were often a few coppers in the bilges and I was always allowed to keep a couple of half-pennies. As we neared either side of the harbour, I was allowed to grab the chain and put a rope quickly through it and pass it to Grandad to hold us steady and allow the passengers to disembark.

On the Melcome Regis town side the ornate metal stairs, known as the Ferry Steps, had decorative holes which allowed the rain and seawater to fall through. They also allowed a clear vision of customers ascending or descending and granted an early awareness of ladies underwear for a boggled-eyed child looking up through them. Grandad, being a gentleman, always averted his eyes and warned me never to tell Grandma about the sights I described to him. Of course I did and after a couple of stern warnings, I learnt all about having one's 'mouth washed out with soap'.

These simple beginnings on Grandad's ferryboat taught me a great deal about the feel of the tide and wind, the need for speed of reaction at the right time, how to keep the boat clean and tidy and how to bail out without soaking your feet! I listened to all the banter and the magical stories that Grandad used to tell the customers as he rowed us across the harbour and I knew, right from those early days, that I was spending time with someone very special and who had an aura about him that commanded respect despite his diminutive size.

When Mother remarried about 5 years later, she was furious that the local paper, The Dorset Echo, carried just two lines about her wedding and then devoted two full pages to Grandad. The story was mainly about his time as Weymouth Football Club's all-time top goal scorer in their 130 year history and who still holds the record for the most appearances for the club throughout the 1919-1931 period. Weymouth Football Club's ground was right in front of our house,, which was set up high, in Chickerell Road on the site that the local Asda Supermarket now occupies. We had a Grandstand View from the attic bedroom window which looked down onto the full length of the pitch. Grandad used to take me to home games and I could never work out why everyone, and I do mean everyone, knew him. It was hard to comprehend that this most modest, quiet and gentle man had scored 253 goals in 476 appearances. Although surely not known back then in his lifetime, Grandad's nickname 'Lutor' was strangely in keeping with my early years in Lagos being a Nigerian word - very appropriate for his control of a football - meaning to 'Be a Ruler'.

My childhood at Chickerell Road, Weymouth, was distinctly memorable. The house always smelt of fish. There would be live plaice in the kitchen sink, crabs wandering around on the kitchen floor, new nets strung up the landing being made , or bred, by my Uncle Victor and Grandad. The part of the net they were currently working on would be in the sitting room and curled out into the hall-way and up the stairs. Grandma and I filled the net needles and made sure the netting was nicely laid out. In the winter, when the open fire was burning, the sitting room air would be full of hand rolled or full strength Capstan cigarette smoke. I was allowed a packet of sweet cigarettes and I was taught to make sure I threw the 'red end' into the fire so as not to burn my lips when I progressed to the real ones.

Everything stopped dead for two main events in the household. The football results with Grandad listening intently to the radio and checking off his football pools and, of course, the Shipping Forecast. All four of us were huddled round the radio at 1900 hours to listen. The forecast told us if we were going to work the next day. It was God's word coming out of that old valve radio set and instilled my love of the magical language used in the broadcasts.

'Wight, Portland, Plymouth. Winds South West or West increasing 4 to 6. Smooth or slight at first, occasionally moderate later. Fair. Good'.

It was a secret code for us seafarers and I was privileged to be in the company of two of the best of them.

During this time, my uncle Victor was running an open boat called *Silver Foam*. He had started to take out holiday-makers mackerel fishing. I was allowed to go along as crew. I was 6 years old by now and I loved being at sea with him. We used thick cord mackerel hand lines with 2lb leads on to keep the 20 foot heavy mono trace and mackerel lask bait at the correct depth when being towed along by the boat at 2 knots.

I went on many trips and was often allowed to steer *Silver Foam* using the tiller at the stern which allowed my Uncle to freedom to assist the customers with their endless tangles. Like Grandad, Vic was a superb story teller with a natural sense of humour and that wonderful ability with words that held the listeners spellbound in their nautical grip.

I also discovered that I had the sensitivity in my fingers as a youngster that allowed me to detect if the hook had picked up some weed on it. Bear in mind that we were chugging along at walking speed and dragging a hefty lead before the very long trace back to the hook. But I really could tell if there was weed on the hook and I would ask a customer to pull his mackerel line in to clear it and, if he didn't, Uncle Vic would give him a good bollocking explaining that, "If the boy says there's weed on your hook, then there's weed! And you will catch nothing until you take it off."

The customers would go home with their mackerel strung up by me and as they wandered off through town they were the best advertisement for mackerel fishing that we could wish for. Some days we caught a lot of mackerel; too many for the customers to take away. I was given the job of selling them right there on the harbour side out of the fish box. If I sold a whole box, Uncle Vic used to give me six pennies. Some days I would sell four boxes and earn 2 shillings which is now the equivalent of 10 pence and what was a lot of money back then especially for a little boy just six years of age.

When we returned to Grandma's after a day at sea, I would proudly show my Mother what I earned on a Saturday or Sunday. Uncle Vic had installed in me right from those early days the importance of 'thirds' with money. A third will be given to your Mother! A third will be saved in a tin, under the bed, for a rainy day. And a third can be spent. A third of six old pennies...two pennies...could buy a packet of sweets and entrance to the Saturday morning picture show at the cinema in town. I was indeed wealthy!!

It was during these times of sharing out the money that I realised I actually had a Mother. She detested the fishing life. She hated the smell. She hated all the smoke and nets in the house. She was forever screaming when she discovered live fish in the kitchen. She hated the fact that the only toilet was outside in a closet in the back year. She hated how we spoke and my increasingly Dorsetian accent. Mother's name was Elizabeth and she really did think she was the Queen. This was a truly terrible time for her as much as it was a colourful and wonderful time for me.

I knew this wasn't going to last for much longer!

A Sunday Walk into Conflict.

It was very hard for my Mother during the two years we lived with her parents and brother, my Grandparents and Uncle Vic, in their fish-smelling house in Weymouth. It must have been a massive and unbearable contrast to her married life in the Army, enjoying spacious Colonial marbled accommodation in Lagos with servants and parties. Now here she was, returned to a life she thought she'd been forever whisked away from and surrounded by gasping fish, cigarette smoke and enduring the delicate aromas of a cold, damp outside toilet.

Mother was doing her best to make me civilised whilst Uncle Vic was teaching me how to stand with my back to the fire and fart loudly. I often think back and wonder why she acted in the way she did, with her exaggeratedly 'posh' mannerisms and accent, knowing it would result in yet more raucous laughter at her expense and even more exaggerated immodesty on the part of her brother.

I believe it was the 'Sunday Walk' that finally brought matters to a head. Mother would dress me in my Sunday suit. I seriously detested dressing up and that short trousered suit in particular. I wanted to be with Grandad on the ferry boat *Daisy* or out mackerel fishing on *Silver Foam* and earning some money by getting tips for helping the holiday makers and for selling the spare mackerel. I had learnt that people on holiday can be very generous to a little boy who spoke with a 'genuine' local accent and could string up fish to be carried proudly through town.

And, to complete my utter disgrace, Mother made me wear yellow, woollen gloves! We left home on Sundays as if we were off to a Church Parade but the further we distanced ourselves from the comforting sanctuary of Grandma's house, the more nervous I became that one of my young school chums would see me and my reputation as a wild seafarer would be instantly destroyed.

The momentous Sunday in question saw our lengthy walk taking us along the inner harbour-side and away from the sea making me feel even more uneasy. We were heading towards Radipole Lake and then towards Weymouth Promenade and getting into territory where I would be recognised. The next phase of our journey required crossing the railway bridge at Radipole Halt, the last stop before Weymouth for the steam trains bringing holiday makers to the seaside or taking them along the harbour towards the Channel Island ferries and the recently launched State-of-the-Art, *Caesarea* and her sister ship, *Sarnia,* for an exotic voyage southwards to the mysterious Islands of Guernsey and Jersey.

Steam trains are dirty creatures bellowing masses of black smut laden smoke into the air. If one is unfortunate enough to be crossing a metallic bridge just as one of these beasts were to pass through and be even more unlucky to lean one's head so as to be directly over the train's funnel, the results could be quite dramatic.

Mother was in despair as her smart little boy disappeared into thick smoke only to reappear as some blackened, dishevelled urchin and whose gloves were no longer a dainty colour of yellow but filthy black. I apologised profusely for my innocent mistake and thought by the time we'd got back to Grandma's that I'd convinced her that her little darling had endured a terrible accident and deserved great sympathy and not the tantrums he was currently observing from his Mama.

Uncle Victor opened the door to us and burst into laughing and laughed and laughed and laughed driving his immaculately attired younger sister into speechless fury and then a heart rending torrent of tears. Grandad, always quietly observant, had to depart to the outside loo to recover and Grandma's face was also soaked from tears but of uncontrollable merriment. It was a turning point and I realised I had made a big mistake. Not only would there be no more Sunday walks but I feared we would move away from the fun filled home of my Grandparents because I had pushed Mother too far.

We left soon after this event but it wasn't so bad. Mother rented the first in a row of Coastguard Cottages at the end of the Weymouth Beach Road. These cottages were right by the sea and now the first few have actually collapsed, tumbled down the clay cliffs and been swept away. My bedroom looked right along the beach and back to Weymouth. It was a wonderful view. I could see the ships in the Bay and the boats leaving harbour. I had all of Furzy Cliffs and miles of coastline off to the east to explore with Bowleaze Cove leading on to Osmington Mills and then Ringstead with White Nothe, Bats Head and the famous Durdle Door with its alluring 'Man 'O War Rocks' all within sight.

We were poor. Mother worked in a shoe shop in town. We walked the beach wall together; with me stopping first at St John's Junior School which back then was opposite the now shortened Pier Bandstand and Mother continuing on into Weymouth High Street to work in the shoe department of Marks and Spenser's. If the weather was grim, with the sea crashing over the beach road, we could catch a bus but this was to be avoided if at all possible.

Our timings were different in the evenings as I finished school first and would walk home before Mother arrived. I was maybe 8 years old by now and thought nothing of this fairly lengthy walk and getting home first to make a fire and get things ready for Mother's return. And, if I knew she was working late, I could run down to the harbour and see what was going on without her knowing. Luckily, I could still go to sea at weekends and continue selling the mackerel.

It was at this time Uncle Victor had obtained a new vessel. Instead of the open boat, *Silver Foam*, *Atlantis* had arrived. Not only did *Atlantis* have a forward cabin but also a cuddy within which to steer and, being dry exhaust with an air cooled engine, she had a funnel which was warm to lean against on chilly days and the nights when we started trawling in Weymouth Bay.

About this time a large and very well dressed man had started to appear. His dashingly smart military looks and his size...he towered over everyone in our family...had Grandmother swooning all over the place. There was instant animosity between him and two of my uncles who became very protective towards me. There was clearly something mysterious going on between him and Mother and her brothers did not like it. He and I were very wary of each other and I feared the worst. Fortunately he wasn't around too much to start with, so I was able to continue my downward spiral away from further attempts to civilise me and to be at sea as much as possible.

Once again my behaviour drove Mother to despair and brought about her regular desire to chase me round my bedroom wielding a wooden coat hanger with which she wished to thrash me. And, on one occasion, she succeeded.

What had happened was that I had persuaded her I should return to Grandma's house whilst this large man was visiting. She agreed that maybe it was a good idea and my uncles were in full support. I stayed with my fishing family for the school's September to December Autumn Term. When reports came out at Christmas, my attendance record showed that out of 90 possible attendances (we had two attendance marks per day) I had managed to be absent 89 times having attended just once throughout this lengthy term. This was because I had been 'very poorly' and the hand-written letter sent to my school explained this.

Mother threw one of her most eloquent and exquisite tantrums. The presence of the large man gave her support and I was threatened with every imaginable horror a child could possible think up. Mother told me I was 'ruining her chances of happiness' with the mysterious man and that totally confused me.

Where had I been? Trawling of course and working on the boats every day and many nights. When this had all been revealed, I recall my teacher at Saint John's Junior School making me stand at the front of the class and telling my classmates what a stupid boy I was to be throwing away my chance of an education and for everyone to do their best not to be like me. I could see the other boys wishing they could be like me and that glint in the eyes of the more adventurous girls who were starting to get interested in my piratical life.

We had a Student Teacher that term. She was from Scotland. She was a strong and rebellious lady. She asked me to write about my life at sea and trawling and so I did. As a result of my essay...which was monstrously long for an 8 year old....she rewarded me with a Chinese Take-Away which none of us had ever heard of let alone tried. I was asked to read my essay out and to bring along anything that might make it interesting.

So I did. I brought faded charts of Weymouth Bay and Portland and talked about the Shambles and the Adamant Banks, The Cow and Calf, Durdle Door, land-sightings so that we could avoid hitting submerged obstructions that we had previously snagged the trawl net up on, compass bearings, night navigation by stars and depths being recorded on the old graph sounder. I spoke of all the various fish we brought up in the nets, the plaice, dabs, various rays, whiting and angler fish and how to handle them and where they went.

I described the various war-time munitions that were being regularly trawled up at that time; the shell casings, the bullets, fragments of bombs, pieces of aircraft and parts of bombed ships. Sometimes we would have to buoy off the trawl some distance outside of Weymouth Harbour and leave it there for the Navy to investigate as there was every chance it might be an unexploded bomb which needed to be towed further out to sea and detonated for safety.

Uncle Vic had allowed me to take along a complete roll of the carbon sounder paper which had the profile of Weymouth Bay taken from a multitude of trawl headings and was long enough to go round two classroom walls. We looked at the fish markings, the bottom soundings, the bearing marks and reciprocal calculations.....and I could see my classmates were totally non-plussed about this strange maritime world I lived in.

At the end of what was a long presentation, my rebellious red-haired Scottish teacher stood up and explained to the class that I 'had indeed wasted a whole term and learnt nothing'. Her smile hinted at the world of double-meaning words could convey and the door into irony cracked open.

I walked back along the beach road towards the Coastguard Cottages and home. I was busting with happiness and pride. I open the door to be confronted by Mother who looked at me with utter contempt and hissed: "We are leaving this Country. This week".

I looked at the mysterious man and he looked back at me and we both knew this was going to be a posting full of conflict.

Tripoli...Navigating by Stars

*A brief history: Tripoli is the Capitol of Libya. It is right on the Northern shores of Africa and pretty well directly south of Malta. Italy controlled Libya from 1911 until 1943 when the city fell to the British Eight Army. The British governed up to independence in 1951 when t*he United Libyan Kingdom was formed under King Idris until Col Muammar Gaddafi seized power in 1969.

My overall memories of Tripoli are as vague as my recollections of childhood in Weymouth were vivid. It amazes me that I cannot even remember the flight from Heathrow to Idris Airport, Tripoli, or the first few days in a different country. It's as though I refused to acknowledge what was happening and must have gone into a mental lock down. I did not want to leave Weymouth and my family and the local Dorset men I was privileged to experience that idyllic time with.

And now here we were in Tripoli, North Africa, in the early 1960's, aged 9, and it appeared that I had a new 'Father' who I rarely saw.

We lived in an area called Garden City, appropriately named because of the pink and purple vines that grew up the walls of the white, square buildings, in a secure flowerless compound consisting of four large three-storey blocks of flats. Garden City bordered the Italian City with its Mediterranean style architecture stretching right back in history to Roman Times. The daily busy ride to school skirted the edge of this area with its wide roads, well planned streets of shops which bustled in the early morning with smartly dressed Italians sitting out on the pavement cafés for breakfast. We could easily have believed our school bus was travelling through a stylish city on the Italian coast itself if it were not for the many date palm trees and long white robes of the Arab men and absence of their women.

The Italian sector, with its Colonialist lifestyle, bordered in turn on the Old City, Medina, ,with its busy narrow lanes and squat sandy coloured buildings which led into the ship filled port of Tripoli with its mixture of oil tankers and colourful fishing vessels and famous fish market. Amongst the many hints of its Byzantine/Roman/Islamic past, the Old City contains the splendid Marcus Arch built to commemorate Marcus Aurelis' visit in the 2nd Century AD along with its many Mosques and several churches reflecting the various architectural influences of the time of their building. The wide promenade had a sandy beach and strikingly blue Mediterranean sea on the one side and a spacious road lined with palm trees and which was full of mainly stylish Volkswagen Beetles.

Tripolitania consists of the three ancient towns, hence its name, of Oua, conquered by the Arabs in the 7th Century but granted total autonomy and which remained inhabited throughout its own history and the coastal trading ports of Leptis Magna and Sabbratha with their fabulous World Heritage ruins. It would have been a wonderful place to explore but I was an Army Brat and was thus mainly 'Confined to Quarters' and unable to experience the wonders of this city and country except by fleeting glimpses through the sun shielding curtains of our school bus.

If not attending school my life in Tripoli, with a few notable exceptions, was limited to our compound on the edge of Garden City. There were no other British children of my age living there at that time and The Uniform was away at work so it was very much a case of entertaining myself for the most part.

The flats themselves that we lived in were enormous with marble everywhere creating a roomy and cool environment. We were fortunate to be on the ground floor so that our kitchen opened onto a very small garden in which nothing grew. Mother had a daily house maid, an Arab girl called Sadie. Sadie enjoyed living with us. As soon as she entered the flat, Sadie would pull off her all engulfing, black Shufti-Shawl and reveal herself to be a fun loving young lady who delighted in giving Mother exotic dancing lessons and who taught me what little Arabic I know. Sadie saved Mother from what would have been endless hours of loneliness in a country that promised so much but to which we had no access on our own.

We were walled in. We could have been in any one of a multitude of countries such was our isolation and it was difficult to imagine that behind our tiny garden, which was little more than a sandpit, and the 10 feet high mud wall, there was a bustling Arab compound on the other side full of shops and families living their lives which we were never able to see let alone take part in. On the opposite side of our flats ran a large and high stone wall with wire along the top which led towards our compound entrance. The security gates were hefty and towering with armed Military Police and Alsatian guard dogs in evidence. The weak point in our mini-fortress was at our end of the compound where a much lower wall gave potential access to a dirt road and the Arab Street vendors. This wall could be easily scaled but was not a good idea for any outsider to try and enter our fortified compound especially with the armed MP's presence and their very large dogs.

No-one ever thought that anyone living in our compound would be stupid enough to try and climb out…until I did!

This place was totally different to Weymouth with its sea and cliffs and friendly community. Here, the view was limited to the walls. The flats were situated on what was desert and so everywhere was arid sand. There were a couple of palm trees within our compound but that was it. In the time we were there, I spoke to hardly anyone except Mother and Sadie. I always wondered why I was the only child there but it was explained that other families preferred to send their children to boarding school in the UK as Tripoli 'wasn't safe'. Even Sadie agreed with this and shook her head vigorously when I expressed a desire to leave the compound for a short exploratory walk.

As we were home from our short school day by early afternoon, I spent a lot of my time just kicking a football against one of the compound walls. I was startled one day by a very high pitched screaming and crying. On the second floor of one of the blocks of flats a girl of maybe 12 years old was out on her balcony. She looked tall and skinny to my inexperienced eyes and was completely naked. She was running around her veranda, banging on the closed glass door into her flat and then gripping the balcony rails and trying to shake them as if she were about to hurl herself over. I stood there transfixed as this was somewhat of an unexpected sight, especially as I thought I was the only child living there, and then heard an adult male voice roaring at the girl from inside the flat. The door was opened and she was grabbed and dragged, squealing, back inside.

This was a very unsettling experience and even more confusing when I tried to approach the subject with Mother who refused to answer and disappeared into the bathroom in floods of tears which she usually reserved for when The Uniform was at home. I tried to ask Sadie who kept shaking her head and telling me 'Tripoli…very dangerous place'. I dare not ask step-father so it was and has remained one of those unanswered mysteries but one I have never forgotten. What it did do was to reinforce my own complete lack of presence in this strangely insular existence I was experiencing.

My escape was the roof. It was flat and large and easily accessible through a stairway and a door leading on to it. From here there was a commanding view of the surroundings. I could see the Arab families in the compound beneath, socialising and with children playing together. Sometimes I caught someone's attention and tried a friendly wave. No-one waved back. From another part of the roof, I could see the dirt road and the simple shops. This was not a busy area. There was very little traffic apart from an occasional horse and cart.

The way to that area was over the back wall…the one that I planned to escape by.

My Uncle and Granddad had always taken great pains to explain things to me. They delighted in telling stories about the sea and boats. Just before we left for Tripoli, my Uncle Victor had started taking motor boat trips to Portland Harbour to see the many Royal Naval ships anchored there. With more local boats taking advantage of this money making opportunity, there were even more wonderful characters to meet and much more to learn such as the recognition of those various Naval ships and the History of Portland Harbour. I was able to marvel at men like the RNLI Coxswain at the time, Fred Palmer, Alf Pavey who took over as Lifeboat Coxswain in 1962 to 1979. and became one of the few recipients of the 'Men of the Year' awards for his bravery at sea and featured on one of Eamon Andrews' 'This is Your Life' programmes. There was Bert Legg who was the courageous Lifeboat Bowman who jumped from the Weymouth Lifeboat onto the plunging foredeck of the yacht Lafita in 'Hurricane Force winds and 65 foot seas and several other well-known local boat skippers with massive characters such as Bert Randal and lifeboat radio operator, Lionel Hellier. I was 'the boy' amongst them and those generous men included me as one of them regaling me with tales of the sea in peace as well as in war-time. And as ever there was overriding presence my Uncle Vic who became the Weymouth Coxswain 1979 to 1986 and who had skippered the Lifeboat in that dramatic silver medal rescue in 1976 of the Lafita.

These were the men that I had been extraordinarily fortunate to spend my childhood with. They had been generous enough to include me, a small boy, in their company but right now, exiled in a fortified compound in Tripoli, none of that existed. There was no-one to listen to and admire. Yes, I was regularly shouted at and threatened with the 'heavy hand' but no explanations ever offered as to where we were on the planet or why on earth we were there.

As night fell, the roof of our block of flats was my favourite place. During our night-time trawling, Uncle Vic explained and pointed out the basic star systems. I knew where the North star was from a very early age. I had been taught how to line up the Great 'W' of Cassiopeia and the correct stars in Orion to double check the Pole Star position. Those nights installed a great and continued fascination with the night sky. I particularly enjoyed 'star gazing' years later when I was alone at night moored up in non-light polluted harbour of Braye, Alderney, aboard one of the Offshore Rebel boats.

Looking up at the stars, I knew the direction to the nearby Mediterranean sea and thus all the way to Weymouth, some 2000 miles to the North-northwest. If I turned a little to the North, the various star patterns emerged that I had followed when being allowed to steer Atlantis slowly across Weymouth Bay and brought back those memories. I was still at sea when on top of that roof.

The Army recommended that people stayed indoors for the first week of a posting to a hot country and then over the rest of the month gradually expose themselves to the heat and sunlight. So, apart from the roof, I was in isolation which suited me fine. I was happy to escape into my memories of Weymouth and blank out this strange place I was now in.

The Uniform did occasionally take Mother and I out to visit nearby places and I apparently attended School...but I recall nothing of those school days apart from discovering that my real Father had passed on his ability to run to me. It seemed I was quite fast and I'd inherited some of Granddad's footballing skills. I recall playing in the school team against an Arab school team. This was supposedly going to be a great moment when two communities met in friendship through the sport of football as played by the young. No such luck....I learnt then in that game just how much the Arabs detested the British...and by the end of the match just how much the feeling was reciprocated.

The Military Camp of Kassala was 10 miles off to the east of Garden City, Tripoli, where we lived. This is where my new Step-Father was based as an officer in the RAOC (Royal Army Ordinance Corp). This was a pretty exciting place with plenty going on and lots of vehicles to explore. My particular favourites were the British armoured personnel carrier, the Saracen 'tank' and the Saladin six wheeled fast moving 'armoured cars' which were known for their excellent performances in desert conditions. The army men that I met were friendly and they understood that I was in a similar position to them in having to contend with a very aggressive and difficult new officer. Thanks to them, visiting the Kassala Army Barracks became fun and enabled me to experience riding in these various vehicles at speed through the desert.

Mino was one of the many Italians working at the Kassala military base. He was a large, flamboyant Italian man in his mid-thirties. He loved fishing. He had a small boat in the nearby harbour. He took me under his generous Italian wing and I met his wife and family. Fishing with Mino was a real lifeline for me. He introduced me to several Arab commercial fishermen but I was banned from going to sea with them for my own safety. But, thanks to Mino, I learnt a little bit about fishing in the Mediterranean and how to catch bream. Even way back then in 1962 the fish were small!

Mino also took me snorkelling in the crystal clear waters near the famous Roman ruins of Leptis Magna and Sabratha originally built in 300 BC and then rebuilt by the Romans in the 2nd and 3rd Centuries AD. That first snorkelling experience was amazing! I could not believe what I was seeing with the vast variety of colourful fish and corals in what was then an absolutely crystal clear sea. I see that look of astonished wonderment now on the faces of people that I am able to introduce to scuba diving when their eyes are popping out in total amazement at their first look into our truly fascinating underwater world.

Trying to communicate with the Arab children in the compound next to our house was not easy. I tunnelled my way bit by bit through the mud wall that separated us and when I could see light inserted a bamboo stick through to the other side with the words written in Arabic, not by me I hasten to add, that I would like to be friends. I waited to see if anyone would reply and send the message back.

Well…someone did. My new little Arab friend, named Sadikki by me as it is Arabic for 'friend', and I set to work to cut a bigger hole out from either side of the wall. We made a hole big enough for a football to go through and we kicked the ball back and forth into each other's compound. Nothing was said about this so we went ahead and enlarged the hole so that I could wriggle through. I went through into the compound and was met with a mixture of friendly smiles from the children ranging up to utter hostility from the older youths who clearly hated the intrusion from a Brit. and a Brit Army Brat child at that! I was not welcomed and many Arab fingers pointed back towards the hole.

Before I departed the Arab compound, Sadikki showed me a dried out well which three little kittens had been thrown down. They were still alive and plaintively meowing in the way cats have perfected to elicit human sympathy and assistance. I indicated that I wanted to climb down the well to rescue them and although the Arab children could not understand why I would wish to do this, the kittens were retrieved by a couple of older boys and given to me. Our brief flicker of friendship soon disappeared when they realised I had no money to pay them for their efforts. I thought they were going to thrown them and me back down the well but Sadikki came to my assistance with some plaintive wailing of his own.

The kittens were covered in fleas and it took me some time of holding their starved bodies underwater in a half-filled bucket of warm water, with just their heads poking clear, to drown and then gently remove the fleas and ticks. Within a week there were three happy kittens dashing around our enormous flat, feeding well and gaining weight. And then, whilst playing with them in our sand-pit of a garden, a stray dog which had somehow got into our compound, jumped over our low garden fence and set about each kitten as well as me when I tried to stop it savaging them.

The kittens all died that night, their fat little bellies full of puncture wounds which the nearby Arab Vet said he could do nothing for. I was very upset but what really shocked me was the way the uniformed step-father reacted. He shouted at me in his best aggressively military manner, telling me to 'shut-up' whining and get rid of the 'damn things' straight away. Mother tried to intervene and was similarly yelled at so that she ran to the bathroom, locked the door and sobbed loudly refusing to open it despite the increasing level of threats from her new husband. Our small dog, Sally, was hiding under the stereogram squealing in terror as the Uniform attempted, unsuccessfully, to reach under to drag her out and beat her.

I learned then, in true Brat fashion, that it did not pay to become attached to anything or anyone during our military life. This was a lesson that was reinforced many more times over the years in Tripoli and then Malta as treasured possessions, pets and friends were left behind without further discussion. If something of real personal value was boxed up, the chances are it would be broken by the time it finally reached its destination. My prized collection of 78's containing the complete rendition of Sparky's Magic Piano had 6 inch nails driven right through them instead of the wooden crate framework they were meant for and my valuable first edition Marvel Comics, purchased at the massive American Wheelus Airbase, arrived in Malta as papier-mache.

The anger I saw displayed that day regarding the kittens and our pet dog became a regular part of our lives and signalled the complete breakdown of any chance The Uniform and I had of having any kind of amicable relationship.

Sadikki's and my brief friendship was also sadly doomed to failure as the M.P.'s explained that this couldn't happen and that not only was I in danger by going into the Arab area but I had created a weak point in our walled compound which could be penetrated by the 'hostile forces'. I hadn't got a clue as to what all this meant. I was still naïve enough in my Weymouth way to believe in friendship between people but the hole was refilled…with concrete this time, not mud.

That belief in the possibilities of establishing friendships with our Arab neighbours finally came to an end when I foolishly climbed the back wall and dropped onto the dirt road running behind our compound. I went across to one of the little shops and was met with instant aggression. Before I knew it, I had been kicked and punched to the ground with a load of very angry young local men threatening to kill me. A knife was produced. A very firm kick to the head made the stars arrive and I experienced that total rush of adrenalin that told me I was about to suffer…badly. At that moment two large Alsatians appeared with several MP's brandishing machine guns. I was hauled back over the wall into the compound and later experienced the kind of parental retribution that makes up your worst nightmare.

Just before leaving Tripoli, I did manage to befriend one adult Tripolitanian. He was the local rubbish collector and our compound was part of his round. He drove a horse and cart and he taught me a few more words of Arabic. I learned enough to indicate I would love to ride on his cart and help him on his rubbish collection round. I knew that this would cause even more trouble if I was found out but I worked out the timings and believed I could be home before the return of the Uniformed One. My new Arab friend was surprised that a young English boy would want to do this but as we rode along on what was a very smelly rubbish cart being pulled by a horse whose rear end was covered in flies, the reaction from the nearby Arab community was surprisingly friendly. And, during our short time together, I learnt how to shout out the Arabic for 'Go Backwards' which made the horse reverse the cart towards the piles of rubbish in the small alleyways.

We were getting further away from the safety of our compound and the initial friendliness of the Arabs was changing to that look of hatred that I had become familiar with although no nearer to understanding. We returned to the main road which offered much greater safety and it was indicted that I should leave now and go home.

It wasn't far to run and on the way I met a small, white dog. It was shaking. Many dogs in Tripoli seemed to spend much of their life shaking from fear of the regular beatings they received. I picked up this dog and despite the angry reaction that I knew I would incur and to which I was rapidly becoming stubbornly immune, intended to take it home.

Arriving back inside the compound, I put the shaking dog on the ground just outside our flat and rang the front doorbell. Mother opened the door in what was becoming an increasingly nervous manner. She saw the dog, noticed it was starting to foam at the mouth and dissolved into shrieks of terror announcing it had got rabies. She dragged me inside and slammed the door.

A sink full of the hottest water I could stand with lashing of Dettol was made and my hands and arms held in it whilst I squawked at what I though was a severe over-reaction. The Uniform had returned home and listened with mounting fury as Mother explained my stupidity. A Military Police jeep took us to the Army Doctor at the Kassala Army Barracks 12 miles away and where I had the first of three enormously painful anti-rabies injections in my bum. A few days later, after being kept indoors and shouted at on a regular basis, which meant I needed to make frequent trips to the roof to escape back out to sea, I was returned to the Doctor for my second injection and told that this next week would be the one that would show up any symptoms if I'd contracted rabies or not. I was told by various people that if I had got rabies then I'd die…very slowly and extremely painfully. I explained that I hadn't been bitten but was assured the virus would be transmitted through the animal's saliva.

In-between the second and third injection, we were having a very rare 'family break' along with other Army families at the Kassala Beach Club. The Kassala Army Barracks was well known for the very pretty Italian girls that worked there and there were several helping at the Beach Club on this occasion. After a day on the beach, it was time for us youngsters to go to bed and one lad, Freddie, older than me, had climbed into bed and pulled up the sheets only to then start screaming.

The sheets were pulled back and there was a scorpion which had stung the boy on his big toe and which was now scuttling towards my bed. Luckily, amongst the flip-flop wearing adults, was a soldier in uniform wearing hefty Army boots which he bought down onto the scorpion, squashing it.

This was another potential killer as anti-scorpion sera was always in very short supply.

I remained in bed, fearful of yet more death-dealing scorpions scurrying around the sandy floor and the distressing howls of pain from the casualty. With a general display of panic all around, one Italian girl stepped forth and grabbed the boy's foot. A sharp knife was produced and a blood drawing incision made. I will never forget how the look of initial agony on Freddie's face soon disappeared as this beautiful Italian girl took his big toe into her mouth and started to suck the poison out. The change from anguish to a look of pained ecstasy made me wish I could have been stung so that I too could experience this unusual torture.

I asked if that might also be a cure for rabies rather than the third injection I was to endure but came close to my first slap. Many years later a famous Royal was photographed caught having her toe sucked and I could only imagine she too had been stung by a scorpion.

Mercifully I showed no symptoms of rabies over the next few weeks and it seems that I did not die Thankfully we were about to leave the horrors of Tripoli after my third and final buttock jab to be 'posted' to Malta just a short flight across the Mediterranean.

Lost Tunnels

Brief History of Tigne Point, Malta.

Malta has a lengthy history with the first recorded defences of the Island being positioned on the peninsula known as Tigne Point in 1417. Between 1878 and 1886, when Malta was under British rule, a new Fort Tigne, possessing a single 100 ton gun, was in existence and in the 1890s, further additional Batteries and then a military barracks was built. When the British forces left in 1979, the barracks and the whole area fell into decay and neglect. Parts of both Fort Tigné and the British barracks were plundered or vandalized and now the area is unrecognisable being covered in new hotels and shopping malls built from 2005 onwards.

It is only 220 miles as the plane flies from Idris Airport in Tripoli to RAF Luca, now named Malta International Airport. Our journey was at night and when we landed after a very short time in the air, I imagined Malta would be just like Tripoli and I had no desire to leave the plane. I remember the Air Stewardess talking to my Mother and asking her what was the matter with the sulky looking little boy with her and how her answer of 'He wants to go home to Weymouth' bringing scowls of unconcealed scorn from the smartly uniformed Officer sitting in the row of seats alongside us.

After landing at Luca Airport, we were driven off to start our new life in some Transit Hotel I imagine but I was back in mental lockdown and refusing to take any interest in my surroundings.

We moved into our new flat in Tigne Barracks, Sliema, again at night. Military accommodation is furnished and we travelled very light with the bulk of our luggage coming over by sea and due to arrive at a later date. My bedroom window had bars outside it and peering through them into the darkness, I could see nothing except a dimly illuminated square of what looked like yet more sand. I had hoped the plane would have just kept flying Northwards back to England but here we were again in some strange and no doubt hostile place. I had not recovered from the physical or mental effects as a result of my attempts to befriend the locals in Tripoli. Now I realised I had to be a lot more careful as I had been very fortunate in that instance to have been so speedily rescued.

The first morning in our new home started off in the same way as most days of the previous year in North Africa with the sun burning through the curtains and into my bedroom. I found my way into our new lounge which opened onto a veranda and I stepped out to see what horrors lay before me and if a mob of angry locals were waiting below to finish off the job their brothers were prevented from doing in Tripoli.

What a wonderful sight met my eyes. We were on the second floor and beneath me was a rocky shore line and a beautiful blue sea. I could see away just to the right of our building a path that led through a small gate down to the shore. There was nothing to prevent me walking out now and being in the sea within literally minutes; no security dogs, no Military Police, no barbed wire, no high walls…just the most magnificent view across what was Sliema Creek towards the Capital , Valletta. There were a couple of US Naval ships moored onto enormous metal buoys directly in front of me and a number of brightly coloured wooden open fishing vessels heading out to sea. On the rocky shore was a small wooden beach café with the owner already putting out a couple of chairs and a colourful umbrella. There were a several locals walking along the shore towards the café and I saw no sign of hostility or aggression anywhere. Off to my left I could see the rocky shore heading out to sea and then curving away to the left forming what I soon discovered to be the seaward end of Tigne Point which is the peninsula on which I now lived. The shoreline initially headed away in a loosely easterly direction and paralleled the peninsula on which Valletta is built. Sliema Creek separated the two peninsulas by about half a mile of deep blue sea.

I just could not believe it. What a difference. I knew immediately that Malta was going to be a wonderful place to live and my immediate surroundings were both welcoming and very exciting. And, as Malta was further North than Tripoli, we surely wouldn't need to go through the 'Acclimatisation' period…would we???

My Mother must have woken up but I was so entranced at what I was seeing that I hadn't noticed her standing by me. But, looking at her, I could see the relief on her face as well. There were things we didn't talk about when in Tripoli but I knew she was as excited as me at what now presented itself to us. What an incredible and uninterrupted sea view. What a way to start every day.

The Uniform had already left for work so I headed straight outside and down the path to the sea. The Maltese couple, Cikku and Mary Manduca, who owned the beach café were immediately friendly and welcoming and highly amused at the joyous leaping about by this already very sun-tanned British boy. Moments later, stripped to the pants, I was in that sea. Unlike the sandy beaches at Tripoli, this rocky shore line gave access to immediately deep water and I knew this was going be a snorkelling and fishing paradise!

Again, my memories of going to school are non-existent. I don't know how old I was when I paid any real attention to school but, as in Tripoli, we only attended schools for half days in the summer term because of the heat. The School was called Tal Handaq, which was a name I liked, and it released us all at 1pm. By 2pm I was home with all of the Army Barracks of Tigne Point, the very long rocky shoreline, the fishing and the sea to enjoy. It was a Paradise. Sliema, I discovered, is a Maltese word meaning 'Peace' so it's a very well named part of the world.

Snorkelling was a wonderful experience in Sliema Creek. There was much to see with masses of different species of fish but also a lot of octopuses hiding in the rocky crevices. Maltese people like eating octopus. There were also a lot of Coca Cola bottles in the sea. Back then they were glass bottles and there was money to be made by diving for them and returning them to a shop or café.

Cikku encouraged me to retrieve the bottles and he and Mary would reward me, either with a full bottle of cold coke, some money or a dish of fried octopus. Octopus is delicious and, in retrieving those discarded bottles, I was beginning to discover where the octopus hid themselves. A deal was struck with the friendly café owners and I was back to earning from fishing. The Tigne Point shore line was very lengthy and an excellent hunting ground for me. It meant those school half-days were spent in the water for most of the time with the justification in my mind that I could be of some worth and return to my 'One Thirds' earning days back in Weymouth with the mackerel. I also started getting a few 'private' orders for the octopus which paid more than the Café. Catching octopus required a lot of diving and was pretty exhausting for a 10 year old but I certainly became fitter from doing such a lot of swimming and more adept at spearing my quarry. Turning their heads inside out to kill an octopus was at first very difficult but as the summer progressed I was able to do so without leaving the water. A good session would get me between six to ten octopus and a few Coca Cola bottles. It was a wonderful way to spend the long, hot afternoons.

The Nothe Fort in Weymouth, Dorset, is a fascinating building to visit so living in a whole fortified peninsula in Malta with its gun emplacements, military buildings looking like castles, arrays of military vehicles and air raid shelter entrances going into mysterious depths presented endless possibilities for adventures and mischief. The air-raid entrances were either walled up or had heavy gates across their entrances but there were voices coming out of them whispering, 'Explore Me'.

My increasing knowledge of the rocky shore line had led to all sorts of discoveries. There were walled off areas of sea with the walls about a foot under the surface at high water and then standing proud at low water having retained a swimming pool size of rapidly warming sea. These man-made pools would often hold an octopus or two and were included in my hunting ground. I also discovered caves cutting into what were ever higher cliffs as I progressed further seawards. I entered those caves and in one discovered a concealed entrance with a rusted metal framed gate leading further into the cliffs. It was one of the many entrances to an air-raid shelter.

I was always on my own during these octopus hunting trips. I was never questioned in detail as to where I went as my answer was always that I was just going snorkelling but I couldn't move the gate on my own and I needed help and a bar of some sort if I was to have any chance of 'breaking in'.

This was when I met Raymond. Raymond was Maltese and a year older than me. He was much stronger than I and he liked to balance and walk along railings set in dangerous places. A slip could result in quite a fall. I met Raymond when he had just had such a fall and had dropped a fair way down a stairway. He was hurt but refused to admit it, holding back the tears. I had seen him slip. I went down the steps where he was now sitting very quietly. I knew, because of all those whacks at sea that I'd had, that there is a time to just shut up. I sat with Raymond for quite a long time and at the end of that silence a bond of friendship and understanding had been formed between us.

Back then English was spoken by most Maltese and maybe it still is. When I sensed Raymond was ready to talk I asked him if he fancied doing something guaranteed to get us into trouble if we were caught. He readily agreed and I explained what I'd found. He asked how we were to get there and when I explained that we would swim, he turned white. Raymond, a strong athletic Maltese boy of 12 who lived on an island surrounded by a stunning sea full of so much to discover couldn't swim! This was indeed a problem. But he could and would climb to where we needed to go and his balancing and daredevil skills would take him to the cave entrance by the shoreline whereas I would arrive by sea.

Raymond had found a couple of lengths of metal pole and arrived with them. We met by the cave I'd found and going further in came to the metal gate door. The metal bars were thick and rusted and I imagine they'd been there since the end of WWII. This was now 20 years later but they were still a formidable barrier and we were unsuccessful in gaining access. Over the next couple of weeks, we found several other bits of pretty useless equipment to try and prize open the gate. We finally discovered that we could insert one of the poles we'd found into another one and thus lengthen our leverage. Together we managed to move one bar of the gate enough to just slip our slim bodies through although getting our heads to follow was the really difficult and painful bit with the fear that we'd never get out again.

Behind the gate was an enormous and very dark tunnel. There were rail tracks so this must have been a supply entrance. There were thick strips of rubber tubes on the floor which we realised were parts of electrical cable coverings with all the wire now stripped out. The ceiling was high and it was like we were in a train tunnel. We had no torch! Raymond had a lighter...because he smoked! My admiration of him leapt upwards again! We lit one of the strips of rubber and it burnt fiercely and brightly. It also dropped big globs of molten rubber which had to be avoided because it hurt like mad if any landed on bare skin. And the smoke was awful but it worked and we had an endless supply of old rubber to light our way.

I have often relived this moment. As we walked into the enormous tunnel we saw the most amazing carvings in the sandstone walls. Aerial combat over Malta was some of the most ferocious of the Second World War and the Island of Malta was heavily bombed. We were looking at carvings of peoples' sufferings and fears. The depictions of the dive bombers, fighter planes, the ships and the death were all there to see in amazing detail. Whoever carved these was extremely skilled. There were many religious scenes featuring the Virgin Mary and Christ. Some carvings were small concentrating on just one head or facial expression but other scenes were panoramic and depicting what could be seen from the cave entrance with great attention to detail.

We were seeing carvings that nobody had seen for years and we were awestruck. We both sat there in silence for a very long time and we decided we could not go on any further that day. We wriggled our way back through the bars and it wasn't easy. Our fears of getting stuck were nearly realised. We knew we had to widen the gap next time.

On exiting we discovered we were black. Our clothes (I was only in my trunks) and bodies were black and there was thick soot up our nostrils and in our ears. And we stunk of burning rubber. But we had made an amazing discovery.

Over the next weeks and months, Raymond and I explored those tunnels. We used my octopus money to buy good torches. We discovered that a network of tunnels with offshoots for rooms, maybe a hospital and some classrooms, sleeping and cooking areas lay beneath the army barracks above. This was a gigantic air-raid shelter, almost an underground town, which ran underneath the whole Tigne Point peninsula. There were exits on the hillsides, on the other shoreline and several within the barracks including some that came out inside buildings still being used by the military.

One room was clearly an Ops room. Malta was depicted in miniature with vehicles and people positioned in various strategic locations on a large model map laid out on an enormous table. It was an amazing underground and secret world. I returned on my own several times into these buildings. I had discovered that by repositioning the military models on the large 3D model map of Malta so that tanks appeared in shopping centres and outside churches and people were seen to be doing naughty things to each other on the various serene Maltese beaches, I could create a dramatic and furious reaction in my step-father. He was convinced it was all being done by the Maltese workers and he would find out who they were and Heads would Roll!

I could only stare at him in wide-eyed innocence at the awful things that were happening to his toys in the Ops Rooms. He never found out it was me until very recently when I explained over lunch in his local hostelry what I'd been up to all those years ago. He stared at me in utter disbelief and mounting fury and his hands shook to much he dropped his cutlery….and he did not pick up the bill!

A Canoe and a Hammerhead.

Step-Father was always a mystery to me. Our communications were extremely rare. Then, one day, at the slipway by our house, a brand new homemade red and blue fibre glass canoe appeared which I was told was mine. The other kids and I looked at in amazement. Bearing in mind how young we were, my friends urged me not to go out alone in it. Moments later I was off in that canoe on its Maiden Voyage. I had a boat again! I could go anywhere within the safety of Sliema Creek which led into Mdina Creek, the marina and the town of Mdina with the stunning St. Paul's Catacombs. The first time I saw the artwork in the Catacombs made me wonder if the carvings I had seen in the secret tunnel were by the same person. I remember Mother looking at me as I stared transfixed at the artwork asking me why I was so fascinated by it and recall the strange light that came into her eyes when I explained that I'd seen this before….somewhere else. Being of a deeply religious nature, I'm sure Mother must have believed I'd had some spiritual communication from on high. I'm sure if she knew what I'd been up to the wooden coat hanger would have reappeared.

This canoe took me across the Creek to the towering walls of Valletta and alongside the various warships that came to use the Sliema Creek moorings. I saw that the enormous mooring buoys had ladders up them and that they could provide a substantial fishing area. There were shoals of large fish hiding under those buoys so this all looked very promising. Obviously I couldn't access a buoy when there was Naval shipping attached and to tie my canoe to one would no doubt encourage the wrath of the Military and I'd be grounded. So this had to be a secretive sea-borne operation in which I could use my snorkelling skills. Even though the buoys were a long swim away, they were well within my range having spent so much time in the water, albeit always close to land.

I had prepared a plastic bag for my tackle and another plastic bag for various baits, mainly bread and thinly sliced octopus. I was going to use a bamboo stick for a rod with no need of a reel. My mainline would just be tied to the thin end of the stick and I would use a small piece of cork for a float and the simplest of rigs.

The right day had arrived. Sliema Creek was quiet of shipping, the sea was calm and it was mid-afternoon. Collecting my fishing items together, I gently snorkelled out to the nearest buoy which I recall taking at least half an hour to reach. The Creek is deep. I hadn't swum in this depth before. The uneasy feelings that come with not being able to see the seabed or what is behind started to escalate. I was near the buoy and then, just as I was within an arm's length, a large fin broke the surface close to me. I was out of that water and up the ladder onto the safety of the buoy in what were probably nano-seconds but what seemed to take an eternity. And there, swimming around the buoy was a large hammerhead shark. Now what to do? Nobody knew where I was!

I stayed out on that buoy for the rest of the afternoon. No boats came near. The shark seemed to have lost interest and had long gone but I was too frightened to go back into the water. I had nothing to drink and it was hot although luckily I was used to that. The sun started to drop and evening was approaching. I was convinced I would be there for the night and could only imagine the hysteria of Mother and the anger of the Step-Father. It would be even more of a mystery as to where I was as my canoe was still ashore....so I reasoned that any search would work on the assumption that I must be lost somewhere on the land rather than out at sea.

These mooring buoys were directly in front of our accommodation block. I could see Mother on the veranda and could imagine her shouting my name out in that semi-hysterical two-syllable manner that came so readily when she was upset. I waved and shouted but was convinced she could neither see nor hear me. She disappeared and I resigned myself to a night at sea. Well, it wouldn't be the first, I reasoned and it was warm out here. I considered catching a fish and eating it raw but settled for the bread in my plastic bait bag instead. I was just wondering how many years I would be marooned on this large metal island when a boat came chugging slowly towards me. Mother had rushed down to the

Beach Café and squealed quite a lot to Cikku and Mary who she had never spoken to before.

Fortunately Cikku was able to decipher Mother's strange language and frantic pointing so organised a friend's fishing boat to go out to get me whilst Mary calmed mother with a 'Good Cup of Sweet Tea!' I was rescued. Mother was so relieved that she did not tell 'Father'. Cikku delighted in retelling Mother's dramatically emotional melt-down much to the amusement of the locals and myself. Cikku clipped me round the head quite a few times in a friendly Uncle Victor manner over the next week or so and I could see he thought it all highly amusing.

I asked The Uniform if sharks were known in Malta. He told me not to be so stupid. Later that month shark nets were strung across the Creek entrance as a number of sharks had been sighted.

Malta in the 1960's was a good place to be. The explosion of the British music scene, The Beatles and Tom Jones in particular, was very well received in Malta. 1960's music was played everywhere on the beaches. Cikku loved it and was a good singer and party man. The Beach Café became increasingly popular and many young people, including me, were wandering around with a guitar in hand. My guitar had 3 strings and was wildly out of tune but it was OK as a drum. The Maltese community that frequented the Beach Café was welcoming and fun and I was included as part of the large family, especially as I was still bringing in Octopuses.

Raymond, my Maltese friend, had two older brothers. They formed a band of four called *The Boys*. I was taken by Raymond's family to watch them win a 'Battle of the Bands' competition in Valletta. They played mainly Beatles songs along with Chubby Checker's *'Let's do the Twist'* which was a Beach Café favourite and the Ventures' massive instrumental hit *'Walk, Don't Run'*. Elvis was already King. I clearly remember their sound and being astonished that just four people could make such great music. I promised myself that one day I would be in a band!

Tigne Point is now completely changed. It is covered in big hotels and a sleek shopping centre. I wonder if anyone knows that underneath the hotels is that Underground World of delicate and emotional carvings. I doubt if anyone ever went in those tunnels again. I often wonder if I was the last person to see all those beautiful carvings or if they were never seen again and are now lost forever.

Malta was a wonderful experience and all too soon two years had flown by. One of the memorable events I experienced before leaving was Malta's Independence in the September of 1964, the year before we returned to the UK. I've always enjoyed fireworks and this was indeed a wonderful firework display set in Sliema Creek with the magnificent yellow-orange colours of Valletta's cliffs and walls as the backdrop with Malta's Prime Minister, Dr George Borg Olivier, presiding over the Independence Celebrations.

The end of that two year posting also meant the end of my friendship with Raymond, Mary and Cikku. We swore that we would meet up again knowing that we never would. Mother had managed to bring her small mongrel dog, Sally, with us from Tripoli and it had endured a six month quarantine in Malta. Despite being segregated in the kennels, Sally emerged with pups, presumably by Immaculate Conception, one of which I was allowed to keep. The Army Brat knows he can keep nothing that is cared for when it is time to change countries and under the reasoning that it was unfair to subject the young dog to a wintery six month quarantine in the UK, Rusty was given away along with my guitar to Raymond.

It was time for The Uniform to return us to the UK....and hopefully, Weymouth!

Full Circle

We'd been away to Tripoli, North Africa, and Malta for just over 4 years returning to England in 1965, a year after Malta gained its Independence. When living in such arid countries what really hits home is the sparkling greenness of our fair country as seen when looking down from the aircraft windows. I remember marvelling at the rectangles of immaculately hedged fields stretching away across the land with miniature neat farm buildings and clusters of what looked like identical homes into small, well-ordered housing estates. This colourful landscape was in dramatic contrast to the sandscaped Libyan desert and dry rocks of Malta that I'd grown used to.

We landed at Heathrow and I was hoping my Weymouth family would somehow be waiting to greet us and take me home but of course that was not to be. After a brief stay in Richmond, London, we moved northwards again and moved into our new Army quarters. I couldn't believe it. We were back at Donnington in Shropshire! We had gone full circle and back to where we lived before the Overseas Postings and were certainly not returning to Weymouth.

To my surprise, I had passed my 11+ examination when we were in Malta. I really cannot recall taking that test or even realising that I had been in the Secondary Grammar section whilst at Tal Handaq senior school. Because of this 11+ status, I was to attend an interview at a nearby School, Adams Grammar School, which has often been described as a Rugby Club with a school attached.

I took a series of tests and due to my miserable results was told that I was so far behind in my schooling that I would have to start all over again. The half-day schooling abroad had given me masses of freedom and time to swim, fish, canoe, explore and to infiltrate and confuse the carefully planned Ops Room at Tigne Army Barrack but it had left me with large gaps in my Education for which I was now going to pay.

I joined the school half-way through its Autumn Term. A Brat is used to being the 'New Boy' knowing that this position will not last long in a Military School with so many Service families continually on the move. Because I was so far behind in my schooling and demoted by a full year, I was by far the oldest in my new class and because I had spent so much of my time in the sea or playing football for the army junior teams, I was at a distinct physical advantage. I was tested out only once as to who I was due to my dark appearance which encouraged my challenger to use an insultingly appropriate description that Brats who have 'returned home' do not like. In Malta, at Tal Handaq school, disputes could be settled by a properly refereed boxing match in which the offended party could request that option if so desired. It was desired by me on this occasion but no such tradition existed in my new school and was thus immediately refused. When the bell for break-time rang and the Master had left the room it was misinterpreted by myself as being for the start of a boxing round. It only took one solid blow to my insulter's nose for me to realise how much difference our age gap made at that particular age and I should have 'risen above' the challenge. However, it resolved the situation and allowed me immediate acceptance into my new situation.

Military Schools can be quite keen on discipline and politeness with, as mentioned before, the need for The Brat to use 'Sir' and 'M'am' readily and with frequency, preferably when standing to attention. My new school had a compulsory CCF (Combined Cadet Force) Unit and several of the Masters were granted honorary ranks as commanding Officers. Without realising it, my instinctive reaction to any form of address by a Master was to leap to my feet and stand to attention and respond in the military manner that had been previously expected.

It took several weeks for me to get through this particular phase and although the Masters were clearly impressed by it, as shown by the comments on my first term's report, it was inappropriate behaviour in such a school. I needed to break the habits that had been drummed into me and return to 'normality'.

A few years later The Uniform left the Army with great reluctance but did so to appease Mother who was fed up of continually moving. It was extremely difficult for him to come to terms with life and work in Civvy Street and he lost job after job for a number of worrying years until finally working as a Civilian attached to the Royal Navy, ironically back in Portland. Surprisingly, because of how I initially reacted to non-military school life, I found I understood how hard this must be for him or for any ex-military man who had served for many years and was used to giving orders and having them obeyed.

I had never heard of Latin but this was a compulsory subject at Adams Grammar School. The Latin Master was a splendidly kind and humorous gentleman, named Mr Baker, who supported Tranmere Rovers and who referred to boys' farting noises in class as being 'Thunderous and Atomic Explosions' when quizzing the class as to the culprit's identity of the latest eruption. Explaining that I'd never heard of Latin, I was presented with a text book and told that I must endeavour to catch up on a half term's work completely on my own.

Anyone confronted by a completely new language and told to learn it without assistance will appreciate how difficult that is to do but the Latin phrases held a certain fascination for me with their many references to soldiering. I learnt the famous phrase 'Quis custodiet ipsos custodies?' (Who will guard the guards themselves?) in my first week and it's a phrase that often came to mind at sea. I regarded my crewman as my first line of defence in guarding me from the deliberately inane and insane questions that a skipper must endure from his customers. I suspected that Fishing Clubs set aside a period of time at their monthly meetings to construct such questions in order to see how far a skipper could be tormented until his defences were broken down and his steady descent into lunacy began.

The school motto of *'Serve and Obey'* was also surprisingly military in spirit. On the rare occasion that any pupil was to foolishly question anything a Master instructed the class to do, he would be told to stand and repeat the school motto and then to explain it to the rest of us.

Boys always stood up when a Master entered the classroom. Whilst at attention, Mr Baker asked me in my second week of school if I had managed to learn any Latin at all. The military habits from the last four years were still firmly embedded and so the response was clear and carried out at attention:

"Yes, Sir. Quis custodiet ipsos custodies, Sir."

"Excellent, Boy. And have you by any chance learnt anything else?"

"Sir, Servient ei et obedient," I offered in a poor imitation of how I imagined a Roman Centurion to have answered. "Sir, the school motto here is the same as the one in my school in Tripoli which we were to repeat every morning after assembly. To Serve and Obey, Sir."

Mr Baker beamed in appreciation at my efforts and declared that I had all the makings of a future Latin scholar and I stared around the room daring anyone to express any form of disagreement. That was, however, to be the zenith of my Latin achievements because after that I retained very little Latin much to Mr Baker's profound disappointment although I always remembered the vitally important Latin words for *pollack* as in *Pollachius pollachius* and *Tagetes erecta* for *marigolds*.

Squeaker and Skipper

At the end of this first school year, it was announced that we would be having a holiday in Weymouth. I hadn't seen my Weymouth family for five years now and it was during this period that I ended up 'skippering' my first ever Charter Trip and it all happened by accident. Five years of growth makes a lot of difference to a child and I returned to Weymouth already considerably taller than my Grandparents and Uncle who I realised, like my 4' 11" Mother, were very small people.

In the 1965 to 1985 period, the Weymouth charter boats were mainly Ron Berry built boats or similar. Ron Berry was a very skilled boat-builder based in Chickerell, Weymouth whose boats were made of wood, usually iroko on oak, and were extremely well made with many still working around the country today. Uncle Vic's boat, *Atlantis,* was not a Berry Boat but was constructed by Dicksons in Brixham. It too was a wooden vessel with a typical speed of 6 to 7 knots cruising. Because the boats were slow, they tended to take their anglers fishing in and around Weymouth Bay and not far from the harbour. The tides had to be exactly right for going on the great adventure westwards round Portland Bill as pushing a hard ebb tide which ran at speeds in excess of the boat's best efforts on the return journey was to be avoided. A lengthy trip 'out over' the Shambles Bank was a special treat and one which always promised good fishing.

Uncle Victor was one of the Weymouth Lifeboat crew and what tended to happen back then was that the Lifeboat, on the way out to a rescue, would pick up crew members who were already at sea. Some kind volunteer would come aboard from the Lifeboat to take the Charter or fishing boat back to Weymouth.

The Lifeboat, the *Frank Spiller Locke* built in 1957, had been called out and we headed towards the designated rendezvous point to meet it. On board *Atlantis* were a group of Somerset Farmers headed by Lofty and his side-kick, Squeaker. There were a lot of nick-names about in those days!! Needless to say Lofty was extremely tall and Squeaker had an extremely high-pitched voice which he told me encouraged the milk to flow easily from his cows.

With *Atlantis* stopped, the lifeboat eased alongside and Uncle Victor leapt off. The *Frank Spiller Locke* then continued on its way leaving us drifting about with no-one to replace our departed skipper. Lofty towered over me and demanded to know if I knew how to steer the boat and if I even knew where Weymouth was. Squeaker was talking rapidly in an even higher pitch that I could not comprehend but I could see he was concerned. Then the VHF came to life with Vic asking me if anyone had come aboard *Atlantis*. On hearing that no-one had arrived to take over, he quietly told me that now was the opportunity to show what I remembered from all those nights of trawling and to take the boat safely back to Weymouth and to do it calmly and with the confidence he expected of me. He acknowledged that I was just 13 years old but that I had already spent more time at sea than many men who were considerably older than me.

Feeling very nervous with the weight of my first command, I informed Lofty that all would be OK and I would head us back in. I also explained that we were not far from the wreck of the *SS Binnendijk*, a large 6800 tons Dutch steel cargo ship which sunk in 1939 after hitting a newly developed German magnetic mine. Of course I did not know such wreck details back then but over the recent years of skippering a Portland based Dive Charter Boat and listening to the divers, I have learnt a little bit about them.

I suggested we try a drift or two over the wreck. The farmers were very surprised by this. Here was a child with a voice not that dissimilar to Squeaker's saying they should go and drift over a wreck that they never even imagined existed so close to Portland before taking the boat back in to harbour. I explained that there were some big pollack on the wreck. Back then the *Binnendijk* held masses of pollack with many weighing into double figures. I showed the anglers how to tackle up as shown to me by Uncle Victor and I explained that I would use the land marks to drift the wreck. I explained that 'when I was young' land marks had been drummed into me in order for me stay clear of obstructions if I was steering when we were dragging a trawl. The farmers were laughing and clearly did not believe a word of what I was saying.

Whilst they were talking about the implausibility of what I was suggesting, the sharp eyes of the young, mine, had picked out the appropriate land marks and watched to see how the drift would line up. We had no Decca Navigator in those days because of the cost and no-one had ever even heard of GPS as it wasn't launched until the early 1970's. Lofty announced they were ready and they watched me with enormous grins on their sceptical faces as I headed up tide to set the first drift. The *Benny* is a very large and scattered wreck and difficult to miss. Back then it was not even necessary to actually go over the wreck but to just be somewhere close to it as there were so many fish around. As we neared I gave a countdown and, as luck would have it, we did start to climb onto the wreck. I called out the depth and that there were "fish showing" when we were right on top of the mark and then let out a big sigh of relief when nearly all the rods bent into fish. They could not believe it....and nor could I really.

We stayed and drifted a number of times which resulted in a lot of good sized pollack coming into the boat and then we needed to head for home chugging along at 6 knots as I could see the Lifeboat already making its way along Portland Harbour's southern breakwater and returning to Weymouth with a vessel in tow.

As we entered Weymouth Harbour, I remembered the drill. Slow down. Go into neutral to check everything was OK. Go up onto the cabin to drop the long VHF aerial so that it wouldn't be snapped on the bridge. Check the tide marks to see what the Town Bridge head clearance was and then proceed. Everything was going OK as we very slowly edged our way up the harbour.

We gently ticked under the Town Bridge and I went to put *Atlantis* into neutral....and nothing happened. We were stuck in forward gear. The gear stick, operated by sticking your leg out behind you and pushing back on a big gear lever, was firmly stuck. I turned the engine off with the boat still in forward gear. We retained some 'Way' on the boat even though I had been going as slowly as possible under the Town-bridge. There was still enough forward momentum to reach *Torbay Pearl*, the fishing vessel which belonged to Uncle Victor's brother, Clem Pitman. Fortunately Uncle Clem was on board along with Vic and several other men. Despite all their efforts, I still hit *Torbay Pearl* a glancing blow.

Atlantis was tied up. Lofty and his friends were extremely happy at this amazing catch of pollack filling several fish boxes and told Uncle Vic they didn't want to go with him any more as they wanted me to be the skipper. Once they had left the boat I received the biggest bollocking of my young life for disobeying my Uncle's trust and not coming straight back to harbour, for taking people fishing when I had no right to and finally for crashing his boat into his brother's boat. I pleaded my innocence and when the engine hatch was removed there was the ancient length of rope that acted as the gear linkage dangling frayed, broken and useless. Many vessels back then were, literally, held together with string!

Another possible overseas posting that had come through prior to our holiday in Weymouth was confirmed which was to mean another upheaval and move. This time The Uniform and Mother were to be sent to Dortmund in Germany and I was not to be accompanying them. The Army had in place an Educational Grants Scheme to help service children continually of the move to remain in a school, usually as a border and I was to become one of these. It had all been pre-planned without my knowledge and that was why we'd come to Weymouth so that Mother could see her parents for what would be another three or more years Overseas.

It seemed that I was not to return to Weymouth and the sea. Some children were allowed to leave school at 14 years old and because I'd been 'put down' a year, I was nearing that magical age and was expecting to leave. I knew what I wanted and could not understand why I was being denied my destiny. There were some furious disagreements with The Uniform and surprisingly, for me, Mother supported him. It was settled. I was going to boarding school. I was going to stay there until I'd finished my A levels which meant I'd still be at school by the time I was 19 years old. This was a disaster and certainly not part of my plans.

I had hoped that my Uncle would understand and support me but he too wanted me to stay at school and not become a 'low-life fisherman' like him. My remonstrations that that was exactly the life I wanted and had dreamed off ever since I was taken away five years ago did not impress him. I was clipped round the head a number of times and it wasn't done in that friendly manner that I'd known previously. I stayed with him for the day's work and no matter how hard I tried to show that I was happy on the boat and repeated that this was what I wanted, he wouldn't change his mind. He also told me that I was not forgiven for that incident with his boat and that I should return to school after that summer and be grateful for the opportunity the Army and my parents were giving me of obtaining a good education from such an excellent school.

Grandma and Grandad were also furious and now the whole family was united in keeping me from the sea especially as my first attempt to show my worth was deemed such a failure. The success I'd had with drifting the wreck and finding the fish counted for nothing after my display of disobedience and poor boatmanship! It was a good lesson to remember.

I could sense The Uniform's enormous pleasure that not only had I lost my Uncle's trust but that he was, for the first time, supported by my fishing family that I thought would always be on my side. I was ordered into the back of the car and told to keep 'extremely quiet' until we reached the Army Barracks 200 miles away in Donnington, Shropshire.

I re-entered school for my second year as a Boarder. On the one hand it was a massive relief that I no longer had to live with The Uniform. Our opinion of each other was as low as it could get and as my naïve plan to leave school at the earliest opportunity was now thwarted ….short of running away to sea which I seriously considered…Boarding School was, for me, a very good option.

There were a few more visits to Weymouth over the next 5 years but school holidays tended to be spent either with school friends at their homes or in Germany with my parents and their newly increased family which now contained a daughter and son.

Looking back over our lives, many of us can pinpoint the place we were and even exactly what we were doing or who we were with when a memorable song came out. I remember the summer of 1967 being in Germany at the Army barrack's swimming pool in Dortmund along with many other 'Service Brats' waiting for the first European playing of *Sgt Pepper's Lonely Hearts Club Band* album and being confused by the complexity of some of the tracks like that masterpiece *A Day in The Life* and the simplicity of the original *With a little Help From my Friends* before Joe Cocker got hold of it and changed it into an all-time classic.

I lay on the warm grass with an impressively build German girl of my age who spoke in riddles seemingly wanting me to do something to her and then drawing away with a look of pretend shock when I did, a performance I noticed occurring frequently throughout my life.

Of greater concern was that I seemed to be growing ever more distant from my dream of being at sea. The school's compulsory Combined Cadet Force offered the chance to be in the Airforce or the Army section. There was no Naval option. From the age of 15 onwards I was being paraded, marched, shouted at and shown how to make my boots glisten with blacking and my brasswork to shine after a good work out with a helping of Brasso. We were taught how to use the 303 rifle and later a machine gun. We attended 'summer camps' in Wales, where we tried hard to shoot and hit our designated targets and not the nearby sheep, and also in Thetford in East Anglia.

I have to admit that I enjoyed all this. It came quite naturally because of my background and I was able to follow orders without them affecting me. I saw many sensitive boys crumble under the barrage of shouting and bullying especially when cadets were promoted and they then started to lead the playground drills. As we became older the earlier advantages I had over pupils in my own year group lessened. Boys grew taller and bigger than me but I retained that early advantage I had by staring back at any challenge in my best robotically military manner.

I knew from Tripoli and Malta that the firmer the framework of discipline became the more room there was to manoeuvre within it and the more that framework could be used to one's advantage. At one Summer Training Camp, there was an 'Officer Training Section' for boys that were showing some promise or tendency towards the Army as a future career. I had not expressed an interest but it was assumed that there was one and Sandhurst became a word increasingly used when the CCF officers spoke to me. On this occasion, I was put in charge of a 'raiding party' that was to infiltrate the 'enemy' camp and blow up, using thunder flashes, an 'important piece of the enemies' military equipment'.

My raiding party and I entered the enemy camp at night simply by replying to any issued challenge with a very polite and firm, "Yes, Sir. Patrol returning from scouting, Sir." This would be said to young cadets from other schools who found it most amusing that here was some idiot calling them 'Sir'. We strolled in and proceeded to tie the enemies' tent guy ropes together so they would pull on each other and collapse should the inhabitants attempt to break free and confront our raiding party. We found the target which we were to 'blow up and destroy' and chatted amicably to the boys on guard duty who must have assumed that we were on 'their side' having reached the centre of their camp without any kind of disturbance.

A couple of our raiding party sauntered over to the target, planted the Thunder Flash and returned to chat. There's wasn't much of a delay before the 'explosions' went off and we started shouting and pointing into the darkness that we could see infiltrators running into the woods. Our new chums rushed off in pursuit. Young cadets tried to get out of their tents and several were pulled down in the effort. We wandered back out the way we came in and strolled back to our 'base' leaving the confusion behind.

The next day the debriefing revealed all that had occurred and we were declared as successful with no casualties in our group. The Commanding Officers were highly amused by it all but to me it just proved exactly what I'd realised in the first few days of our CCF training that the firmer and tighter the framework of discipline and supposed order there was, the easier it became to recognise and skirt round that framework using it to one's own advantage. Simply by addressing everyone as 'Sir' had allowed us free and easy access to our target.

I know this was all very simplistic but at the time it worked and it seemed another step had been taken towards me proving myself as potential Army Officer material. If I continued down this route, I could see my chances of a life upon the sea getting ever further away.

Israel and a Good Pick-Axe

Fate is very strange. When it happens it does so completely unexpectedly and the whole course of one's life and future can be changed in a second. I loved soccer. I was playing a match at that Summer Camp in Thetford. The pitch was terrible being full of divots and holes. I was tackled, badly, from opposite sides. I spun at the same time. The resulting double leg break and knee dislocation meant agony and operations with months in plaster and what back then, compared to modern advances, was very amateurish physiotherapy.

That was the end of my military career before it ever began. I wasn't worried about that but greatly concerned that my days of playing soccer were finished. The Uniform was back in the country and had to drive all the way from Weymouth to the hospital in East Anglia to fetch me on my release from hospital. He was not happy. I'm sure he thought I'd done this on purpose just to confound his military aspirations for me. The accident occurred on July 20th 1969 which was the day Commander Neil Armstrong and Buzz Aldrin landed on the moon; a day few of us will ever forget.

Boarding school carried on until my final release in 1972. Summer holidays were spent in different places now as Father, who had left the army after the pleadings of Mother to do so, could not hold down a job in Civvy Street and they were constantly on the move. I understood that it was often very difficult for military men who were used to giving orders that had to be obeyed to settle back in to the world of civilians who simply would not co-operate when instructions and demands came to them as a torrent of orders.

Uncle Victor had a new and excellent young crewman, Andy Sargent, who went on to enter the Lifeboat Service full time and is the current Weymouth Lifeboat coxswain since 1999 thus continuing Victor's early influence. I was no longer invited to be crew and by now my parents were living in Somerset. It was very easy to get causal work back then. In the summer of 1972, I walked into the labour exchange in Yeovil and asked for a temporary job; I didn't mind what it was, just whatever paid the best money.

Like so many youngsters, I went labouring and in my case worked for Tilbury Construction based in Yeovil, Somerset. I spent that summer of 1972 using a pick axe and shovel helping to lay Hepsleve soil pipes throughout various Somerset villages. I lived in a caravan in a mate's garden in the little village of Tintinhull and when I had saved enough money, I went to Israel as a volunteer to work on a Kibbutz, a Hebrew word meaning 'Defensive Settlement'. There were plenty of European volunteers turning up in that summer in response to Israel's offers of Kibbutz Working Holidays and there were many who really had no idea what hard physical graft was and what the Israelis were expecting them to do. My time on the boats and on the end of a pick-axe really paid off and I was fortunate to be selected to work with a group of young Israeli men rather than the Volunteers. We were doing the various jobs, such as vehicle maintenance, building repairs, tending the fish farm and laying irrigation pipes around the Kibbutz grounds.

As I was able to stay in Israel, having no commitments back in the UK, I was invited to join a small group of Kibbutzniks who were going to meet up with other Israelis to work further south at Eilat at the northern end of the Red Sea. The Negev desert was immediately to our north and the Sinai Desert to our south and the project was to lay the first water pipeline all the way down to Sharm El-Sheikh and through the Sinai Desert that Israel had taken in the 1967 six day war. We were making a lot of money back then with nothing to spend it on and I was with a great team of hard workers.

The water pipeline followed the Red Sea coast and so in the evenings I was sometimes able to snorkel our immediate coastal area. I was very aware that I was probably one of the first to do this and enjoyed a pristine, totally untouched sea area jammed full of fish life.

And then, in early October 1973, Israeli jets started to fly over us and we heard that war had been declared with a coalition of Arab States led by Syria and Egypt against Israel. This was the Yom Kippur War that lasted less than a month but it resulted in our workforce being bussed out of The Sinai and back to the safety of the Kibbutzim. The current year's volunteer Europeans had already been flown home and as I was one of the last to still be around and I was asked if I would like to stay.

Adams Grammar School's compulsory Combined Cadet Force and the years with The Uniformed military step-father had given me a background that appealed to my Israeli Kibbutz 'father', Eli. All Kibbutz volunteers were given 'Fathers' on arrival to be our mentors during our stay and Eli, an officer in the Israeli Army and a Tank Commander, knew about my background and tried to persuade me to stay.

But this was not my war and I reluctantly decided to leave. That was one of those turning point decisions. I often wonder what would have happened if I have stayed at Kibbutz Negba and committed myself to assisting in their defence, not that Negba was ever attacked as the Yon Kippur War was over within the month. I was thoroughly searched when I arrived at Tel Aviv airport. It was one of those unpleasant deep searches that we hear about and hope will never happen to us. The worst thing to happen is that the Israeli security stripped out all the films from my camera so that I have no photographic record at all of my 14 months in Kibbutz Negba, the Sinai Desert and Israel in general.

An Important Fish

By the time the Yon Kippur war was over, I was back in the UK and had gained a very late entry admission to a four year Education Degree course which was to take me even further away from my long held desire to return to Weymouth!

This section could be devoted to the horrors and tribulations of being in what was previously an all-female College and which had very recently opened its doors to males. This meant there was a 7 to 1 ratio of gals to us poor innocent chaps. When I attended my College Interview, I was asked by Professor Sidney what my first impressions were. I said that it looked like I'd landed in Heaven. He smiled and said, "Sign here."

So, without going into the details about College Life which would be of little interest to fellow seafarers, I had one particular experience that was very important for me and was to help me with my future Angling Journalism work. Like many Undergraduates, I had to write a Special Thesis. I had written mine and had been summoned to meet my tutor, Dr Della Fish. Doctor Fish- a very appropriate name for me - was a formidable lady. She did not take kindly to wimpish students and had a fierce reputation for giving them a ferociously hard time if they didn't match up to her very high standards.

We got on very well...usually. I entered her study with an air of quiet confidence after having handed in what I thought was a good thesis and was expecting a congratulatory pat on the back. That was a grave error of judgement on my part. Dr Fish was glaring at me as if I was beneath contempt. She told me that she had made a decision and that she was going to give me a choice, one that she would not normally extend to a student. She would give me a pass Grade for my work as it stood or, if I could take it - and she believed I could - she was going to rip my work to pieces and explain to me in excruciating detail why my thesis was utter trash. She told me if I took the second option that I could possibly come out of this experience with a completely different level of understanding of the English Language but equally, I could fall before the challenge and end up as a miserable wimp of a weak-kneed failure (my interpretation of her words!). She was quietly seething! I didn't dare say I'd take the Grade as it stood. I agreed to be shredded.

And shred my work she did. It was revelatory. She took me into the depths of what was then the Academic Buzz-Word of *Deconstructionism*. She ripped everything I had written to pieces. She questioned me at length of what I had written and what I thought it really meant and by the end of a very lengthy assassination of my pathetic thesis, I left her study with a totally different outlook on my writing.

And so, I set to work and offered my first pages which were again annihilated. And again and again until in the second week of rewriting she looked at me and smiled and said, "At Last!" and pointed to a single sentence that she regarded as being good! A lonely sentence! But that single sentence unlocked what she was trying to get me to do and then I was able to write what she considered to be a worthy offering.

I have never forgotten that lesson. It stays with me all the time. It is hovering over my shoulder now. It sat by me through the 20 years of angling journalism and, when I was tired after the demands of a five day Alderney Fishing trip and two demanding days of weekend wrecking trips with the knowledge that we'd be off again early Monday back to Alderney and I had publishers' deadlines to meet, she would be there scathingly telling me to stop grizzling and get on with the job...and, "Write with your audience in mind and not to fulfil some selfish aspiration of your own."

Well...she was tough and I have a lot to thank her for.

When I was a teacher in Weymouth, I had a very dry Head of English. One cold January morning, she produced our local paper, the Dorset Echo, with my weekly angling page open and she congratulated me on being a true journalist as I had managed to fill up a whole page and say nothing of any worth.

It was high praise indeed and, Dear Dr Fish, I thank you for showing me how to do that.

Having finally gained the qualifications necessary to apply for my first teaching job, I applied to everything on offer in Weymouth and got absolutely no-where. I discovered that Dorset was a County many people wished to work in and no school was going to take a completely inexperienced first time teacher when they had the pick of experienced applicants from all over the country. No, it had to be somewhere where nobody in their right mind would wish to go.

I knew where that place was...and I applied.

Fishing through the Classroom

I always thought that it would be difficult to get a teaching job in Weymouth, Dorset, but did not realise it was all but impossible. Having applied for every post going without even an Application Acknowledgement, it was time to reconsider my approach.

I had read about the opportunities for teachers in the East End of London, particularly in what were then termed SPA areas. SPA stood for Social Priority Areas which would mean that this could be a 'Challenging' situation. There were stories of teachers lasting even less than an hour in their new appointment before fleeing in distress. Surely, with this sort of staff turnover, there might be a job opportunity for me.

Because of my earlier unsuccessful applications to Dorset, I'd missed the start of the Autumn term for that year so decided to get some work and start applying for the Spring term of the following year. I was in Hereford having completed my Teaching Training there at Hereford College of Education.

Bulmers Cider Company was based in Hereford and they were a very fine family run Company to work for. They had helped me through my final year by giving me a Night-Shift job in the Pectin Department of the factory. This was a 10 hour shift and it paid well. They allowed me to stay on for that September to December 1976 period knowing that I would be trying hard to get a teaching job in London. The Pectin Department was like a steam filled weight-lifting gym. The big heavy wooden presses need to be stripped and cleaned out on the hour. It was hot and hard work maintaining the steady flow of pectin through the 8 presses and noisy centrifuges and it meant that all of us working there developed an upper body physique out of all proportion to our legs.

It was of course important to prove one's masculinity by being able to shift the heavy wooden frames and clear the press on your own when it should have been a two man job. This meant, once one had reached the impressive level of being a 'Filter Soloist', that the right hand side of one's upper body then developed even further than the left hand side (unless you were left-handed, of course).

This made the purchasing of shirts difficult with one side hanging loose and the other side fitting with blood stifling tightness.

It also meant that when I finally arrived at my first Teaching Post, I was extremely fit albeit in a lopsided manner which I did my best to disguise under my suit. I am sure that I had been offered a job when I attended my earlier Interview because I wore a suit. In fact that was one of the all-important, job-clinching questions. "Do you think it is important to wear a suit in this job and will you wear one?" My answer in the affirmative led to a firm nod in my direction and I knew I was in with a chance.

I walked into my very first lesson. A large, heftily built boy of 15 years in the back row of the classroom stood up and said: "Who the Fucking Hell are you then?" and thus my teaching career began.

It was true. Staff turn-over was pretty rapid but the English Department was staffed with some exceptionally strong characters and the Deputy Head, Mr Dargon, was superb. He was an ex-Rugby player and it showed. The boys in particular had a good deal of respect for him. After the battles of the first term, I found that I really enjoyed working in this school and discovered that Mr Dargon was very supportive in my requests to form a fishing club and take the lads out fishing at the weekend. Also, because of the rate of staff turn-over, those of us who remained working at the school had more of a choice of the classes we were allocated. I recall a class of amazingly motivated and talented students, some of which have remained in contact with me until this day and who were a rewarding joy to teach.

Back then, the National Anglers Council, the NAC, was the representative body for fresh and saltwater fishing. They had an award scheme, Bronze, Silver and Gold for Freshwater and Game Fishing. They had managed to construct only the Bronze award level for Sea Fishing and were hoping to progress with further development for this section. The scheme, sponsored by Swan Vestas Matches, included a detailed theoretical side as well as practical work. Because the questions made sense to a lot of the students, I soon had a flourishing sea fishing club on my hands. The Deputy Head made sure I had access to the School mini-bus at weekends and several Dads who were Black Cab Taxi drivers gave their services freely and helped me take the students to places like Clacton, Walton -on -the -Naze, Southend and Deal including Sandwich Bay. We even made it to Weymouth on several occasions and I was able to take them out to sea and find them places on friends' trawlers and potting boats for a day so they could have an idea what commercial fishing was all about something that definitely would not be allowed these days.

THE National Anglers Council ran a training programme for would-be Instructors. I attended the course at Grantham Reservoir, East Anglia. It was assumed that if someone had applied to be an Instructor, then they knew something about angling. This was a course designed to help non-teachers to teach in an imaginative and informative way. As a teacher already, I remember being very inspired by the NAC techniques and could see how they could also apply to my English Teaching.

Many shore anglers will have tried to improve their casting skills in a field. My School Fishing Club were out practicing in the School Fields once a week, much to the bemusement of their non-fishing mates, and we had two 'Theory' sessions a week at lunch-time in my classroom. The structure the NAC provided with their Course Booklets, handouts and exams was excellent and a lot of students who normally had little interest in reading could relate to this subject matter and enjoyed the discussions and multi-choice questionnaires.

After 5 years in London, it was time to leave and this time I was able to offer enough experience for a Weymouth School to consider my application. I was advised by Mr Dargon that I was making a big career mistake in returning to Weymouth. He was keen to point out the qualities that I possessed that made me a very suitable teacher for an SPA London School and which would not be recognised or appreciated in Dorset. He was correct and had I intended to remain in teaching, I would have needed to return to the 'East End' of London but, without going into all that, I had finally made it back to

Weymouth and my 'plan' to become an angling charter skipper was back on track.

Property in London had escalated in value in the 1976 to 1981 period. The very small terrace house purchased in Waltham Abbey virtually doubled in price during these years whereas the house prices in Dorset had not increased with anywhere near the same speed. The small two bedroomed property in Waltham Abbey, Essex, property had now morphed into a large detached house, not far from the Beach, in Weymouth. This meant that now I had something to offer as collateral when it was time to go grovelling to the Bank for a Business Loan.

I firstly bought a 16' Open Boat with a Yamaha 9.9 HP outboard and a faithful Seagull outboard back-up. This allowed me to apply for a limited local licence meaning I could take 2 or 3 anglers out at the weekend within the confines of Portland Harbour. I had joined the Weymouth Angling Society and met the Society President and much admired local Councillor, Mr Jim Churchouse, who had been writing the Sea Angling reports in our local paper, The Dorset Echo, for a long time and wanted a break. Thanks to him talking to the Editor, I was allowed to take over the weekly Sea Angling page.

This was an important step as it provided me with the excuse to regularly phone all the local clubs for their competition reports and stories and let it drop that I now had a very small licensed boat and could offer light tackle fishing close to shore. This became popular option and I started to build up a few regular customers.

I started a fishing club at my new school using the NAC Course material again. It was extremely popular and quite a few of the students were also members of the Junior Section of the Weymouth Angling Society. With the help and expertise of the Weymouth Society Committee, an Inter-School fishing competition was established with Senior and Junior events planned. It became so well supported that we needed to hold competitions on separate days as literally hundreds of youngsters were becoming involved from schools throughout Dorset.

The Mysteries of Water

By 1983, my small open boat had been sold and had been replaced with an Islands Plastic vessel of 24 feet called *Purbeck Star*. This was a real chugger of 7 knots top speed but it allowed me to take up to 6 people on it and it had a good sized forward cabin for its size with a cooker for the all-important facility of tea making, an essential service on a charter boat. *Purbeck Star* had a converted and ever reliable Gardner bus engine in it. The problem with the engine was that the starter motor was set very low and vulnerable to any sea water collecting in the bilges. Water is a mischievous creature and can find its way into boats from all sorts of unseen and unpredictable places especially when the boat is under way and pushing through the sea forcing water into the smallest entry point. That 'entry point' is usually a very long way from where the water eventually accumulates and can be all but impossible to find.

Sometimes the boat can run along happily for a week without any water ingress and it seems the leak has miraculously healed itself only to find a bilge full of water on another day after a relatively gentle trip. Engine designers like to put the electrics in the most vulnerable position in order to expose them to water and also, knowing that a marine engine will be confined within the restricted area of an engine box, like to fix the components in the most difficult position to access. This means that even a simple job like removing a starter motor will result in lost tools and impressive cuts to the hands and arms. *Purbeck Star*'s starter motor was in such an inaccessible position that a specialised tool complete with a backward looking mirror on it had to be invented and constructed by our local marine mechanics. Then, by laying full length on top of the engine and reaching down to the very limits of arm stretch the socket extension bar could be manipulated into position to release the three holding bolts and extract the starter motor.

Boat skippers have to become mechanics as often they are at sea with no-one but themselves to call on when a break-down occurs and it's why there is often a reluctance to turn an engine off even when anchored. Lifting an engine hatch at sea when there are customers on board is also a hazardous occupation. A surprising amount of customers enjoy falling in and landing heavily on the engine thus causing themselves injury to add to the complications of the breakdown situation.

Like water, gravity also starts to play tricks when at sea. If a spanner or other such important tool is accidently let go when fixing one's car, it will fall downwards and mysteriously get lost within the complications of the engine. Sometimes it will drop right through the engine and need to be retrieved by crawling under the car. In theory this should happen in a boat but against all the laws and theories, tools can often shoot upwards and somehow go straight into the sea through the nearest available scupper. I've even watch a socket disengage itself from the socket bar under pressure and leave the engine room only to leap over the side of the boat to be lost forever into the watery depths. How these things occur is a great mystery but anyone who has worked on a boat, especially when under pressure of customers looking down upon them and offering well-meant advice, will know it happens.

Purbeck Star was a jinxed vessel. It would go for weeks with nothing untoward occurring and then on a gentle ride in calm seas the bilge alarms would start up and on opening the engine hatches a full bilge of seawater would be discovered with the water sloshing onto that ever vulnerable starter motor. On eventually being sold, the vessel was taken by sea to to its new home port of Poole Harbour and, after several months of remaining bone dry, filled up and nearly sank in the unpleasantly unpredictable waves of the St Alban's Race, 15 miles east of Weymouth

Without me even travelling all the way to Cornwall to view it, a 26 foot Task Force dory was purchased on the strength of a photograph and advert in Fishing News and arrived in Weymouth on a low-loader. It was quickly given the name, *Vanishing Trick*, because of the speed I was assured it could reach if correctly engined. Colonel Gaddafi was very much in charge of Libya at the time and had ordered thirteen Task Force craft to be built. Twelve of these boats were to be fitted with explosives and were to be guided towards 'enemy' shipping by remote control, basically being used as unmanned missiles. Being superstitious, the 13th boat was not to be taken from the UK builder's yard and had been left rotting, under Gaddafi's direct orders so the story goes. It had found its way to Cornwall and there I was able to purchase it for a very low price. This was to be my Commercial Bass boat and, with a shiny new 120 HP Mercury outboard was able to reach an amazing and scary 38 knots.

I started commercial bassing whilst still a teacher and was able to choose crew from my students, many of whom were extremely keen to become commercial fishermen. When the the timing was right, we would occasionally be able to fish the very early morning tide before school. After fishing, we'd race the boat back into Portland Harbour to unload the bass. A taxi would be waiting by Copines Fish Market waiting to whisk me and my young crew along the beach road to school. I headed towards the Men's WC where my suit would be waiting whilst my school-boy crew hurriedly changed into their school uniforms hanging up in the boys' changing room.

The Deputy Head was very understanding and ensured my form register was completed if I was running a bit late. This might have been because his son plus two other 15 year olds were working for me. It's hard to imagine this scenario occurring now with all the various rules, 'correct' behaviour models and the need for compulsory sea going certificates for crew members that now apply.

As the final bell for end of school time approached everyone knew to stand clear as I needed to be first out of the classroom door, back into the Staff WC to fast change into my boat clothes and then meet my half-dressed crew lads racing to from their respective exit points towards the taxi waiting in the car park and back to Portland to meet the boat to fish the evening tide. This didn't happen every day of course. It was only when the tides were right to do this.

One of the young school-boys, named Lee, out-fished all of us all the time. I never worked out how he did it because he looked like he was fast asleep standing up but somehow he never missed a bite. In the long School summer holidays, Lee stayed on as crew and we were joined by a young James Davies who went on to have a dazzling career, supposedly for three years, in the Army where he still is now 30 years later.

Portland Race and Bass Fever

Fishing the Portland Race is not for the faint-hearted. The flood tide tends to be safer than the faster flowing ebb with its high standing waves easily capable of overturning a small bass boat drifting into them broadside. We tended to fish the flood tide but there were many occasions when I looked at the towering seas that we were drifting towards wondering if we would come out the other side in one piece. It was actually safer to stay in The Race than leaving it and trying to get back in as it was the first waves that were usually the most dangerous.

We caught a lot of large bass in those days and crews tended to catch 'bass fever' during the bass season when the exhilaration of working at speed in the sort of seas that sensible people would avoid, the fierce competitiveness between the crews and the reward of a good income depending on how many bass the boat caught drove us on to go fishing at times in insanely life threatening conditions. Boats were forever breaking down and not just because of engine failure. There were a number of occasions when the se would punch its way through the wheelhouse window shattering the crew with glass and sea. The electrics would flood and the engine might die leaving the vessel in a perilous position, drifting without power or steerage through a very angry sea. It was not unusual for a boat to be hit by several waves at once thus the crew off their feet and flooding the deck so that crew and bass were helpless on their backs on a boat full of water which would be pouring out through the scuppers. But, no matter what happened, it was vital in such situations to never let go of your fishing rod!

Fishing on what appeared to be a very pleasant day by Portland Race standards, *Vanishing Trick* was driven too hard by the over-excited adrenalin filled skipper out of the flood tide standing waves that guarded the northern end of the Race. We left the top of the waves at a good 20 knots and suddenly there was no sea between us and what looked like a considerable drop back to the nearest water. The three of us at the time hung on for dear life in expectation of what was going to be a very heavy landing. It seemed we were suspended in mid-air and I looked out and down from my small wheelhouse to see the crews in the nearby bass boats looking up at us with mouths wide open in appreciation of our high and seemingly sky bound trajectory. Time stood still as it often does in such intense situations and then we were falling to crash onto to the sea with a worrying loud fibre glass cracking crash.

My crew were on their backs and once again joined by the bass we had caught being flung out of their fish boxes onto the deck which was actually bone dry, our two second airborne fight forcing the seawater out of the scuppers in pressurised jets. I was holding onto my steering wheel in the wheel house and as we hit the sea, I fell backwards taking the steering wheel with me with the steering morse and throttle cables arching back into the wheelhouse as I fell. The wheelhouse, which was more like one of the phone booths that were found everywhere at the time, collapsed inwards and lurched back towards and over me before disintegrating. I was on my back still holding the steering wheel with my crew looking at me with a mixture of disbelief and humour on their faces. We didn't do fear in our days of fishing The Race….or if we did, it was never shown.

We scrambled to our feet. *Vanishing Trick* had come to a temporary halt although the engine was still running but thankfully in neutral and then the 4 knot tide grabbed us and started taking us back into The Race. We knew we would just have to hang on and be bounced through a mile of turbulent sea before we could access the damage and see what was to be done. Before we hit those first waves again, another bass boat had sped alongside us containing the wildest bass skipper in the Fleet and probably in the whole Northern Hemisphere. His surname rhymed with 'nutter' and it was difficult to know if he was nuts or a bassing genius as his was so often the top catching bass boat and his crews were driven on by their skipper's demonic fury.

Drawing alongside he shouted at me in his always monstrously loud, heavily accented Dorset voice

"You alwight yung 'un?"

"Yes," I reply looking at my trashed boat, my befuddled crew, the fish still bouncing around the deck and the approaching standing waves. "All good, thank 'ee."

"Here's a hamma," he bawls above the noise of the increasingly near wall of water we were now drifting at speed towards. "Knock it all back together and carry on, young 'un!"

He shot off to reset his drift. We clung on until we reached calmer seas at what we called the 'Back of the Race' and set to work. It's amazing what three keen young men can achieve in a very short time. The fish were re-sorted, the fish boxes stacked properly, the tackle retrieved and untangled and the wheelhouse held in place while I hit everything back together with the help of items from my enormous tool kit that contained a bag of nails, some screws, a couple of very rusty screwdrivers and useless spanners but also an invaluable second hammer.

We rejoined the bass fleet having missed a number of fish producing drifts. After the flood tide we used to all head back into Weymouth or Portland to offload the catch. The ebb tide was rarely as productive as the flood tide and, after weighing in our bass at the local fish market we had time to have breakfast. This was often a period of great friction between the crews when inter-boat insults could easily escalate into fights. On this occasion, I was expecting the worst but surprisingly the bass crews were in surprisingly sombre mood. We all knew that we were vulnerable when bassing and anything could happen to any of us at any given moment, such was the unpredictable nature of the waves inside The Race.

The acknowledged Admiral of the Fleet, Commander Mutter, came over to our table. He was known as being a violent and unpredictable man and I was expecting a black eye or something like that but instead he shook my hand and said well done for getting the boat back together and re-joining the fishing. He actually smiled at me before grabbing my arm in what really was the 'vice like grip' we read of in action stories and staring into my eyes and growling; "And don't forget to give me my F**king 'ammer back, young 'un."

Sea Ahoy

Prior to finally leaving teaching, I had a slow chugger of a boat for chartering, with Lee also crewing on that, a fast commercial bass boat for the big tides and I was back crewing aboard Uncle Vic's latest Ron Berry built boat, *Valerie Ann*, whenever I could. Vic decided I should start taking the boat out on evening sessions and a few day trips to give him a break. This meant I needed to take the local Waterman's Licence. Another of the local skippers, Ken Leicester, *Bon Wey*, gave me a lot of help with this. I used to go to his home in Portland and he took me through the Waterman's syllabus. It was very much a licence based on detailed knowledge of the local area as it covered 3 miles out to sea and 15 miles either side of Weymouth Town Bridge.

The Harbourmaster at the time, Captain John Whitney, was a very helpful and encouraging man and very easy to work with. He took me for my Waterman's examination. I remember his opening 'question' and from this can be seen the depth of local knowledge expected. Sitting in his office looking towards the Lifeboat station, I was told to imagine that I was to leave my mooring in Weymouth Harbour and go to the West Shambles Buoy, then head north westwards onto the Kidney bank, return to Portland Bill and head towards the East Shamble's buoy, then the Adamant Bank and back towards the Chequered Fort, North-east passage and thence to Weymouth Harbour entrance and back to my mooring. At each stage of the trip, he wanted compass bearings and depths and tide directions based on him giving me the time of High Water Portland for that day. As well as this, he expected me to tell him every buoy, cardinal mark and light I would see including every light as I came up Weymouth Harbour and to tell him what I needed to look out for in the harbour. I recall Granddad telling me from an early age that the wooden rowing boats operating the cross harbour passenger ferry were the most important vessels to be looked out for as they were carrying a lot of passengers including babies and elderly people. If a collision occurred or a capsize was caused by a large boat's wash, then a terrible accident could occur. The Harbour

Master was very pleased when I related Granddad's words of cautionary wisdom and I passed.

The first person I told that I'd managed to pass was Uncle Vic. He told me that nobody passed first time and refused to believe me. After much protesting, he came with me to see the Harbourmaster to demand why an idiot such as me who knew nothing had passed the examination. Captain Whitney knew how to deal with men after years in the Royal Navy and asked my uncle who was it who had taught me. On admitting that it was he, Captain Whitney was able to congratulate Vic on being the finest teacher anyone could wish for and that my passing the examination first time was testament to the thorough training he had given me. This was the perfect approach and allowed Uncle Vic to proudly present me to everyone as having become a Professional Waterman thanks to him and his endless patience in trying to instil some proper sea-going knowledge into my knuckle-head. I could tell he was pleased as he clipped me round the head on a number of occasions thereafter.

I was becoming involved with an increasing amount of Angling Journalism. *The Dorset Echo* was now expecting a full page with four photographs every week as did the Somerset *Western Gazette* along with submissions to the *Angler's Mail* and the *Angling Times*. New monthly magazines were appearing and I was writing reports and articles for *Sea Fishing* and *Boat Fishing*. There was money about in those days for sea angling and TVS (Television South) ran a well-supported annual event whereby south coast Angling Clubs sent their Club Champion to represent them at local heats and then on to a Semi-Final concluding with 10 Finalists being taken away to fish in some very exotic places such as The Azores, the Great Lakes in Canada, Tunisia and Iceland. TVS liked to invite a journalist to the Finals from an area where one of the anglers who had made it through came from. The area I was covering in the newspapers was all of Somerset and Dorset so for several years in a row I was fortunate to be one of those invited journalists and met people like the multi-talented Trevor Housby, writer of that wonderful book 'Dream Fishing' and technical adviser at the Azores Final and Mick Toomer, Daily Mail journalist and superb angling photographer who played a very important part in the start of the *Offshore Rebel* adventure.

I was still in full time teaching but it was nearing the time to make the break to go full-time chartering. The journalism had given me a lot of extremely useful angling contacts. Running the various boats was helping me to gain the experience I needed for the next stage in my plan. And I was able to raise a loan thanks to offering our house as security, a move that made me extremely nervous.

I had placed an order in the summer of 1986 with a now defunct company, Port Isaac Workboats , for a brand new Offshore 105 fitted out for angling. It was due to be delivered to me on May 1st 1987 and be ready for its first trip on June 1st. I had coverage from Television South lined up, Sea Angler Magazine and a number of Angling Journalist contacts arranged for this auspicious date and the boat builder had assured and reassured me that everything was going to be on time.

My buddy, Pat Carlin, of *Channel Chieftain* and now owner of Carlin Boat Charter Company which includes a fleet of very impressive Wind Farm vessels, told me he'd been to the boatyard in Wadebridge and had taken a photograph of my new vessel. Pat then produced his photograph showing a number of large cans of fibre-glass resin and told me that this was far as the boatyard had got with my boat! It was now February 1987 and there was the serious concern that the new boat was not going to be built in time for the proposed launch date. I feared my carefully constructed plan was going to be thwarted at the first hurdle!

PART TWO

The Seadog Longitudes

Explanation

The Seadog is a person who spends their life as far away from land as possible and who exists in a world of salt spray, face weathering winds, unpredictable seas, impenetrable fogs and dazzling sunrises. Failure to learn the language of the sea, revealed through the natural phenomena listed above, can result in severe and painful punishment which is often out of all proportion to the initial mistake. The sea will look after those that learn to listen but cause great suffering to those who remain deaf.

A seafarer must learn these lessons well if progress to the auspicious level of the Seadog is to be achieved. Part Two relates some of the adventures at sea that can take the Army Brat and change him in a Seadog without his knowing it was happening.

The Launch of the *Offshore Rebel* adventure.

With the very real prospect of me achieving my ambition of becoming a charter skipper coming closer, the question to ask myself was why would anyone wish to go sea fishing with me when there was an already well-established charter fleet in Weymouth with outstanding skippers. Men like Vic Pitman, Burt Randle, Lionel Hellier, Alan Boreham, Bugsy Bugler and Ken Leicester were already very well-known and highly regarded throughout the south coast, Wales and the Midlands. There was also the trail blazing *Peace and Plenty* skipper, Chris Tett, who was an established   star on the UK wrecking scene having been featured in National magazines and who had built up a fearsome reputation for himself as 'something of a Captain Bligh figure' who would stand no nonsense but put you over more fish than could be imagined.

With this in mind, I needed something different to offer people. There was no way I could compete with these experienced and exceptional men. I needed a gimmick; something different that I could offer which would put the emphasis on the boat and what it could do and the skills of the anglers themselves rather than me being any good as an unproven skipper.

The Weymouth boats were travelling at speeds of 6 to 7 knots. I wanted a boat that could do double that speed and cruise at 14 knots. A wrecking day back then was 12 hours long starting at 0600 and finishing at 1800. Basically the day was divided into 4 hours travelling out to the wreck, 4 hours fishing it and 4 hours returning. The rewards for this lengthy steam could be huge with catches often in the 1000lb range.

The Offshore 105 Sail-away version came with a massive 8.2 Litre Iveco 320 HP engine which was advertised as offering speeds well in excess of what I was looking for. If I could offer a vessel that cruised at twice the 'normal' Weymouth cruising speed then I could advertise and offer double the amount of fishing time or 'Two Days in One'. Also, the slow boats struggled to reset their drifts in the bigger tides and tended to go wrecking only on neaps whereas I could work any tide with a fast boat. The wooden vessels also tended to stay clear of the Portland Race as 4 knots of tide was just too much work for a 6 knot vessel and the confused seas were dangerous for a wooden boat.

Much of the charter fishing trips was inshore but it was my intention to concentrate on being as far offshore as I could. I wanted to appeal to the anglers' Pioneering Spirit and Sense of Adventure. Yes, the talented anglers would have to initially put up with an inexperienced skipper but the advantages would outweigh this and, with their help, I would improve and hopefully become worthy of their bookings.

In the year before my boat was due to arrive in Weymouth, a visit to our local library in Weymouth and found a massive list of many the angling clubs in the UK, both freshwater and sea. Everyone Club, every person and every possible address received a letter setting out my aim to provide a fast modern charter boat out of Weymouth which would offer a wide range of angling right from light tackle inshore trips which would be good fun for the freshwater anglers in particular, right up to the multi-day Channel Island trips which were rarely occurring back then, especially to Alderney which is where I had set my sights.

Alderney is 54 miles from Weymouth and is the shortest crossing with Guernsey being another 20 miles further. The already well known Geordie Dickinson of *Artilleryman* fame from Plymouth was running trips to Guernsey and it would be madness to consider competing with him. Also, I had taken my commercial bass boat *Vanishing Trick* to Alderney several times to get an idea of the bass fishing and it all looked extremely promising with some excellent early results.

In addition, the advantage of writing the sea angling reports for the local papers over the past five years meant regular contact had been established with the Angling Club secretaries and I was invited to come and explain my plans at their meetings. The NFSA (National Federation of Sea Anglers) were also very helpful providing a list of every Angling Club associated with them to whom letters of introduction were sent.

So, a mass of contacts and ideas had been established and were all pursued with enthusiasm. The new boat was written about and advertised as if it already existed and was in action but was already 'so heavily booked up there were no more available trips or even individual spaces until the following year'. This was much more of a risk than I realised because I had naively put my complete trust in the Offshore 105 boat designer/builder to produce my new vessel on the date we agreed.

As another way to make the new boat be part of the 'New Way Forward', angling journalist and photographer Mick Toomer, who I'd met at the various TVS competitions over the past five years, came up with a superb idea for naming the new boat. Mick made up 10 catchy boat names and then ran a competition in his Mail on Sunday Sea Angling Page, asking readers to vote on the name they liked best for this new and exciting project happening down in Weymouth.

The name *Offshore Rebel* comes from the make of the boat, an 'Offshore' 105 with the 105 numbers just relating to the boat's length of 10.5 metres. The *Rebel* part was because the boat was going to double the speed of any other charter boat in the area and thereby offer a whole new range of exciting, action packed angling adventures. The skipper was also referred to and described as 'a rebel' having given up a safe and steady career in teaching for this unpredictable and risky occupation of Charter Skippering! So, boat and skipper were going to make a perfect couple!

Mick had a marvellous way with words and the name *Offshore Rebel* was overwhelming voted for 'By the people and for the people'. The pen is mightier than the sword and that then became the name for the ensuing 30 year, four boat, *Offshore Rebel* Adventure.

Interest from a Navigation Company at the Earls Court Boat Show in London produced a new sounder and a plotter with the agreement that complimentary reviews would be written and published about these two essential items. A plotter is an electric chart which superimposes one's own vessel on it making it very easy to see whereabouts you are and where you are heading. The early plotters were nothing like today's super sophisticated and accurate machines. The old cartography was terribly simplistic and inaccurate with the machines also being extremely user-unfriendly and thus very difficult to write an encouraging equipment selling review about. When going round around Portland Bill, for example, the plotter had *Offshore Rebel* firmly positioned in the car-park at the end of Island.

One of the major Tackle Companies, Daiwa, also agreed to help out equipping the boat with a few rods and reels, again under the agreement to review them in the various magazines I was writing for. It was not easy to give positive reviews to items that broke very easily yet they were gratefully received in those early days. The idea with sponsored fishing tackle is that it can be offered to customers to try out in the hope they will be impressed enough to purchase their own but it often had the opposite effect and put them off. It seemed short sighted to provide inferior equipment to promote future sales and anglers soon know if a rod or reel is any good and capable of withstanding the punishment that they were going to get on the mid-Channel cod stocked wrecks.

An enormous amount of preparation had gone into this project and, thanks again to the journalism, there were contacts at TVS and several magazines including the then current Editor of Sea Angler, Mel Russ, ready to come and experience the boat on her Maiden Voyage but it was now late May. The boat was supposed to have arrived on May 1st to allow me a month of getting used to it before I started on my new career.

The boat was obviously not going to come on time. The designer, Rod Baker, had managed to persuade another Offshore 105 owner to lend me his boat until mine arrived. This was a boat fitted out for private use and was a stunning piece of workmanship well above the standard Offshore Sail-Away level that I was getting. The first tentative inshore trips went out on that 'borrowed' boat it was was disappointing that after all the big build-up to *Offshore Rebel's* arrival the event had fallen flat.

Offshore Rebel I arrives in a Blaze of Breakdowns.

By early July 1987, the new boat had finally arrived. A few trusted friends and I took it for a gentle ride down the harbour and between the Town Bridge and the start of the Pleasure Pier the rudder had fallen off and the propeller had come loose and was rattling away sounding like it was going to burst through the hull. With no steerage we managed to crash into the Weymouth Pleasure Pier and secure a line round a dangling chain and hung there in shame and ignominy. What a start! Luckily the rudder was found by divers and the boat was lifted out again for a refit of rudder and propeller plus a very close inspection of the hull.

At last the boat was really ready and already there was a backlog of cancelled bookings because of these various late arrival and teething problems. Mick turned up with a full camera crew an at last all was ready to make the introductory film of this amazing new technological marvel that was going to revolutionise the offshore wrecking out of Weymouth.

The intention was to fish on a genuine, previously unfished 'virgin' wreck that the Hydrographic Department had recently discovered. We travelled a long way offshore to our chosen wreck, in fact exactly half way across the English Channel to Alderney on a wreck now fondly known as 'The 22'. I was asked to turn the boat's single engine off so sound checks and recordings could be made. I remember having a terrible feeling about doing this but did as told. And then, after all the voice work was completed told to start the boat up and begin the fishing.

The key and the starter button pressed. There was an almighty bang. Smoke was coming from the engine room. The mountains of Camera gear were hurriedly shifted and the engine hatch open. Smoke poured out and there was the hint of a flame. The new powder fire extinguisher was bought into play and fired off all over the shiny new starter motor which was on fire and we were now well and truly dead in the water. Talk about a feeling of despair. The Lifeboat was called and it was a very long wait for them to come a full 27 miles out to the wreck and then tow us all the way back to Weymouth. One of the camera crewmen fell asleep in my helm seat and dropped his beer all over my new VHF radio and totally destroyed it.

When we arrived back in Weymouth Iveco, the engine suppliers, were waiting. When I explained what had happened, I was informed that, "Yes, there seem to be a few of these starter motors catching fire" and a replacement was provided and fitted. I couldn't believe it! This problem was known and I'd been allowed to go to sea with this starter motor failure very likely to happen.

Anyone owning a boat will know all too well what this does to your confidence. How can you go to sea if the trust in your vessel has been lost? Rudder lost, propeller loose and now a fire all within a week and I hadn't even taken one proper trip out yet. This was not what I had expected, hoped or put myself into serious debt for.

Uncle Victor had already told me that I was a complete twat for buying a boat like this and for giving up the security of teaching. He was very angry about the Lifeboat having to come all that way to tow me in and all in all, it seemed like I had made a terrible mistake.

The next few days of trips were cancelled and I took the boat out to sea on my own and did everything I could to break it. I smashed through the wild seas of the Portland Race and I mistreated in every way I could to make it show up anymore faults and I cursed and raged at it. Boat owners have a strange love/hate relationship with their vessels and tend to talk to them as if they were alive. A boat is not called a 'She' for nothing. 'She' and I had a serious falling out over these early disasters and I had established a firm hatred and distrust of the boat which I needed to resolve by pushing it to its limits and seeing what else could possibly go wrong.

But *Offshore Rebel* performed brilliantly. I learnt a lot about the boat over those few furious days, what it could do and how it would perform in rough seas and what it would allow me to get away with. And we developed an understanding between each other. I was now ready for the first full-on proper charter trip and when the anglers came on-board they must have wondered who this wild-eyed madman was before them who was still furious with his new boat and doing his best to contain that anger.

We rocketed straight out to sea in a southerly direction. It was a big tide and no-one in their right mind back then would go south to an offshore wreck. A big tide meant you'd at least head west to lose the effect of the tide. But this was Weymouth's new fast boat and it could handle the tide and, after last week's fiasco, it was going to have to prove itself to me.

We lined up the first drift and I shouted out the distance to the wreck and the fact that we were screaming along at 3.5 knots but the flood tide was at its peak and we were going to fish it down. We closed in on the wreck and then mayhem with everyone doubled over into fish.

It was 1987 and the year of the cod ban. There were more cod in the English Channel than had ever been known in the History of Man. There were so many cod that whatever method was used to fish, including using mackerel flappers at anchor intended for conger, cod took the baits. Cod, cod and more cod. So many that a total cod ban was soon implemented in the Channel that year complete with MAFF spotter planes flying overhead. Back then, a commercial fishing licence was issued for free if you wanted one. I had a commercial licence on my boat with the regulation size registration letters and numbers on my cabin roof which were large enough so that aircraft could spot and record my position. Not only did the cod ban certainly apply to me but whatever we did and wherever we went that year we caught cod and stacks of them and whenever I looked up there seemed to be a Ministry of Forestry and Fisheries aircraft heading straight for us.

1987 was a summer of insanely productive fishing and it gave me an instant reputation of being a fish finding genius which of course was not true but which I obviously used to my benefit. When new (they were all new to me) customers boarded the boat they would ask me if it was true about these monstrous catches they were hearing about and I was able to say that they would soon be able to judge for themselves.

The 1980's were plagued by wreck netting with the wreck netters travelling up from the West Country, Devon and Cornwall, to set their nets were over the wrecks just west of Portland and would do this on the gentle tides, known as neap tides. This was where the wrecking trips out of Weymouth tended to take place. It could be very difficult to find a wreck to fish that didn't have a net on it. I was taking angling customers to the wrecks south of Portland on the big tides and then travelling even more to the south east when the tides eased to maintain the speed of drift that seemed to be working best for the fish. This meant I was never faced with this wreck-netting problem and the catch rate was maintained thanks completely to the capabilities of the Offshore 105. There were a number of very despondent charter boat skippers working the slower boats about during that time because of the intensive amount of wreck netting taking place.

It was an amazing stroke of good fortune for me that all these fish were around and that I had the boat with the speed to stay away from the areas being fished by the wreck-netters. Anglers will remember how we were good little boys during this period and kissed our cod affectionately on the nose and released them back to the sea in deference to the ban.

The hours that I was working at sea meant that I rarely saw the other Weymouth skippers. This was another stroke of good fortune as I needed to keep a low profile. The *Rebel* was moored out in the middle of the harbour on a buoy mooring opposite the Weymouth Angling Society HQ so I was out of the way which again was very useful.

Because of the mass of letters I'd written, clubs that I was in contact with for their reports for the newspaper and all the publicity that journalists like Mick Toomer had given me, I was actually very heavily booked in that first season and well into the following year. My Uncle never ever came onto my boat and during that busy summer I hardly saw anyone outside of my customers. One evening sitting in the Sailors Return, I met up with Lionel Hellier, the skipper of *Just Mary*. There was a lot of rivalry between the skippers back then. In the summer, when the boats were taking individuals on holiday fishing, numbers would be counted and that would be a great cause for concern if there were less customers on their own vessel than on a rival's boat. Lionel was very supportive and highly amused that I was working every single day and never needed to be involved in the summer holiday trade as my boat was always booked by Angling Clubs. He was always very complimentary about what I was doing and he would express his uncontained amusement in front of the other skippers whenever he could which did not go down well. I was able to explain that this was all just a novelty and soon the anglers would lose interest in belting around the sea catching fish that all had to be returned and that they would soon come back to fish on the traditional Berry boats.

I'd spent several years commercial bass fishing with my fast bass boat, *Vanishing Trick*. Offering bass trips was something else I wanted to try. In 1987 the bass decided they didn't like the big tides and it was the small tides that fished best. These smaller tides were ear-marked for conger fishing which was very popular in the 80's and conger men don't want to be drifting for bass especially with the conger tackle they brought with them. So, this first year did not go totally to plan and we lost out on an excellent bass season off Portland but that could be something to develop next season.

Alderney Ahead

The Channel Islands trips started off as three day ventures and concentrated on Alderney which was the nearest Island to Weymouth at 54 miles distance. The trips were accommodated close to the harbour in the Braye Harbour Hotel which back then was cheaply priced, chaotically run and remarkably like Fawlty Towers. The 'package' included breakfast but I was often the one in the kitchen cooking for the anglers as there was no sign of 'early morning' staff. The hotel offered us great deals such as taking all our cod and pollack in exchange for reduced rates, pack lunches and dinners. It was a great hotel to stay in; very relaxed and a lot of fun.

Opposite the hotel was the restaurant *The First and Last* and that is where I met Rita and her staff. Rita was and still is a very glamorous, incredibly well spoken lady and the rather grand atmosphere of *The First and Last* restaurant made many of my early customers feel rather intimidated. I remember going to see Rita and explaining how I felt and I couldn't have wished for a more delightful response. Rita was and remained one incredibly special lady and our backgrounds were not that dissimilar. Rita became and remained a very dear friend for 30 years. She was always there to offer a consoling ear and give friendly and knowledgeable advice and over the years, I and my customers spent many delightful evenings there. In fact, for a tiny Island, Alderney always had amazing places to eat.

Reaching the dizzying heights of St. Anne's town involved a trek up what was affectionately called Heart Attack Hill. It was very steep and what made things worse and the heart pound faster was the tightly track-suited derrieres of the young keep fit ladies of Alderney. Watching them race past us inspired a firm, three second spurt of energy in a futile attempt to extend the motivating vision for a few more precious seconds before returning to the struggles of the climb.

Many of us could not make it up that hill and the Island's Taxi service run by the affectionately named Dollop and his sidekick,

Mad John, would be hurtling up and down Heart Attack Hill to pick up the steady stream of sufferers attempting to reach the delights of the town's impressive selection of pubs. Halfway up the cobbled street of St Anne's Town was the *Albert Pub* which boasted a large, bushy bearded Landlord named Richard who made outrageous offers of truly gigantic meals that could be eaten for free if the diner could finish it all. There was the very occasional Hero that could eat every last pea but for the majority of us, the mountains of chips and everything else before we could even find the 32 ounce steak was too much.

There was also the *Mari Hall* at the top of St Anne's town. This hostelry fed our anglers with superb food for all of the 30 years we based ourselves in Alderney. And, unlike other eateries which stopped serving at 2030, we could phone up if we were going to be late in from sea and the staff did everything they could to accommodate us. It quickly became and remained a favourite place. There was also the famous *Harbour Lights* where the well-known *Sundance* skipper Roger Bayzand and his teams used to stay. Howard, the landlord, was a wonderful and generous host and we enjoyed many late nights there. And then the *Mai Thai* restaurant opened on Alderney and remains the very best Thai restaurant I have ever experienced even after years of being based in Thailand for the UK's long winters .

The sea around Alderney to me was fascinating. The tides and the multitude of under-water obstructions that affected the currents, the wild and fast waters of the *Alderney Race*, the dangers of the *Blanchard Rocks*, the tumbling tidal overfalls in *The Swinge*, the drying horseshoe of *The Rhone*, the rapidly changing depths of the pollack-holding *Pommier Banks*, the intricacies and vagaries of the channels running through the Island of *Burhou* and the raging flood tides of the tope holding grounds of *Verte Tete* along with *Ortac,* that looked like a fast approaching Condon Ferry when viewed from afar, and many more places fascinated me with each area producing its own individual seas and back-eddies. What an amazing and challenging place Alderney was for someone who loved the sea.

At this point, it should appear clear that it was the sea itself that I loved. I was not personally all that bothered about fishing. My aim was to try and find fish for my customers but I had little interest in fishing for them myself, apart from bass that is. When I worked for Uncle Victor as crew he would always tell me that I could not expect to fish other than for bait. My job was to help the customers in any way that I could other than catching fish for them. There are skippers who inspire by being superb and keen anglers and there are crewmen who are expected to fish and boost the overall catch rate. Uncle Vic was never like that. He believed in providing a service and part of that service was having a crewman who made the tea, cut the bait, netted and gutted the fish and did whatever he could to assist the customer. I always tried to instil that into the crews that worked with me.

During the *Offshore Rebel I* years, I had several excellent crew. My first full-time crewman was an ex-pupil, Tom Williamson. Tom was a very big and strong young man who, like Lee on my bass boat *Vanishing Trick,* could fall asleep standing up. He would head-butt the cabin door frame as we crashed our way back and forth to the wrecks and Alderney but still manage to remain asleep until needed. He was often concerned that he had some sort of illness because of the bruises on his forehead that seemed to mysteriously appear when he was at sea. It was no good putting him on the helm as he also fell asleep there. I remember one day 'down below' hearing the increasing throb of a big engine and coming back up into the main cabin could see we were heading straight at an oil-tanker with Tom fast asleep in the bouncy helm seat.

But Tom was perfect as my first crew. He loved fishing. He was totally loyal and hardworking and was able to throw the anchor so far away from the boat that we were able to consistently miss the wreck I was trying to fish and would have to re-haul, by hand, the anchor and shoot it away again with a bit less enthusiasm. Anglers may recall another small person who came along as crew after Tom moved on to a commercial crabbing vessel. Mr Ivan -6 foot 6 inches -Wellington joined me and I will always remember his uncanny ability at navigation. Bringing us back from mid-Channel to

Weymouth, he took us to the west and not the east of Portland. When I emerged from 'Down Below' to see if we were home, we were just passing the wreck boil of the *Salsette* which is well off to the west of Portland. We were bound for West Bay and not Weymouth. When I queried this strange detour, Ivan announced, "Well, it begins with a *W*, doesn't it?"

Alderney made my business a success. As it is an Island with many smaller islands around it, there was usually shelter to be found. When the winds were howling in England and the Weymouth Fleet was storm bound, I would still be working and in comparative shelter. The inshore fishing around Alderney was very productive for pollack so if all else failed, they could be relied upon and back then pollack were very acceptable.

After the various problems of the first couple of months, *Offshore Rebel I* proved itself to be a remarkably reliable vessel. The big 8.2 litre Iveco engine matched with what was a light vessel handled the demands of regular Channel crossings with ease. After a shaky start, my first season was looking set to be a remarkable opening success. But, as we all know too well something unexpected always seems to happen to our detriment and bring us back down with an almighty crash.

Hurricanes Hardly Happen

October 1987 was the time when the BBC Met Department got the forecasts horribly wrong with Michael Fish taking the brunt of the criticism as he was the main Weather-Forecast frontman on TV at the time. Southern England was hit by winds of Hurricane Force that very badly destroyed Kew Gardens and generally wreaked havoc along the South Coast.

Weymouth Town Bridge was undergoing major maintenance and had scaffolding all over it and could not be raised. The scaffolding came down to nearly water level so it was impossible to get under the bridge except on dead low water on a Spring tide. *Offshore Rebel* was fully booked right up to the end of the year so I moved her down to a new mooring in what we call The Cove area of Weymouth Harbour so that I could continue the trips. But the winds never let up that autumn. By Christmas I had been to sea just twice in two and a half months and I was spending nights down on the boat worried about the force of the winds and what damage they might do to my unattended boat. The Bank Loan back then was charging very high interest rates at 18% and I could see that what started out so well could soon disintegrate into a financial disaster. I had to go back to the classroom as a Supply Teacher...something I promised myself I would never do but this became necessary for survival. In fact, I decided that I would have to do this for the next three winters as our weather was just too unpredictable. The trips in the January to Easter time would need to be restricted to weekends and school holidays with journalism and teaching taking over. I counted myself very fortunate to have these extra ways to bring in an income and it is something that many charter skippers need, that being another 'string to their bow' in such times as it was not possible to go to sea.

The locally issued Waterman's Licence did not, in theory, allow vessels to go more than 3 miles out to sea from the shoreline. Alderney was considerably further and so another licence was needed. This was the Department of Transport Licence. The examination for this was much easier than that for the Waterman's

Licence but the demands made on the boat were ridiculous. We all talk of people sitting in offices, far removed from the reality of everyday working life and constructing unworkable practices apparently designed to destroy peoples' livelihoods. This is a regular occurrence in the Charter Boat world where regulations for large vessels are passed down to apply to small ones and simply do not work. The DOT Licence required major alterations to be made to vessels which were dangerously impractical and made them, in some cases, unseaworthy. It is happening again with the latest dictates being passed to charter boat owners that they must cut great big holes in their boats to let the water out in the case of a massive sea landing on the deck and flooding it. The size of these new holes will weaken the structure of the boat and make it much more vulnerable to mishap.

A long list of requirements was given to me to comply with in order to be awarded my new Licence. These included making thick wooden window protectors that could be quickly affixed to the outside of the wheelhouse window in a storm to prevent the sea smashing the windows in. Goodness knows what seas these people in their offices thought we went to sea in on our family fishing trips. They must have thought we had easy access to these windows so that in a storm of window breaking ferocity, with one of the windows already stove in and the seas pouring into the tiny wheelhouse, we could carry these big heavy sheets of wood onto our foredeck and happily screw them into place whilst carrying out what would be one of the most superb balancing acts on the bow of a wildly bucking boat in order to do so.

The engine room was to be clad out in inflammable Rockwool, which was stupidly heavy even when dry, overlain with metal sheeting all of which was to conform to the thickness decreed but which of course was not available to purchase just to make things even more difficult. Double sheeting of the metal was needed and then the boat was even more unnecessarily heavy because the two sheets came to more than the designated required thickness. We were assured it was fine to be 'over' but not 'under' the specifications. And so it went on with a list of very expensive and inappropriately applied regulations which resulted in an overweight and unwieldy vessel and all in the supposed name of safety. There was so much extra safety gear, wooden window protectors, extra metal sheets and larger life-rafts that there was no roof to move. I was considering the need to tow a large rowing boat behind me that could carry all this unnecessary nonsense.

The DOT licensed skipper and boat could then travel 40 miles to sea from their Home Port. This meant there was another 14 miles to run to Alderney and even further to Guernsey. The wording in the Licence allowed, in emergencies and break downs, to limp into the nearest port for repairs. This meant that on every Channel Island trip, having travelled 40 miles, I either needed to turn round and return to my Home Port or limp into Alderney. The 'limp' speed on *Offshore Rebel 1* was often miraculously faster than its normal cruising speed as it was important to reach safety before the predicted problem or breakdown occurred. Once in the safety of Alderney Harbour, the necessary repairs would last the same time as the planned trip which always needed gentle sea-trials to take place allowing the customers the opportunity to fish whilst the boat was carefully checked over whilst at sea.

After three whole trips, I could no longer live with the dangerous insanity of DOT conformity. The boat's cruising speed had decreased dramatically to 10 knots, it was difficult to steer, it could no longer 'lift its bow' into head seas and there was no room anywhere for all this additional 'safety gear' that I was carrying. The boat was stripped back to its original state when we were in Alderney and everything distributed amongst the commercial fishermen who could use it on their much bigger vessels. This had all been a costly exercise but I ran with that worthless licence for the next two seasons. It was because of the farcically inappropriate demands and conditions of the DOT Licence that the Royal Yachting Association Code of Practice, COP, came in which then allowed correctly equipped charter boats to travel up to 60 miles from a designated Safe Haven. Crossing from the 'Safe Havens' of Weymouth to Alderney meant that we were never more than 30 miles from a Safe Haven and so now the same boat was miraculously 'legal' all because of the paperwork and sensible changes in the previously outdated rules.

This was all less than 40 years ago but seems like we were doing something outlandishly daring and unusual in crossing the English Channel in our increasingly powerful vessels. Her Majesty's Customs Office also issued a procedure which was all but unworkable but if not adhered to could result in the vessel being impounded and the skipper arrested.

On our return trips to the exotic and far off unexplored, self-governing Channel Islands we were required to hoist a yellow Q flag upon crossing the 12 mile territorial limit into UK waters. This Q flag was the size of a yellow duster and could just about be seen by the customers on the boat as it fluttered wildly from its expensive bamboo stick in the boat generated wind. As we approached our Home Port, Weymouth in my case, I was to notify Customs that I was entering port and then wait at my moorings with all my customers remaining onboard for up to two hours. If no Customs Officer had arrived in that time, we were free to leave. Imagine that scenario! It is rare to experience a flat calm sea when crossing the Channel in a small boat and our total time at sea, because we fished on the way back, would be about 10 hours. Customers often then had a very long way to drive home adding anything between 2 to 4 hours extra travel time and we were all expected to sit patiently on the off chance someone from Customs had time to turn up and clear us.

It meant that two hours out to sea, thank goodness for that analogue 'mobile' boat phone with its ever present signal, Customs would be notified that the vessel was in harbour now and was awaiting their arrival. By the time we actually pulled in to our mooring, the two hours was up and we could just unload and clear off. I never saw a Customs Officer waiting for us and it wasn't long after that the whole system was scrapped and we were advised that as long as we filled out the paperwork everything would be fine. Well, it was in UK but not in Alderney which maintained a fanatically keen interest in our arrival and demanded our Customs Forms even before we had finished tying up.

On one occasion, Uncle Vic came rushing to my newly returned boat telling me that the Police Drug Squad was around and awaiting my arrival. Apparently Customs Officers were also nearby and hiding in the nearby carpark. When we pulled in and tied up, the Police Drug Squad arrived and everyone was told to stay on the boat and all communications to be switched off. One by one the anglers and their luggage were taken off the boat and searched. It took a very long time especially with so much fishing tackle and fish in black plastic sacks to rummage through. It was dark by the time they finished and released my crew member leaving just me.

My engine hatch was raised and the compartment searched. I was asked why I needed such a big engine. I was made to feel like I'd done something suspiciously unusual in having a 'Sail-Away' boat that supplied the appropriate matching engine that was deemed 'so big'. I explained that the boat could only travel at 14 knots cruising, about 16 mph, even with such a big engine, and we regularly visited The Channel Islands which were 54 miles to the nearest one so that engine was not oversized by any means. It seemed to me that my boat was being regarded as some kind of alien spaceship that had travelled through time to provide the ultimate high speed Cross-Channel drug carrier, obviously operating under cover as an angling boat.

Parts of the engine were dismantled and inspected as potential hiding places for the suspected drugs stash with the large air filter and even the turbo unit removed. The hollow handrails round the boat were taken off and torches shone into their tubular depths, every locker and smelly fish box, still containing slushy ice, was thoroughly searched and even the radar dome was removed. When the search had concluded and my Customs paperwork copies inspected, the Drug Squad and presumably the hiding Customs vehicle departed. Nothing was said and nothing was put back. I was left with a boat in bits and it was now late into the pitch black evening and I had another trip booked back to Alderney the next day.

I turned on my trusty boat phone which then rang immediately.

"Skipper. Thank Goodness you've answered. We thought you'd forgotten us. We're with you tomorrow. We're already down here and staying at The Sailors Return. Is it OK if we put our stuff on the boat now as we're worried it might get nicked from our cars tonight. What did you catch? What time are we leaving? Where do we park our cars??"

Silence.

"Skipper. Are you OK? Speak to me."

Over the next three years, *Offshore Rebel I* made regular trips across the English Channel, mainly to Alderney and occasionally to Guernsey. These trips were always exciting because of the 'middle days' around the inshore marks. The trip across the Channel always concentrated on fishing several of the many ship wrecks that lay between Weymouth and Alderney and which provided the bulk of the catch, cod and pollack, to sell on the first day and for the anglers to take home on the final day.

Particularly amusing when we were mid-Channel and on our way to Alderney was the passing of The Concord. Sometimes, when the tide was right, I would anchor a wreck directly under the Concord Flight path. This particular wreck fished best on the ebb tide which meant the current was running from East to West. Anchoring on the ebb tide meant the bow of the boat was pointing east with the anglers concentrating on their lines dropping down to the wreck in a westerly direction. They could not see the approaching Concord coming up the Channel from the East. On a calm, still day the noise of Concorde breaking the sound barrier directly overhead was a magnificently deafening double bang followed by a lengthy thunderous rumbling. It caught many a customer off-guard and, as the daily occurrence could be anticipated to the minute by me, the perfect timing of the distribution of hot drinks could take place. It is quite surprising how fast hot drinks can leave their receptacles and how far the liquid can travel into the air inflicting superficial but initially painful damage when landing on exposed skin can cause. No customer ever actually suffered a heart attack but there were what appeared to be some very close moments and certainly there were regular and highly original post sound-barrier -breaking song and dance sequences which graced the decks. The lyrics were somewhat repetitive though and contained many 'F' sounds.

Because I initially knew very little about the Alderney marks, I used to try and seek information from the Islanders. It was extremely difficult to find anyone who would be prepared to share any of their local knowledge so I spent a good deal of time looking at charts and plotting out Latitudes and Longitudes of interesting looking submerged rocks and banks, mindful that my plotter was very inaccurate and that I would need to use my Alderney charts with great attention to detail..

I enjoyed building up my own records. I always kept the sounder on and was constantly scribbling untidy maps with the GPS positions placed over anything that looked vaguely interesting. The whole sea area around Alderney is fascinating with so much diversity that it would be a lifetime's work to explore it all and that was how I presented the trips to customers. We were pioneering! Every day was an adventure where we experimented with drifting and often anchoring for the fish. There was so much fish around that we rarely blanked although I was 'caught out' by the rapid change of tides of a few occasions and had to leave my anchor behind with a buoy to mark its position so that we could retrieve it at slack tide. I carried three anchors in the boat all set up and ready to go back in those heady days of exploration.

I thought that the people I asked for help on Alderney just did not want to assist me which was fair enough as I was not a local and I was seen to be 'taking their fish' but when they started asking me where we found the sandeels, how we fished for them, how did I know what time to be there, where did all these pollack come from, how did I discover the method to catch turbot and a multitude of other questions, I realised that they really did not know. This was hard to believe; to live on such a tiny Island and to be surrounded by the most amazingly fascinating sea full of fish on so many different marks which were often very close to each other was a complete mystery to me.

For the first couple of years I was the only visiting UK charter boat that tried to fish inshore around Alderney and although it was fun discovering everything on my own, I could see that there was so much more than I could possibly uncover without assistance. Fortunately it was not too long before Chris Tett realised he had to get a faster boat and start offering some of the fishing that his customers were telling him that I was doing. Chris sold his big, solid trawler and brought an Offshore 105. He hated the light boat right from the start which was understandable after the sturdiness of his roomy trawler and sold it within the year to another local skipper. Chris then took us to the next level of boats by purchasing and fitting out his 38' Lochin which dwarfed my Offshore 105.

The Lochins were formidable vessels, strong and stylish. I had to have one if I meant to 'keep up' which meant selling my trusty *Offshore Rebel I* and commissioning Chris to fit out *Offshore Rebel II* in the winter of 1989 to be ready for the 1990 season.

Offshore Rebel II is launched

Changing boats for a bigger one is a costly business for most people. At the end of 1989, my trusty Offshore 105 and I were to part company as it was necessary for me to 'go bigger'. I was very fortunate to sell *Offshore Rebel I* within Weymouth Harbour and so was able to use the boat right up to the launch date of *Offshore Rebel II*.

Offshore Rebel II was fitted out over the winter of 1989 into the spring of 1990 inside the large Kingfisher Marine workshop on Weymouth Harbourside. It came from Lochin's workshop as a bare hull but with the cabin and foredeck shell already in place. The name Lochin comes from the designer's surname, Frank Nichols, a well-known racing car entrepreneur, spelt nearly backwards. This was to be a twin-engined craft powered by Iveco 250HP x 2 engines installed with the shafts running out and supported by 'P' brackets. The 'P' brackets meant that the props were very exposed and managed to act as debris collectors over much of the English Channel for the next 9 years and enabled me to dive regularly in places that I would have normally avoided!

The Lochin is a very smart looking vessel and looked gigantic inside the Kingfisher workshop. I am utterly useless at practical work so I spent the Autumn '89 and 1990 Spring Terms working as a Supply Teacher again to keep the money coming in along with the weekend trips and angling journalism. The boat came out at over four times the original price of the Offshore 105 which meant a huge Bank loan which remained at 18% right throughout the 1990's. I was to pay this loan back during the 'working' months of May to October each year which basically meant at the end of October I was pretty skint and relying on the weather between the Novembers and Aprils to be kind enough to give me enough days at sea to cover all the winter costs and outgoings.

That is probably how my rather dubious nickname of 'All-Weather Whittall' came about because it had to be pretty fluffy (some might call it more) to stop the boat from going to sea. Any boat owner knows how stupidly expensive owning a boat is and it has become a lot worse over the years with costs such as engines, maintenance, **mo**oring fees, life raft hire, insurance all rising out of proportion to income and of course servicing a merciless Bank Loan at the crazy rates they were back then. There's nothing for it but to buckle down to it and work as much as possible and not give in to the various inevitable set-backs. It is a job that you really must want to do in order to retain the energy and motivation required to do it. That big white Lochin was motivation in itself...just looking at it being built was enough to fire up enough enthusiasm to want to keep going. It was indeed a truly splendid boat and I couldn't believe it was going to be mine.

Launch Day arrived on a bright spring day in late March. The vessel had been supported by a huge trolley throughout the work and this was going to be pushed out onto the road for the crane to take over and lift her in. With all the new cabin top fittings, it was going to be a very tight fit to actually be able to exit the workshop.

Chris Tett skipper of charter boat *Peace and Plenty* had masterminded the vessel fit-out. He had now put out the word that as many of us available that day should assemble at the workshop to assist in pushing this massive trolley loaded with a very large and heavy boat out of the building. A lot of men turned up and we pushed and heaved....nothing happened apart from a little squeak from one of the trolley wheels.

Someone started singing, " Right said Fred; 'ave to take the roof off. That there roof is gonna 'ave to go!" This ditty inspired our leader to even greater efforts of truly Herculean strength and as he charged the trolley like an American Football Star and bent into the job, there was a large expulsion of air from his nether regions and an impressively long rumble echoing round the shed. "F###-it", he said. "I've followed through. Someone phone for a taxi".

Our leader had now waddled off outside leaving the rest of us in hysterics and rolling around the floor. I fully understood that day the phrase 'helpless with laughter'.

The crane helped drag the trolley out and then gently lifted the boat into the water. The Master had returned and was soon on the boat checking for leaks and any other obvious problem areas before the Iveco engine experts took over in order to start the engines for the first time. Everything was working fine and we went to sea for the first timid test ride and have engine alignments checked and rechecked. Everything seemed OK and both rudders stayed on and neither propeller came loose!

On our return to harbour we held an official launching/naming ceremony with my son Tom swinging the Champagne bottle to smash against the bows followed by drinks on board for everyone who had assisted that day. The *Offshore Rebel II* adventure had begun.

The Lochin was fast and easily capable of 24 knots so well over the 14 knots I aimed for with the Offshore 105. Now we could comfortably cruise at 16 to 18 knots and at only 9 pence a litre back then for fuel, speed was not an issue as regards fuel consumption. I worked on the rough assumption of a galleon a mile and the fuel bill worked out about one seventh of the gross earnings back then as compared to the unsustainable 40% of the gross it became several times in the 2010 onwards era.

I had always been told that a working boat should aim to gross its own value per year. The locally built Ron Berry Boats were still very much about and at a cost of about £12k to £15k for them, the equation was attainable. The Offshore 105 cost £23,500 and so once again the equation was reachable but now we were into a whole new ball game. The value of the Lochin was a lot more than a decent house in Weymouth would cost in 1990 and seemed like a monstrous target to reach. My Uncle shook his head in despair at my lunacy.

I was still very much working on the premise that it is the boat that attracts the customers. This fabulous charter boat was surely going to maintain the edge for me and indeed it attracted many new customers along with those that had stayed with me during the Offshore 105 period.

There was no way I could compete with Chris Tett on his catch rate. He was extremely good at the job and to him the success of the day depended totally on the quantity of fish landed on the deck. We still had Commercial Fishing licences on these boats and selling the fish, particularly in Alderney, helped offset the cost of the trips for customers. Pete Jenkins owned the Harbour Side chip-shop in Alderney and he really was the most welcoming friend we skippers had there. Our first night would be spent at his restaurant with a magnificent amount of food to eat and Pete would be out the back very skilfully filleting his way through the masses of pollack we had brought in. Back then he paid us £1 for 1lb of fillet or 50p per pound for the whole fish. We aimed to arrive with 500lb+ pollack on the first day which covered the cost of the day's charter and dinner as well as a few drinks. There was also the added attraction of Pete's highly attractive daughters and I'm sure quite a few return bookings were made if I promised the group that the first meal would be in the chip shop.

Because I really could not compete with Chris Tett's wrecking catch rate, I decided we needed to concentrate on what I was better at which was the bassing. Bass commanded a far better price than pollack being worth six times their amount for whole fish. I'd spent quite a lot of time now over the past years searching out the mid-channel and Alderney bass marks and that became a major part of our trips. It meant that we could catch a lot less quantity of fish but end up being able to offer a much better reduction on the trip price for the anglers.

This all sounds very mercenary and not in the spirit of angling as it is today but many skippers back then came from commercial fishing backgrounds. Our vessels held commercial licences so it was perfectly legal to sell our fish. Alderney was able to benefit by buying at a much cheaper price direct from the commercially registered boats than from imported fish. I was then bringing a regular order of fish such as plaice and sole over from Weymouth Fish Market to Alderney and in return was able to access the local fish-mongers supply of ice.

The extra speed of the Lochin and the large fuel tanks meant I could aim for five day rather than 3 day trips. The English Channel was ours to range over and discover some of its many secrets. I was operating between 3 degrees West (roughly in line with West Bay) to 1 degree East which is right on the eastern side of the Isle of

Wight and between Weymouth and the Shoal Bank which is between Alderney and Guernsey. This gave a 60nm x 60nm or a massive 3,600 square Nautical miles to explore.

It was not easy getting wreck marks. These were obtained by purchasing them from the Hydrographic Department in Taunton and it was an expensive but essential outlay. The co-ordinates were often very inaccurate and so a good deal of time went into pin-pointing the wreck and recording the accurate numbers in the boat's 'Black Book'. It was no wonder these wrecks were often guarded and stories of charter boats leaving a wreck if they saw another vessel approaching in the distance are true. Nowadays the plotters are extremely sophisticated and many wrecks are already available on them with a remarkable degree of accuracy. The hard work that went into confirming those wrecks is no longer required and the unspoken code of never intruding on a wreck if a boat was already there working it or asking a skipper than you didn't know well for some wreck marks just didn't happen back then.

Chris and I had been the only two vessels out of Weymouth regularly wreck fishing and we were able to 'farm' the wrecks by going to each one just once or twice a month. It's not uncommon in recent years to see anything up to 4 or 5 vessels working a single wreck and having to line up to take turns on the drift.

Apart from all the wrecks, there were masses of reef marks to explore such as the so-called 'French Banks' well off to the East-Northeast of Alderney with fantastic pollack and cod fishing and the very productive reef on the northern edge of the Hurd Deep north of The Casquetes where we could pretty well guarantee seeing basking sharks in large numbers. Even fairly recently, the Weymouth boats started using a 'recently' discovered reef north of Alderney that on a certain state of ebb tide allows the drift to go straight over two nearby pollack holding wrecks.

When I had the Offshore 105, I could not afford a winch. We used an Alderney anchor ring at the time. With the anchor and chain balanced dead right and a one way system invented to stop the Alderney anchor ring buoy from travelling back up the anchor rope, hauling became fairly easy and was certainly a way for us to keep fit. But with the Lochin came a powerful winch system and a pot hauling arm which made anchor retrieval very easy.

Anchoring in the 120 metre depths of the Hurd Deep was a challenge but that's what made the job exciting. To take on this challenge I was using three coils of 220 metre rope plus a 20kg weight at the start of the anchor chain. The wreck we used was massive and thus presented a large target area to aim for but the tides there are complex as it does seem that the bottom layer of tide can be travelling in the opposite direction to the top layers. The boat would be anchored perfectly with the wreck behind in the ideal position but the lines were travelling back under the boat as if we were slipping back on the anchor. Many times I used to check and recheck the GPS numbers with the sounder put onto wide beam so I could see the wreck well behind us and we were certainly not moving. The anglers' lines were definitely being taken by a tide running on a reciprocal bearing to the surface layer flow.

One time Mr Ivan Wellington, newly sporting the title of Mr Portland, onboard and aiming to fish the Hurd Deep wreck at anchor for conger and ling. Ivan had put on a lengthy three hook trace and told me he wasn't going to fish 127 metres down for one scraggy eel. He intended to catch three at a time! And indeed he did. His rod would be bouncing about with eels already hooked but he knew when there were three and not just two eels on. I remember seeing the eels come blasting out of the surface first one, then two and then the third all lying there on the surface back behind the boat. Ivan did not really believe in 'playing' conger! But these eels were small. There must have been plenty on that wreck as I never managed to get a big eel out of it...only silly amounts of little ones.

Charter Boat Invasion of Alderney

By 1990 there were increasing amounts of Weymouth boats such as *Channel Chieftain,* Pat Carlin, *Tiger Lily*, Chris Caines, along with *Peace and Plenty*, Chris Tett, coming to Alderney to join Roger Bayzand, *Sundance,* from Lymington, Glen Cairns, *Valkyrie,* from Hayling Island and Colin Dukes, *Smuggler,* from Exmouth. It was much more fun with good friends coming over and a revelation meeting Roger Bayzand. He became a firm friend and we enjoyed 'working' together by sharing our knowledge gained by fishing two very different areas for the same species and at the same time. This allowed us to compare notes and slowly build up our understanding of the complexities of Alderney. It was a very exciting time. We never knew what new things we would discover and what unexplored, to us, at least, marks we would end up on.

The key to Alderney is gaining some understanding of the incredibly complex tides. It was a great day, for example, when we understood that on low water Alderney when the tide is still screaming at 6 knots on a South-southwest direction on the south side of Alderney, there would be a weak flowing North-northeast back eddy that would help us to reset our bass drifts without punching the maximum tide or which would even help us all the way back to the tide-deflecting Brimtides reef on the Northern-Eastern end of Alderney if it was time to go back into harbour.

The Brimtides rocks extend a fair way out to sea and are a dangerous obstruction to vessels. The most famous ship to fall victim here was the sailing ship Liverpool, the largest sailing ship in the world at that time, which ran in thick fog in February 1902. The cargo was salvaged before the wreck broke up leaving behind just a few solidified barrels of cement and a tangle of girders in the shallow, dangerous waters of this area.

Many discoveries were made by trial and error. One very rewarding discovery was made by Pat Carlin on *Wave Chieftain* who was fishing the north side of Alderney on the ebb tide and was drifting tight to the outside edge of Burhou and heading towards the now famous permanently submerged Speedy Rock. Pat's anglers were using live launce and he was telling me over the phone about the massive bass that were grabbing the eels and making unstoppable runs leading to snapped off traces. Grabbing one of the angler's rods in frustration, Pat had managed to play one of these enormous 'bass' to the side of the boat only to discover it was a tope. Thus the amazing tope fishing of Speedy Rock had been discovered...by accident! Those who came to Alderney throughout the 90's and well into the 21st Century will remember those insane tope fishing sessions when everyone of the boat would have a tope on at once and the amazing tangles we were able to achieve during the slack tide period when we were swinging around the anchor rope which was the prime time for the peak of the feeding frenzy.

Anglers who had time to look around at the surroundings will remember how close to the rocks we were. Those rocks made up the Island complex of Burhou with the low water revealing what was an extremely dangerous place. We learnt by cautiously working together that the area was alive with pollack and many of them were well into double figures. The best pollack that came aboard *Offshore Rebel II* from within metres of the rocky entrance into Burhou and the 'lagoon' known as the Little Nannels and which weighed just over 19lb.

At that time the British shore caught record was (and still is) 18lb 4oz caught from Chesil Beach in 1986. Burhou would be THE mark to break that record and anglers were allowed to fish there with permission at certain times of the year. I actually took the photo's when Charles Lowe caught that pollack from Chesil and remember how happy he was as it cheered him up on the day after he'd unexpectedly been made redundant from work. I wrote about these massive pollack in our local newspapers urging shore anglers to come to Alderney and arrange a trip onto Burhou but the only time I ever saw anyone on the Island was when we spied a young, naked couple boinging about on the rocks and they were definitely not pollacking in the way we pure-minded anglers think of the word.

Burhou is a rocky and dangerous area. When we were pollack fishing there and the tide was dropping, the remains of a large boiler block would start to show. This is all that what remains of HMS Viper, a *Viper*-class torpedo boat destroyer for the British Royal Navy in 1899 which was notable for being the first warship to use steam turbine propulsion.

Records show that on 3 August 1901 HMS *Viper* sailed from Portland to take part in annual fleet exercises. By early evening the mist had become fog and she slowed to 10 knots but in late afternoon, at 1730, found rocks all around and grounded losing her propellers, finally drifting broadside onto the rocks. By 18:45, with the engine room flooded and *Viper* heeling over, she was abandoned. The subsequent enquiry found that the commanding officer, Lieutenant William Speke, had failed to exercise proper precautions while steaming in fog.

Over my the years at sea, I have noticed an improper lack of respect given to bananas, the 'R' word and a general 'poo pooing' by the landsman regarding so called superstitions at sea. Those disbelievers need to heed the extract from Naval records recording HMS Viper and another turbine-powered ship, HMS **Cobra**, both being lost to accidents in 1901 and that since then the Royal Navy has not used snake names for destroyers.

There's plenty of fascinating information about Alderney and the surrounding marks. Here's a short extract from the 1915 United States Hydrographic Department publication highlighting the dangers of The Nannels rocks which explains that *'they are always above water with the Great Nannel being 62 feet above high water and is near the southwestern part of the reef. The Little Nannel, the next in height, is only 16 feet above high water, and is at the northwestern end of the reef 200 yards distant from the Great Nannel. The end of the group is Pierre de But.: this rock covers near high water. The Boues de But, two sunken rocks having 9 feet over them, lie 70 yards eastward of the Pierre de But. The Cordonnier, a small rock drying 3 feet, lies 250 yards southward of the Great Nannel. The width between Burhou and the Nannels is just 400 yards wide; the Equet, a rock near the middle of the outer edge of the shoal ground extending northward from Burhou, and which dries 6 feet at low water, divides the passage into two channels through which the tide rushes into the Little Swinge with great velocity'.*

There are little snippets of information from many available sources which reveal Alderney to be such a fascinating place apart from the fishing! Running between the main Island of Alderney and the much smaller Island of Burhou is an area of very fast moving water which generates huge standing waves especially on the ebb-tide called The Swinge. Research shows that the etymology of the Swinge is probably Old Norse, relating to Old Icelandic meaning *swift* or *rapid.* Corbet Rock lies in the Swinge and is said to be named after the ancient Corbet family of the Channel Islands.

Information such as this must be of great comfort to people hanging on for dear life as their vessel careers madly through these extremely fast and dangerous waters.

The very popular old Citizen Band (CB) radio sets used had a much greater range that our VHF radios. In the 1980's we had them on the boats combined with a dedicated marine aerial along with an illegal 'booster' which gave massive range especially when we experienced the phenomenon termed 'skip'. This was when the CB signal could bounce off clouds and cover enormous distances...we even spoke to stations in the USA sometimes.

Some of us also had analogue 'mobile' phones on the boats by the very late 1980's. These phones looked like a proper phone and were held in the solid mounting of a proper 'phone station'. They didn't do text and you couldn't play stupid games on them or even take photographs...they were a proper phone. And again we had dedicated marine aerials for them and a clever gentleman in Somerset was able to boost their output to 25 watts as opposed to a measly 2.5 watts. He also managed to clone the sets so we were able to carry objects that looked like walkie-talkies around with us when we were in Alderney. Because the phones were analogue, the signals were strong and able to follow the curves of our planet so that we always had a perfectly clear signal and could hear each other wherever we were in the expanse of the English Channel. This meant that our inter- boat communications were excellent at all times. Those old 'mobiles' were expensive with the monthly bill never under £200 in 1987-1989 as compared with today's mobiles which are more like a quarter of that cost. This cost meant that only a relatively fortunate few people had these devices installed on their boats.

One day I watched a helicopter hovering over a patch of empty sea just north of the west bound shipping lanes whilst we were returning to Weymouth. My brother was flying helicopters in the Royal Navy back then and I asked him why that might be and his answer really surprised me. Apparently the pretty simple navigation systems on our charter boats were considerably better than the Navy's as regards accuracy on the shorter distances as we needed to be able to drop our anchors to within a couple of metres for successful wrecking. My brother suggested a possible reason was that the helicopter was hovering in a given position because, in theory, a RN ship was directly underneath him. The nearest Naval ship I could see was some way off.

 Shortly after that incident, the Hydrographic Survey ship was in the same area. So I called up the ship and asked them what they were doing. I was told they were surveying the area that I was in and would I like a little job? Over the radio they took my boat phone number and rang me up. We were about 30 miles out so there would be no way our useless mobile phones of today would be able to communicate but my old analogue system was perfect. I was told the ship had found a number of 'new' wrecks in that area and that they were currently stationed on top of one I was asked to come towards their position and check it and then for us to compare our Latitude and Longitude numbers. So that is what we did. As the ship pulled off, I came in close behind and there was the wreck. I noted the GPS numbers and gave the area a good look search and recorded any other targets.

Our telephone conversation then was extraordinary. Our GPS numbers were considerably different to those of the Hydrographic ship, so much so that we agreed to meet the next day and they would station their vessel over the co-ordinates they now had and I would put *Offshore Rebel* over the ones I had noted. On the following day we both took up our positions which in theory should have been identical but were not. We were a good half a mile away from the ship and sitting on top of the wreck! This resulted in me being given another 10 wreck marks to try and find because having found them once, the Hydrographic ship was unable to find them again as their navigation system was so awful.

I couldn't believe this or my luck. I shot off to the nearest wreck numbers but could not find anything and I realised that I would have to carry out a considerable and time consuming search pattern. It made me realise now why the wreck positions we paid for from the Hydrographic Department were no-where near where they were supposed to be.

I headed off into the Shipping Lanes to find Captain Tett on *Peace and Plenty*. I came alongside his vessel and handed over a scribbled paper copy of the 10 wreck positions I had been given and then explained all that had happened and that we had some searching to do over the next few months. I then headed southwards to the next wreck mark in the Hurd Deep and Chris steamed northwards back to Weymouth When I arrived in Alderney that evening we were met by police, drugs squad and sniffer dogs. My customers were taken off the boat one at a time and interrogated. The sniffer dogs were all over my boat and the Police growled at me when I offered them coffee. This search was carried out because French radar had picked up our two boats meeting mid –Channel …and this was way before Automatic Identification System or IS came in… and suspected that we were carrying out a drug exchange!

On his arrival back in Weymouth, *Peace and Plenty* had also been met in and subjected to the same treatment! Skipper Tett was not happy about this but the results of our subsequent wreck searches really paid off and made up for having to endure the drug searches. Several of those 'new' wrecks are still central to today's wrecking trips having been consistently productive over the years.

The early 90's was a very exciting period of discovery. Chris Tett and I had these two amazing Lochin 38's that gave us access to a vast area of sea to explore, good contact with the Hydrographic Department to help us find new wrecks and in Alderney an increasing number of vessels arriving bringing new friends and contacts working together to expand our knowledge of the Island's fishing areas. And for me, the installation of that analogue phone system meant that I was available for customers to contact for 100% of the time which was a massive boost to my chartering business.

To have a job that was you enjoyed so much that when you finally got your head down you were already looking forward to the next day was everything I'd hoped for. Yes, it was very demanding and often exhausting…..but the rewards and unpredictable adventures made it all more than worthwhile.

Tall – but true -Tales from the *Offshore Rebel II* Logbook

Working at sea is to live an unpredictable adventure where incidents take place that are often hard to believe. Here are a handful of 'Tall but true Tales' from the Offshore Rebel II Logbook.

Tall Tale 1.   *The Froggies in the Fog.*

Fog.

The Seafarer's nightmare.

Everywhere on the boat is damp. The windows are smeared on the outside and steamed up on the inside. Despite occasionally seeing the glow of the sun, it is chilly and dank….and, without the sight of land to focus on, it seems to take forever to travel across the sea to the chosen offshore wreck mark and even longer to return to port.

It means a day glued to the radar and watching the plotter for the skipper and for keeping the fingers firmly crossed that the boat doesn't run over something like rope or netting with all the awful consequences this can bring. It tests out your hearing to the utmost and soon exposes any weaknesses in one's sense of direction. It is a day to be highly alert.

In the June of 1992, we were 20 miles or so south-west of Portland Bill. *Offshore Rebel II* was anchored nicely to a wreck in 60 metres and flat calm conditions…the sort of conditions that allow sounds of other vessels to be heard miles away.

We were catching a steady run of conger. We were on the flood tide so the bow of the boat was pointing to the west. I was in and out of my wheelhouse keeping an eye on the radar screen for any new targets; my crewman, Ian (he took over Park Street Tackle in

Weymouth for several years), was on deck unhooking the conger as they came to the boat.

The past couple of seasons had been marked by the presence of the rogue French trawler the *Chrystal Nathalie* out of Cherbourg. Despite the best efforts of both charter boat and UK commercial fishing vessel skippers up and down the Channel, the skipper of French boat refused all attempts at radio communications. He had been causing many problems by trawling up static nets, strings of crab pots and even charter boat anchors! The French skipper would aim straight at an anchored vessel and then cut across its bow allowing his trawl to snag into the anchor and tow the anchored boat away!

This sounds far-fetched. Surely no professional skipper would deliberately do this to another vessel...but, as many will testify, this is exactly what was occurring in the English Channel in the early 90's. It's no wonder Anglo-French seafarers' relations are fractious!

In the mid-afternoon I heard a boat approaching far off to port but in the very thick fog could see nothing. I had the vessel on radar now heading straight at us but showing nearly 3 miles away to the south. It kept coming straight towards us and the distance was narrowing. It had to be the *Crystal Natalie*. I started our engines and warned everyone what might happen and that there might be a need to 'reel in quick'. Standing on the bow of the *Rebel,* I waited to see what would happen. Sure enough it was the rogue trawler. She cut across our bows, veered westwards into the fog but did not pick up my anchor. All was well. The anglers on-board looked at me in complete disbelief and bewilderment.

We carried on fishing.

Clearly unhappy about his lack of success in dragging us away, the *Crystal Nathalie* made a big circle in the fog and headed straight back at us. This time I said nothing to the lads but prepared my anchor rope for a quick release by attaching several large buoys to the end of the anchor rope and made ready to throw the lot overboard if needed. My engines were turned back on. I was back on the bow with an anti-collision flare (not that it would have been much good in the fog) and I had notified Portland Coastguard as to what was occurring and asked them to try and communicate with the French trawler. I also put out a call just in case there was any Fishery Protection vessel around.

Out of the fog came the *Crystal Nathalie*, clanking and banging as only a large trawler can, heading straight at me. Again it veered across my bow but very close this time and turned to the west. I looked at the French skipper who was leaning out of his wheelhouse and leering at me. He wanted trouble.

This time, he was successful as my anglers started yelling at me to 'slow down, skipper' as they had congers on. Anglers and skippers often inhabit totally different worlds and this was a great example of my chaps not having a clue what was going on!

I explained we were now 'under tow' by the French trawler that they could not see ahead of us in the fog and to stop mucking about and get their eels which were now bouncing along the surface in as we were dragged away at 4 knots. Meanwhile I put *Offshore Rebel* into gentle reverse to make life a bit trickier for the trawler. Once the conger were all released and the lads were shouting at me as to what was going on, I released the anchor warp and buoys and then raced towards the bows of the *Crystal Nathalie* aiming to try and slow her down.

Surprisingly she did slow and then heaved up the trawl along with my anchor. This was a ridiculous waste of fishing time for the trawler and no-one was more surprised than me when the net came up with my anchor in it and the French crew untangled it and let it drop…. I was convinced they'd just cut my anchor warp and I'd lose everything.

We retrieved my anchor and buoys. Attempts to communicate with the vessel failed so we headed back to Weymouth with all of us amazed at what had occurred. I gave a detailed report to Portland Coastguard who forwarded it to Fisheries and to the French Coastguard at Cherbourg. We all knew what the outcome would be…..nothing!

Tall Tale 2.   To 'Bob' or to 'Weave'….that is the question.

The next day I was due to leave on a 5 day trip to Alderney. After I passed my details to Portland they though it would be jolly humorous to talk to me in a silly French accent reminiscent of 'Allo 'Allo and 'oped wee wud 'ave a gud weeek in Ol-der-ney'.

I headed out to a big wreck just 20 miles south of Weymouth where we intended to start our Channel Island trip with a conger session. We fished the flood tide down and then it was time to head off further south to a mid-channel wreck ready for the ebb tide and the chance of some pollack. The anglers were relaxing and chatting as my winch pulled in the anchor in when suddenly one of the lads yelled out...."Whale!" as a very short distance in front of us was an enormous spout of water hurtling upwards. Before I'd registered the first explosion, another excited shout pointed to a massive crash into the sea behind us with the shout of,"It's a plane. It's crashed!"

And then came the sound from the first explosion mingling with the second and we were shrouded in smoke. The third explosion took place at the starboard side of us and this time I could see the shell dropping out of the sky and into the sea as I tried to get the anchor in. I was pretty convinced the next one would land right on top of us but I didn't want to do something stupid like heading off at speed as I would surely wrap the anchor warp round my exposed propellers.

The anchor surfaced and by now we were completely enveloped in smoke with me expecting fourth shell to land on top of us.

I called up Portland Coastguard and explained what was happening. They clearly did not believe me. It took an excited voice from *Condor 9* which was returning to Weymouth from Guernsey to break in on the conversation and verify what was happening with a final conviction coinciding with the last explosion that *Offshore Rebel* had definitely been hit.

Tiger Lily with Chris Caines and *Channel Chieftain* skippered by Pat Carlin were also closing in on my position and added to the general melee on the radio. I managed to break in on the conversation and asked Portland to contact Fost (Flag Officer

Training Organisation) Ops and tell them to stop firing but Portland replied that there was 'no firing in our area' for today!!

I notified Portland Coastguard that I was going to break out of the smoke and that I would take a Southerly bearing and go as fast as I could to get out of the shelling zone. I asked if they could offer me any advice.

Remember that the day before saw me having that run-in with the French Trawler, *Crystal Nathalie*, and that in the morning Coastguard had bade me farewell in a jolly bad French accent that they thought was hysterically amusing.

And now....when I needed a quiet and reassuring voice against the escalating panic on the radio from my colleagues who still could not see me through the smoke and the general air of panic on my boat...I am 'advised', in an even more dreadful 'Allo Allo' French accent that I should 'Bob and Weave'.

'Bob' and friggin' 'Weave'!! Great Advice!

We hurtled out of the smoke and didn't look back...hoping that another salvo wasn't coming our way. *Condor 9* took a sharp turn to westwards; *Tiger Lily* and *Channel Chieftain* headed east and we were pointed towards the French coast and travelling at 20+ knots which made the steering heavy and 'bobbing and weaving' difficult.

I felt no further inclination to converse on the radio and left the ensuing VHF chatter to my friends.

Back then I was writing my weekly angling page for the Dorset Echo. I rang them up and told them my story. I did this because I was so angry that the Navy denied all knowledge of any live gunnery firing that day. We hear about mysterious disappearances of vessels at sea and this could have been just such an incident. If we had been hit...and it was VERY close and not the 200 yards that the Navy said....how could they know anyway as they denied any firing...we would have just disappeared and become an unfortunate but soon forgotten statistic.

I maintained radio and telephone silence for the rest of the week whilst we were in Alderney until Chris Caines finally got through to me later in the week and announced in that way of his...'You B***ard.....you left us to deal with all this. We've had the BBC and

ITV camera crews round our houses and every National newspaper contacting me and Paddy for interviews because you've disappeared into friggin' Alderney'.

The Dorset Echo had run my story the next day complete with front page photo of *Offshore Rebel* and me with a particularly glamorous young lady on the bow...which is the reason I am sure the major National papers picked up on the story.

The story rumbled on over the next few weeks and *Offshore Rebel* reach the peak of her notoriety by featuring in the Sun's daily cartoon....now framed and hanging in my house as a much a prized possession.

Friends in the Royal Navy and stationed at Portland told me that *HMS Southampton*, the ship in question was regarded as a 'bad luck ship' and that when the ship and crew returned to Portland and other ports they were greeted in the mess by the other Navy crews with shouts of 'Incoming' and everyone diving under the canteen tables for shelter.

I can understand where that reputation came from as HMS Southampton's first successful attempt to sink something took place in 1984 when she ran over one of the enormous Shambles Bank Cardinal Buoys off Portland during the final Thursday War intended to prepare her to deploy to the Falklands. The collision sank the buoy and resulted in a period in dry dock for repair. Four years later in September 1988, HMS Southampton tried to sink a container ship called the MV Tor Bay by colliding with it whilst it was being escorted through the troublesome Straits of Hormuz.

It's only thanks to the Newspaper media records still being available that the initially denied incident described above is retained for all to read that in 1992 HMS Southampton let loose a live shell salvo onto the unsuspecting charter angling boat Offshore Rebel carrying 12 passengers and crew.

An official enquiry finally resulted in this announcement:

A 'LIMITATION' in a Royal Navy destroyer's radar system led to three fishing boats almost being blown out of the water, it was revealed last night. Three live shells fired from guns on HMS Southampton came within 200 yards of fishermen.

Last night defence chiefs admitted the limitation resulted in the vessels being 'invisible' to the destroyer.

The equipment on board HMS Southampton is installed on ships throughout the Naval fleet but an emergency safety code is to be introduced by the Navy to prevent a repeat of the shelling near Weymouth, Dorset, last June.

The findings of a top-level inquiry were revealed last night by Archie Hamilton, the Armed Forces Minister, in a letter to Ian Bruce, the MP for South Dorset.

He concluded: 'However, as all the safety procedures then in force were fully complied with, there are no grounds for taking disciplinary action against any of the personnel involved.'

Tall Tale 3.　　　　　　We've run out of locking wire.

Before the welcome arrival of braid to make our fishing easier, wire line was used. There was multi-braid and mono wire with opinions divided as to what was best. Wire allowed us to fish in stronger tides than monofilament line would which tended to bow out and stretch in tide so that it was very difficult to feel or see a bite. The disadvantage with multi-braid wire was that it tended to fray and broken strands would stick out of the main body of the wire to dig deeply into unsuspecting thumbs when controlling the descent of a hefty fishing weight. The offending tiny piece of wire was also prone to breaking off leaving itself deep in the flesh and proving extremely difficult to dig back out with a hook or knife.

Mono strand wire had a habit of just parting for no reason. An angler would be happily fishing away when suddenly his taught wire line would come out of the sea towards him in springy coils and his tackle would be lost. Worse, it was prone to 'part' when a good fish was on.

And both wire lines were very expensive.

I was grateful then when 10 very heavy drums of mono wire line appeared on my boat one day with no hint as to which generous person had donated them. One drum would be enough to cater for several years of fishing and so I gave 9 of the drums to the other skippers and set about rewiring my reels which I loaned to people on certain ray fishing trips that always seem to work best when the tide was running hard.

Because of the incident with HMS Southampton it was announced that the Royal Navy would from now on be 'launching heliotropes'- helicopters to us – to make sure the area they intended firing their live shells into did not have any charter boats full of customers innocently enjoying a day 's fishing at sea.

Because of spending cuts (there's always spending cuts!) the Naval helicopters had their flying hours drastically reduced. But now, because of the incident involving me the helicopter pilots were to catch up on their hours during the exercises off Norway. My brother was telling me how excited his fellow pilots were and how everyone was looking forward to this getting back into the air.

About a month later, my brother had returned and I was having dinner with him. I asked how the trip to Norway went and he said it was a waste of time. On enquiring why he explained that the flight mechanics had removed all the locking wire on the various helicopter parts that needed it but then disaster...there were no coils of replacement locking wire in the ship's stores despite the manifesto showing there were 10 new drums available.

It was a mystery as to where the drums had gone but it meant the helicopters were all grounded for that exercise with nothing for the pilots and observers to do.

It was indeed a jinxed ship.

Fact is often funnier and less believable than fiction. I regarded myself as an Angling Reporter for the Dorset Echo. There is a big difference between a Feature Write and a reporter. My job, as I saw it, was to gather angling competition results that Angling Club secretaries would be kind enough to give me and maybe a story or two from the anglers involved. My main job was to insert conjunctions, namely 'and' and 'but' between the lists of names of the successful competitors along with the weights of their prize winning catch with sometimes an adventurous 'hopefully' inserted if I were to make some prediction for the angling future based on the results of the day. It was time consuming but pretty straight forward. This next 'Tall Tale' is a report as best I can recall it...and the recollection is vivid!

Tall Tale 4.   " It's alright….I've dealt with sheep."

We had left Alderney bound for Weymouth. The forecast was good. We were to anchor a wreck for a conger fishing session on an untried wreck just north of the Hurd Deep and south of the East going Shipping Lane. I'd just fired the anchor over and was waiting for the boat to settle when out comes a warning from the Coastguard of an 'Imminent Gale Warning'. I called a few skippers up and asked if they'd heard that warning and yes, much to general astonishment, there was a warning of winds rushing in from the west. Even during that short conversation, a very light breeze had become evident. The wind was due to come out of the Northwest and freshen to a 6 to 7...so, no big deal but not nice. I decided we would abandon our conger fishing and head for the shelter of

Portland and try anchoring again when we reached there….which was about a 35 mile run.

We had a large lady on board. I had never met her before and have never seen her again. I do not recall her name. She was with one of the anglers. As the winds freshened into a developing head sea, the lady started to complain of stomach cramps and nausea and insisted of being allowed to 'go below' and lay out in one of the bunks. I explained that this was not such a good idea as the bow of the boat was going to bear an increasing brunt of the increasing sea.

Anyhow…down she went and the groaning increased. I had at that time a crewman who was fairly well known for his unpredictable behaviour and who came from a small Somerset village called Radstock. He was down below offering comfort to the lady. I also noticed he had put the kettle on and was standing by with a tea-towel draped neatly over his right arm.

I ask you now to read this interchange under the following stage directions. The crewman had a very definite and pronounced Somersetian accent. The lady in question had a strong London accent. I, of course, had an increasingly bemused Dorsetian accent and the Coastguard started with their usual poor French accent when talking to me but which changed into an increasingly professionally agitated one.

"Skipper," says he from Somerset. "We have a problem."

"And what might that be?" I enquired.

"This 'ere fat bird b'aint just big. She'um preggars," continued our self-appointed Radstockian mid-wife.

"What!!!! How pregnant?" I ask.

"Ahhh…8 months and 'oi thinks the bab's a-coming….soon…as in now!"

"You're joking," I squeak.

"Ee F***ing ain't ain't!" yells the Maiden.

"Don't worry," shouts our crewman…standing there with kettle now steaming and T-Towel looking increasingly important, "I've dealt with sheep."

There was an exchange between Maiden and Crew at this time which I avoided by calling up the coastguard. The ensuing conversation is as accurate as I can recall it. Please forgive me; it's nothing to do with me!

"Portland Coastguard; *Offshore Rebel*."

"See-lonce. Casualty working. Call Back later," is the sharp retort from Coastguard although there was still a heavy French accent and emphasis on the word 'See-lonce' as in appropriate phonetic marine radio style.

"Portland Coastguard. *Offshore Rebel*. Apologies. I have a situation developing which could become serious," I humbly offer.

A dramatic pause.

"*Offshore Rebel*. Pass your message."

"Roger, Coastguard. I have a heavily pregnant lady on board. My crewman believes she is very likely to go into labour. We have a North-west strong wind warning and I am now 35 miles from Weymouth with a head sea developing," says I.

"*Offshore Rebel*. Give us your Latitude and Longitude, please and Wait One." The French accent had diminished and I detected a hint of urgency.

A few moments later coastguard explain that they have been in contact with Coastguard Helicopter Rescue and they suggest coming out to meet me and air-lifting the lady off. I explain that I really don't think that is necessary at the moment and that it will be difficult to maintain the speed they will require heading into this ever increasing sea. My call was to establish contact and forewarn them of the developing situation.

A yell from down below from the crew, "Yeah....launch the helicopter."

Coastguard: "There seems to be some disagreement. Who is that calling for the helicopter?"

"Portland Coastguard...that is my crewman. He is standing by with hot water and a towel and tells me he has dealt with sheep. I think it best to ignore him."

A pause.

"Offshore Rebel. Portland Coastguard. We are concerned especially in the light of the request we are overhearing to launch the helicopter. Please clarify the situation".

It may be remembered that I worked in the East End of London as a teacher for five years and learnt that for many people from that part of our fair country it is impossible to string more than three words together without an 'Effing' being thrown into the mix.

"Don't 'effing launch that 'effing helicopter. I 'effing ain't going up in that 'effing thing!" shouts our mum-to-be.

"Launch it," retaliates that mischievous crewman. "Get the helicopter 'ere now".

My ever reliable analogue phone rang. "I think we need to continue this conversation by phone, Paul," says Colin, Coastguard colleague of mine. "Why does your crewman insist on the helicopter coming to assist?"

I explain that he, my friend the coastguard, really does not want to know the sad mind-set of my semi-insane crewman. I was politely asked to spell it out so a proper decision could be made in the knowledge that this was becoming a potentially serious situation.

"My crewman would like to know two things," I explain. "Firstly...if the lady is airlifted and she gives birth on the way up and the baby drops down....can babies Bungy-Jump at birth? Secondly, if the umbilical cord were to give way, would I be able to position the boat underneath fast enough for my crewman to be able to catch a slippery, moving target?"

Sometimes a lengthy period of professional silence can speak volumes and I was told later in ever increasing detail how the coastguard team reacted to my comments being relayed over the Station loudspeaker.

The helicopter was not sent to us but remained on alert. We crashed our way back towards Portland and the sea eased. We entered Weymouth Harbour and I was directed to come alongside the slipway which is by the Weymouth Rowing Club. There was an ambulance standing by as well as the inshore lifeboat, several lifeguard canoes and a police car. Nothing like a bit of drama!

The lady was whisked away and a boy was born that night in Dorchester Hospital. Apparently it was to be called Storm but I sincerely hope not for the little lad's sake!

Tall Tale 5   *Is it a canoe...or is it a yacht?*

I read many people saying that they were out on a charter boat in force 7, or 8 and even a 9! A gale force 8 is scary and a 9 is something to avoid. And if you are in a Storm Force 10 then you could be in deep trouble.

We left Alderney with a forecast indicating that we needed to get a move on. We had a southerly force four 4 to 5 which was the perfect direction to get us home to Weymouth very quickly. With that sort of forecast we would also expect to do some wreck fishing on the way. But, on this occasion, the forecast was for winds to 'soon' be veering to the west then north-west and increasing 7 to 8 and then NNW 9 possible storm 10. This was an unusually bad forecast for summertime but the key word was 'soon' giving us a 6 hour window. With a following sea and easily cruising at 18 knots we could expect to cover the 54 miles from Braye Harbour to Weymouth in 3 hours and be home for 11.00 am.

We set off with the start of the big spring flood tide helping to give us even more speed. We had travelled 20 miles out but already the wind had turned to the west and was increasing in strength very quickly. The flood tide was actually not now to our benefit as with its easterly going direction and the wind now coming out of the west we were heading towards home with a lot more easterly in our direction than I wanted.

I had with me my trusty Radstockian crewman, Troy, who was ex-military and had told me on a number of occasions that he had a 'sniper's eye' meaning he could see a man rolling up a Golden Virginia cigarette on a passing trawler 18 miles away.

Troy (remember him?) yelled out that there was what looked like a surf board off to starboard. I didn't want to go any further east but we were bound to just in case someone was miraculously hanging on to the 'surfboard'. This low lying white object turned out to be a dismasted yacht called the 'Eclat' from Weymouth and was quite a way off to our starboard. When we arrived the seas were becoming increasingly big with Atlantic rollers building. The yacht's mast had snapped with a full set of sails up. The sails and rigging were tangled under the yacht and around the rudder and prop. The VHF aerials and GPAS antennae were on top of the submerged mast so no radio or navigational aids. This was a yacht in trouble indeed. I needed to get up-wind to communicate with the yacht and tell them I could not take them under tow as it was far too dangerous and that I would call the Alderney Lifeboat and stay with them until the Lifeboat arrived.

It seemed like there was an 'elderly couple' (probably a lot younger than I am now!) and two children....although this turned out to be four children on-board the yacht.

Alderney had taken over a new lifeboat which was the very first Trent Class to be stationed on service and this was to be their first rescue. The Lifeboat 14-01 was called the Earl and Countess Mountbatten of Burma and stayed in Alderney until Replaced by 14-04, The Roy Barker 1, in 1995.

Waiting nearly two hours in a very rapidly freshening wind and increasing sea and being pushed ever further eastwards in the knowledge that a NW wind is going to be a very difficult head-sea situation. Once the lifeboat arrived, we were released from 'Standing By' and the lifeboat established a tow to take the yacht back to Alderney which by now as a long way to the SSW against the flood tide.

We headed towards St. Alban's Head. I tried to head more into the north west but it was not possible. My reasoning was by the time we were nearing St Alban's, the early ebb tide would be under way and help take us more into the west despite the wind.

The wind was now a strong force 8. The big swell had breaking rollers on their tops and these were thwacking into the port side of the boat making it difficult to maintain a straight heading. I was thinking that we will have to use St. Alban's Head and the coastline eastwards to Old Harry to offer us protection and go into Poole if necessary.

The change in sea-state from a Force 8 to 9 is very noticeable. Now the foam from the breakers riding the top of the swells was being whipped off in a horizontal manner so that it looked as though we were in a severe snow blizzard. We could see nothing except white sea all around us and that included the driving spray in the air. We couldn't even see the back of the boat from the wheelhouse. I was very lucky because my trusty crewman managed to point out every monster wave that was approaching us and doing a continuous knee bending series of exercises by hanging on to the boat's dashboard edge. His continuous shouts of 'Shamoolie (whatever that is!?) coming...brace!' thoughtfully kept me on a nerve-wracking edge.

We were still some 20 miles out to sea and now more like south east of Weymouth but the tide was starting to ease and I was able to at least now keep the boat headed towards the glimpses of land I could see. We managed to round come to the west of the St Alban's Race area and saw that our speed had risen back into double figures.

I called Portland Coastguard to tell them what was happening and they told me they had monitored the rescue and our slow progress was being tracked by several radars. They noted that I was attempting to line up for Weymouth but by now the Northwest Wind was bang on our nose and was slowly developing into a storm 10. Coastguard told me to remain on Channel 16 and they were going to contact me every 15 minutes from now on to check on our condition....so that shows how serious the sea state was becoming.

And what of my customers during this trial and my 10 year old son, Tom, who was with us on this trip? I was very fortunate that these customers were all very experienced sailors who had a good deal of experience of heavy weather sailing and were actually enjoying the experience. They were doing a very good job of keeping Tom safe as well....so I could not have asked for better men to be aboard. And they were in a small group of 6 which also helped.

From our position west of St. Alban's Head to Weymouth was now about 12 miles but it still took nearly two hours to reach port with conditions on a full blown NNW 10 by the time I entered the harbour mouth. I was drenched in sweat and hardly able to talk and in need of a good strong cup of tea!! The last 5 miles had been horrendous and that was with increasing shelter from the land. The Lochin handled the seas magnificently and it is no wonder the RNLI used the Lochin 33 for its Brede Class Lifeboats. I could have taken the easier route and run for Poole but as the boat was performing so well, I decided to maintain Weymouth as our destination.

Coastguards welcomed us back and said that they bet my customers were relieved. By now everyone was in the wheelhouse and shouting out...'No...we want to go back out and do it again!!'

It was now 1715. We had left Alderney at 0800 so we had endured a 9 hour 15 minute experience of ever increasing sea and wind intensity. Uncle Vic was waiting as I pulled in. I had the distinct feeling that a magnificent rollacking was about to occur but then word came through that Alderney Lifeboat had just arrived in Braye Harbour and the rescued family wanted to convey their thanks to us for finding them and standing by whilst co-ordinating the initial rescue. Two of the coastguard team had come to welcome us back and convey the message. Once Uncle Vic realised that we'd been part of this rescue, his attitude mellowed towards me.....a bit!

NB: Some superb photo's were taken by my crew of all this and one was enlarged to form the backdrop to the RNLI stand at Earls Court at the annual Boat Show A couple of the photo's were included in an RNLI book of Dangerous Rescues published about that time and we presented a framed photo of Alderney Lifeboat and the Casualty which stayed in the Alderney Lifeboat Station for many years.

Thank You to Lochin Marine for building the most amazing 'rough weather' boat ever!!

Politics ruin our Seafood Banquets.

In 1994 it was decided that the UK Commercial Fleet tonnage should be reduced in line with European directives. An effective way to do this would be to sacrifice a few unimportant charter boat commercial licences for the good of the cause by effectively devaluing them to the point of worthlessness. Commercial Licences are valued in terms of Units. The amount of Units are based on the working deck area of a vessel multiplied by the power of its engines. My Lochin, for example, had 500 HP's worth of engine power and a large deck area so the Licence Unit Value was very high. By removing my licence it could be shown that reduction of the Commercial Fleet was taking place but actually having with very little real effect on fishing effort as I sold such a tiny amount of fish.

There was short window of selling opportunity offered so that any such skipper had a month to either sell or end up with a worthless licence. Scottish Brokers were quickly involved buying up licences and amalgamating them into Licences of massive units…just right to sell to the large European Trawlers and Super-trawlers that now required them to operate. Convenient, eh?

This happened all around the country thus denying charter skippers holding such licences to make some small but very welcome income during the winter months by commercial fishing of some sort. I ent to the Fisheries Office in Poole in 1994 and pleaded my case explaining that right back to the 60's I was involved in winter trawling, spratting or even mackerel fishing and that now my winter bass fishing provided a major part of my reduced income for three months… so please could I keep my licence?

But it was no good. It was 'all out of the local fisheries control'. This was one of those mysterious and unexplained high level Government decisions and thus my licence was to be sold or made worthless; the choice was mine. I did at least manage to sell it to one of our local potters who was in the middle of having a new vessel built and had been caught unawares by this latest licensing development so that we didn't both lose out on all the commission and devaluation fees which found their way into Scottish Brokers' pockets or Government Accounts.

The worst thing about this episode was that it was crystal clear what was happening and the effect it would have on small charter boat operators and the fact that there was nothing we could do about it.

The immediate effect for anglers was that we could no longer legally sell part of our catch in Alderney to offset the cost of Channel Island trips. There is always an intermediary period when selling continues but somewhere like Alderney is a very small community and there were people keen to see visiting skippers kept to the new rules.

Looking back, it was a good thing that we could no longer sell our catches. There was a certain expectancy growing about 'refunds' on trips and there's always a few who wish to push the boundaries. One incident took place just before the Licence selling deadline came in when we had a good catch of bass in Alderney. Two anglers wanted to sell their catch and had tagged each of 'their' fish whereas the rest of the group had been practicing 'Catch and Release' keeping just a few over the week for home use. These two anglers argued over the price with the fishmonger in Alderney which was an extremely stupid thing to do. They told him they could get a much better price back in the UK so he told them to go and sell them there then as he would no longer purchase any fish from my boat from that moment on. Up to that point, I had always been able to access the ice-machine in Alderney which was a very important facility. That also stopped from that moment and we just happened to be very short of ice on that particular trip. . The incident resulted in me having to take the boat overnight to Guernsey to stock up with ice early morning at the Guernsey Fish Market which, unlike in Alderney, needed to be paid for. The 50 miles round trip plus the cost of the ice and the fact that our 4th Day in Alderney was now going to start late all added up to a value far in excess of the slight difference in price Alderney would and Weymouth **might** have paid.

My attempt to explain to those two anglers the consequences of their actions and that now all future Alderney trips were to be affected with no more fish selling or ice provided fell on deaf ears. I could see that they really couldn't give a toss about it.....and so that incident softened the blow of parting with my licence.

Apart from the winter bassing, the blonde ray fishing for our local Sea-Life Centre was a great way to keep earning in January and February. The Weymouth Sea-Life Centre provided the boat with two very large circular black tanks, pumps and small oxygen tanks. I was allowed to put a maximum of 5 rays in each tank and then bring them back to port where a fish transporter would be waiting for me. The Sea-life Centre paid £2 a 1lb for these rays and they had to be in perfect condition as they were firstly put into quarantine. If they died in quarantine then no payment!

My crewman, Troy, and I were able to go to sea at a moment's notice depending on the weather and we fished for the rays in some pretty wild and chilly weather. We would prop four rods up at the stern of the boat and sit in the wheelhouse smoking ourselves silly and drinking endless amounts of coffee. We took it in turns to deal with a fish bite and as it was often so unpleasant on deck compared to our cosy wheelhouse there were often disagreements as to whose turn it was to go and bring the fish in!

We didn't want little rays. The bigger the better....but the bigger rays became more easily stressed when the tide was running hard. We were told that if the edges of wings of the ray were pink then they had become stressed and we were to either return them immediately or unhook and tend to them very carefully with plenty of fresh seawater and regular infusions of oxygen. We became better at this and the ray survival rate improved. Our aim was to bring back 10 blonde rays of over 20lb each as this would pay us at least £400. This was considerably more than an an inshore charter day back then cost and so was a good way to make up for a few cancelled trips due to bad weather.

We managed to catch some excellent rays up to 35lb which was just 1lb 8oz off the British Record back then and I was really hoping we might break that record but it was not to be. I landed an undulate ray one day which we took back to the Sealife Centre. It was weighed before going into the Quarantine Tank and was just two ounces under the current record. Micky Quarm, who did so much for the Portland Angling Club, was in charge of the fish coming into the Centre at the time. I asked if we might weigh the ray again when it left quarantine….maybe then it would be a new record. Mick laughed his head off but agreed to do it. He rang me on the great day when the undulate was to be lifted out and sent on holiday to Scotland. When it was weighed it turned out to now be well under the record by a full 12 ounces having lost 10 ounces in quarantine. 'They do that,' laughed Mick.

The Weymouth Sealife Centre also gave me tickets which we could give to any anglers if they agreed to their ray being kept alive and donated to the Centre. I ran special Sea-life Centre Blonde Ray trips aimed at this and they were very popular as a family Ticket to a Sealife Centre valid for anywhere in the UK was worth a lot.

But, with the Commercial Licences sold, I could no longer offer this type of incentive to customers as even being rewarded with Family Tickets came under the heading of selling and was thus illegal.

The First and Last restaurant and *The Harbour Lights* in Alderney would often do a special deal for anglers. By bringing in fish such as turbot, brill and bass the Chefs of the afore mentioned eateries would conjure up the most amazing seafood banquets. Anglers had a price reduction because they provided the main ingredients but these occasions were all the more special because the lads knew they were eating what they had caught and that it would be cooked in such a way that would be difficult to reproduce at home. Sometimes we handed over much more fish than we could possibly eat and that would result in a free meal or an extra round of drinks. It was a great highlight of the week to look forward to.

The selling of the licences put a stop to all that. Whilst the restaurants were keen to carry on, we were very aware that there were those on the Island that would be happy to cause problems over this putting the Fisheries Department of the Island under pressure to prevent us taking our catches to the restaurants.

Rumours abounded at this time about there being a need for anglers to have a fishing licence to fish in Alderney waters. I haven't got a clue as to where that idea came from but there was scope for a wind-up here and it required those of a 'higher authority' to play their part.

We approached Alderney and I asked the lads who were on that trip to make sure they had completed the compulsory Customs Form, got their passport at the ready (instant muttering at this one; some anglers firmly believed they were needed and brought them along on the trips just in case but most, quite rightly, did not) and their 'Fishing Permits that they all knew they needed'.

Utter confusion. "Skip, we didn't know we needed them!"

"What!? You'll be telling me you haven't brought your passports next! Now stop mucking about, chaps, and get your documentation at the ready….just in case we are asked for it by the Harbour Authorities."

Aha…I sensed increasing concern developing on deck.

We pulled alongside the Alderney Harbour wall and the Alderney Harbour Master's Customs launch came alongside immediately. Dressed in full Harbour Authority regalia was the tall and commanding figure of one Mr Tim Hilditch.

"Customs form, please, skipper," requested Tim.

Forms having been duly filled in were passed over.

"Mooring fees, please. How many days?"

Money (£60 curses) was reluctantly passed over for the 4 nights stay.

"Passports," requested Tim.

A couple of lads including me produced them. Pandemonium from the others. "We didn't know we had to bring them," came the pathetic excuse.

Tim swung into action with plenty of stern warnings and reminders but decided in this instance to very kindly let the lads off….but that they must remember them in future.

This was all going to plan. In fact Tim was so convincing that I was actually believing it all. And then….

"Fishing Permits, please."

And now there was genuine anxiety with some of the customers telling the others that ,"we all knew about this and we should have got it sorted!"

Tim's performance excelled itself. He raged in a most professionally cool manner. It was most impressive. He told me off in sternest tones that I should have all this in hand and did I know what the next step was after ignoring the warnings on the last trip? He was good.....I was really believing all this myself now!

"Right. Confiscation. All tackle to be confiscated, as well you know. All of you to be in attendance at the Harbour Master's Office tomorrow morning where Fisheries will be in attendance. Fines issued and Permits to be purchased before tackle is returned."

Wow...scary stuff. The lads started to collect the fishing rods together and were looking very upset. I felt very sorry for them at this stage...but then, thankfully, Tim let up and burst into laughter accompanied by a number of locals who were hiding behind the first landing stage area of the Harbour Wall.

It WAS a superb and wonderfully acted wind-up and really got the lads (and me and it was my idea!!) going. After a calming down period it was decided that Tim's performance was so good that he should be invited along the next day to fish for turbot on the Shoal Bank with us. Tim had never been turbot fishing before and there is only one guess as to who caught the biggest turbot of the day! Tim went on to work for Jersey Coastguard where he still is to this day. It was his voice we have heard for many years reading out the forecasts on Jersey Radio.

1995 was the end of an era really. It did initially affect bookings and in some ports caused a marked reduction in income for a time. It did not really make much difference to our Weymouth Channel Island trips' bookings but what it did do was put an end to those marvellous seafood banquets made all the more special because of the 'eating what you'd caught' concept.

Plaice and Amstrads

The start of 1995 was all about the plaice on The Shambles Bank. They arrived at the very end of February and stayed until the end of March feeding on the little sandeels. We did not know that they then moved to the nearby mussel beds south and west of The Shambles back then or how to fish for them when they were there. That little secret was unlocked much later and by accident as so often happens. The Shambles, unlike the mussel beds, is an easy place to fish with very few obstructions so tackle loss was unusual.

The plaice were large with 4 pound fish regularly caught but also many more in the 5lb right up to a massive 8lb range. It gave the Weymouth charter boats an excellent early start to the season with anglers really enjoying this amazing fishing and particularly benefitted the slower boats that concentrated on the inshore fishing. Ken Leicester's big wooden vessel, the *Bon Wey* seemed made for the job. Whatever it was about that boat made it the top plaice catching boat on a regular basis. I remember being keen to just get into double figures of plaice and on doing so would call up Ken who would tell me his anglers had already landed over 40!

There seem to be more tackle permutations when fishing for flatfish than any other species. There were endless discussions about the colours and amount of the beads, the length and breaking strain of the trace, the all-important hook size and best make and whether single or pennel rigs were best especially as the ragworm/squid cocktails were getting ever bigger to attract the monster specimens that were turning up.

During the 1990's, I would be very concerned if I had even a single unbooked day in March with this month , in my view, offering the very best of the offshore pollacking and for about five years, the superb inshore plaice fishing on The Shambles Bank. On certain days it was possible to do wrecking and plaice fishing both by racing out to a wreck for the spring pollack and then returning at exactly the correct time the inshore plaice tide. I honestly believed that any free day in this prime fishing month meant I was not doing my job properly and I needed to work harder on the advertising.

Throughout the late 1980's and all of the 1990's, Pat Carlin, Chris Caines and I were churning out newsletters. It was a massive job. I tried to get every single customer to put their name and address in my book on the boat and tried to update it regularly but even so loads of newsletters were returned with 'Gone Away; Address Unknown' stamped on the envelopes.

We were using Amstrad Word Processors back then which gradually gave way to what must now be regarded as Steam Driven Computers......they were so slow...to create our newsletters which gradually improved with pictures, competitions and Special Offers.

I used to try and do two newsletters...One in November/December and one in January/February. It was an incredibly time consuming affair. We printed out our finalised Newsletters and took them to a Printers on Portland. There would be 3 x A4 sheets in my newsletters giving 6 pages to fill up with exciting, trip enticing drivel but the all-important thing was the 'Year's Fishing Programme' and 'Availability of Trips' sections.

I used to aim to send out 1,000 Newsletters and that involved a mountain of paperwork, envelopes and stamps and an enormous amount of time entering 1,000 ever changing customer addresses into the limited computer memory. Imagine the cost of 1,000 Second class stamps! Try folding your printed A4 sheets so that you created a little booklet to then stick into the envelopes. Thank the Lord, again, for Mr Chris Caines who had worked out how to make our basic computers print addresses onto sticky labels (I got that wrong....a lot of times!!). We also had 'return to sender' labels made by the printers to stick on the back of the envelopes.

I would try to 'do' 50 newsletters per day. This meant putting the actual newsletter into the envelope, sticking an address label on the front and the return label on the back and then dealing with the friggin' stamp. They were fiddly little things that could get stuck to your tongue and then the roof of your mouth, your lip and even the lower nose. It was a massively time consuming affair....and this went on for at least ten years until the computers improved enough to handle all this stuff.

Every evening during Newsletter Time involved a short walk to the local post box and the posting of 50 newsletters. After a few days the phone started to ring and there would follow many evenings of sitting by the ever ringing phone to try and accommodate everyone. Every day for 20 consecutive days another 50 newsletters would be dropped into that post-box to send on to my customers' doormats throughout the UK and then there would be, one hoped, the flurry of bookings. We were all also paying a fortune to advertise in magazines such as Sea Angler and of course, by the time customers responded to those adverts, the newsletters had gone out and it was too late.

I remember announcing that I was dropping my Sea Angler adverts because of the success of the Newsletters. This was considered an courageous move indeed and it was coupled with me changing the start of wreck fishing from 0600 to 0700 and reducing my trips for 12 to 11 hours! Surprisingly that caused quite a bit of disagreement amongst certain skippers but the anglers seemed all for it.

August was regarded as quiet month for chartering for some of the boats and so it was decided to try and create an event to attract people and thus the Weymouth Conger Festival was born in 1994...once again the Brainchild of Messrs Carlin and Caines. The new Weymouth event was structured in such a way as to be the opposite of the disastrous British Conger club competition which had been held in Weymouth for the first time the previous year, 1993, rather than in its usual venue of Plymouth. The rules of that BCC event were so limiting and obstructive that they succeeded in ensuring hardly anything was caught. Determined to show what Weymouth could do the new Conger Festival, still going strong after 25 years, put the emphasis on catching the best biggest eel. T

he Dorset Echo's Sea Angling page showed the results of that day which make very interesting reading. 76lb 3oz was the best conger in that first ever event as caught by Duncan Gregory from Oxford fishing on Chris Caines' *Tiger Lily* and second place went to an excellent 73lb 4oz specimen caught by Gary Chapman on Pat Carlin's *Channel Chieftain*. From that first two day, two boat event, the Festival has gone on to now include the majority of the Weymouth charter fleet plus vessels from other ports invited to join in on the action.

Andy Selby opened the Weymouth Angling Centre in a small property 'over the Town Bridge' and it rapidly became an outstanding success. Apart from the actual tackle and quality bait, Andy managed from the outset to employ a team of really good, keen local lads and lasses. Many youngsters, including my own sons, worked there in the school holidays and the Centre became more than just a tackle shop but an increasingly important part of our Weymouth angling community. Andy also worked hard to attract a lot of competition fishing into Weymouth and that contribution to the local angling scene is even more important now than it was 20 years ago. Events such as The Two Day Species Hunt, the various EFSA (European Federation of Sea Angler) multi-day events, The World Championships, The WIBAC (Weymouth International Boat Angling Competition) and the Conger Festival plus many more events made Weymouth into the UK's main International Competition Port.

This was not just all due to Andy Selby however. This was the period when a certain Mr Chris Caines was very much on the scene. His tireless efforts at uniting the port, coming up with ideas to benefit everyone and still having the time to come and assist individuals (he spent ages, for example, at my house helping me with my computer) in a whole range of ways cannot be over-stated. Chris is definitely the most missed person in the history of Weymouth....and probably...UK sea angling!

But it would be very short-sighted to miss out where so many of the ideas actually came from in the first place. It was Pat Carlin who had most of the brain-waves. Pat, Chris and I often joked that between the three of us, Pat would come out with the ideas and sit for hours with Chris discussing them. Pat has his own unique language and Chris was adept at interpreting it. Chris would then have a lengthy meeting me with and Pat, usually over dinner somewhere, and I would take notes and then write about it all in the various angling papers I was now connected with. It was a perfect and extremely productive friendship and I for one regard that as the highlight and best time of my Charter Skippering period.

I was also very fortunate during the Lochin period to be moored next to Mr Chris Tett for a number of years. This may come as a shock to those who have read this far! I am reminded of anglers telling me that they 'couldn't do right for doing wrong' when fishing with Chris and forever getting the regular bollockings of their lives when fishing aboard the *Peace and Plenty* and how many anglers were terrified of him!

Sometimes I would be moored up on the outside of Chris' boat. This meant that my customers had to run the gauntlet of crossing his Lochin onto mine. The early morning bollackings were epic. Too much tackle, the wrong tackle, wrong footwear, wrong this, incorrect that….it was hilarious. And these were MY customers…they weren't even going fishing with Chris. And Chris would often glare at me and tell me if I wasn't ready to go when he was, then he'd just chuck my ropes off and let me drift away (he never did!). And, if I was the inside boat and my anglers were already on-board and waiting for us to leave, Chris would still find time before casting his own vessel free to advise us all about how to fish that day but how generally useless we all were anyway so not to worry too much when we returned with far less fish than his chaps.

The most effective way to counteract all this was by the issuing of tea. When and if my customers had survived the inevitable tongue lashing they had received and managed to board my boat, I would ask them in the gentlest way what they would like to drink. And then, steaming cups of selected beverage in hand, we would watch as some poor unsuspecting wretch aboard *Peace and Plenty* dared to ask Captain Tett for a drink and then receive the most formidable bollacking of his life that put anything my chaps had endured to shame.

This is the time when that famous saying of "If you want fish, then go with Chris but if you want tea, then come with me!" I'm convinced that is why some groups deserted and changed ships over the years. This famous saying was later made permanent when Chris and I were having one of our compulsory MCA Boat Surveys. My survey had been completed and I had my usual list of minor defects to rectify (there HAS to be faults pointed out to justify the outrageous charge of the survey) and the surveyor moved on to Chris' boat.

Gas cookers are always a bone of contention. Having such apparatus means it must meet stringent standards of safety and be properly installed by a qualified and certified person. We needed to show our gas Certification safety certificates and demonstrate our gas alarm systems. Something had obviously not met with the surveyor's approval. There was a heated discussion going on and then a few hefty crashes and bangs and Chris' gas cooker flew out of the wheelhouse and into the harbour.

"That's sorted that out then," came the announcement!

It left me the undisputed Master of the Mug and confirmed that famous saying: 'If you want tea, you've GOT to come with me!'

I had a sense of Deju-Vu about the cooker hurling incident whilst relaxing in Alderney Harbour watching some rubbish on my TV when smoke started pouring out of the back of it. I ripped the TV from its mountings, pulling the wires free as I did so and rushed straight out of the wheelhouse and threw the smoking object overboard.

A crew of yachties on the buoy next to me were out on deck waiting for the Water Taxi to take them ashore. One of them shouted across:

"Didn't like that programme, then?"

Well...for a yachtie, I thought that was actually pretty funny!

By 1998, I admit to feeling the effects of the many trips and days at sea aboard the Lochin. There is no perfect small boat. The Lochin was a tank. I always felt it could and would go through anything especially after the wild trip back to Weymouth after the Yacht Eclat incident.

The Lochin had twin engines. There wasn't much space between the engine boxes and the gunnels. The deck was high and with the new 'One Metre from the deck to the top of the gunnel' rule, it meant that I had to have high safety rails. The Lochin rolled heavily, especially on a broadside drift. On one occasion, on the Adamant Bank in Weymouth Bay, we rolled sharply and one of the anglers, the very firmly constructed Geoff Knight of Dorset Police, was propelled from one side of the boat to the other. He hit the starboard side railing very hard and it hurt him. The railing snapped on one of the main supports and was now hanging on half overboard. This is not what we wanted.

I had received an offer to purchase the Lochin at exactly the same price that I had paid for it in 1990 and the prospective purchaser had said that if I agreed to sell it, I could keep it until the end of the 1998 season. I decided it was the time to make the decision and so a parting of the ways was finalised.

We boat owners get very attached to our vessels. The Lochin was my pride and joy. I thought it was an amazing boat but I used to return home totally knackered from rolling about all day and my shins and knees were often covered in bruises from propping myself up close to the very low gunnel.

The season was approaching its conclusion. I didn't have any idea what I could replace this amazing vessel with but I was committed to the sale.

I remember watching *Offshore Rebel II* leave Weymouth for the last time and thinking that was a huge part of me going….and having no clue what was going to happen next.

The *Offshore Rebel* Adventure seemed to overtaken me and left me at a temporary loss as to what the future held.

Offshore Rebel III 1999. Knife attack and Sacred Stones

In November 1998, *Offshore Rebel II* left Weymouth and turned East. I never saw the boat again except in photographs.

I had nothing lined up to replace the Lochin with but had arranged to purchase a 'Stand-In' vessel for the 1999 season and to give me the opportunity to have a good look around at what was on offer. In order to I free up funds for a deposit and build stage payments if I was able to buy a brand new boat, I needed a temporary vessel much cheaper than the Lochin. The last thing I wanted was a bridging loan with the continuing crazy interest rates.

One of the Weymouth Dive Boat skippers, Len Hurdis, offered me his Offshore 105 to buy. Len was one of those talented people who was particularly good at fabrication work and who had constructed a lot of the guard rails and dive hoists in Weymouth. He is one of those quiet, unruffled gentleman skippers who exuded an aura of calmness which is an excellent quality for a Dive Boat skipper to possess as I have discovered over the past three years!

Len's 105 arrived in Weymouth back in 1988, a year after mine was delivered from Rod Baker's Port Isaac Workboats in Wadebridge, Cornwall. . It was a heavier boat than mine had been with a substantial generator and a generally heftier fit-out. Speed was not so important for a dive boat as there was no need to go rushing from mark to mark as we angling skippers tend to do and in-between dives there would be a fairly lengthy 'surface interval' when Len and his good lady, Maggie, used to provide an array of hot meals facilitated by the generator, micro-wave and oven.

And...as I found out...Len's boat *Autumn Dream* was actually my *Offshore Rebel*! Len was ahead of me in the queue back in 1986 when we placed our orders but I'd made such a fuss because of the Press Commitments for the launch date and I had somehow got Rod Baker to agree to a penalty clause for late delivery that somehow I jumped the order position and poor Len had to wait another year for his boat. When Pat Carlin had shown me the photograph of six big blue cans of resin in the spring of 1987 and told me that was my boat he hadn't been joking! Len never told me any of this until I'd actually bought his boat.

And so there we were….12 years later……and I finally got the Offshore 105 I had ordered!

There are still a number of Offshore 105's about and, from a business point of view, they are excellent. Smaller and with a single engine, all the outgoing expenses are considerably less than the twin-engined larger boats we have progressed to. In their day they were THE boat to operate but the need for bigger, faster boats and then the arrival of Catamarans left the 105 behind in many ports.

The 1999 season began and I was fully booked. This was going to be a test for the boat and how my customers would react to it. I kept explaining that this was a temporary measure and the usual response was that 'it better had be!' The 105 was a good deal smaller than the Lochin and very slow, much slower than my original 105. We seemed to be chugging about in the 10 to 12 knots range. It meant that trips had to be planned around the tides and fishing the Alderney Race and South Banks was definitely out of the question.

This meant that more time searching for potential bass marks that were not in the main tide runs became necessary and those searches turned up all sorts of marks in areas that I'd never previously considered. The Alderney South Banks always seemed to need 3.7 knots before the bass started feeding and we'd often still be there at over 5 knots. The new marks I was finding were producing bass at 2 knots and less with some marks fishing best at dead slack tide. This all became very useful in later years giving many more options. It also meant that I spent a lot more time fishing for turbot in that season and exploring the Casquets Banks plus the back eddies of the South Banks with unexpectedly good results.

The South Banks in particular were very productive from areas just metres away from where I'd previously fished in screaming tide. Here we were right on the edge of the tide and starting to drift in an opposite direction to the main ebb and we were catching bass and pollack plus good amounts of brill. This particular bank in question often used to have a lot of Longlines laid across it by the Guernsey commercial boats so there had to be a few fish there.

We also concentrated on the inshore pollack which I'd increasingly ignored with the Lochin. The Pommier Banks to the west of Ortac was an extremely productive mark. I remember a trip with the Bath based Gannet SAC, that on just one gentle ebb drift across the Pommier Bank and heading slowly towards the Casquets lighthouse, the lads caught over 100 pollack using lures and live eels. The Gannets SAC were a very easy group to please. Their main aim in coming to Alderney was to be as close to Ortac as possible so that they could watch the Gannets close up…they loved seeing those birds, the namesake of their club. And they loved pollack fishing….

In-between the fishing trips, the search continued for a permanent replacement for the Lochin. *Find-a-Fishing Boat* became daily reading as did pestering fellow skippers for their recommendations. A trip to Kinsale in Ireland with Pat Carlin resulted in him purchasing *Cara Cara*, a 43' Aquastar which is still going strong today and which my son Tom is skippering. The Aquastar is a fine vessel with very high gunnels offering a great sense of security which I thought customers would appreciate. Our next boat searching trip, which also involved Chris Caines along with Pat Carlin and several other skipper colleagues, saw us travel to the West Country to view a very well known Aquastar that had just come onto the market. I liked that boat very much and asked the skipper to create some wash on what was a very calm day and then put us broadside to it to see how stable the boat was. Just as the boat lay broadside to its own generated wash which was about to hit us, the skipper nudged the boat to port so that the waves hit us on the starboard quarter and the sting of the potential roll was negated. Just that one tiny action made me realise the Aquastar was not the vessel I was looking for.

Glen Cairns in Hayling had a very impressive vessel called a Revenge. They were big, beamy boats and this looked like it could be the one. We drove into a head sea and it was like driving a big

105. It was a hard slammy ride…..nowhere near as comfortable as the Lochin. I was thinking that I had made a terrible mistake selling the Lochin as there seemed nothing better to replace it.

Then a message came through from Roger Bayzand to come and have a ride in one of the new 32' South Boats designed by Clive Jefferies and currently being made on the Isle of Wight. Clive had plans to extend the mould to make a 36 foot craft.

Chris Tett and I met up with Roger and Clive at Yarmouth for the test ride aboard John Kennet's 32' potter powered by twin x 120HP engines in early June 1999 . Every boat handles well in calm sea and we wanted a blustery day for our test run and so we arrived with a nice brisk south-easterly 5 to 6. The first thing to impress anyone getting onto a Catamaran is how much deck room there is and then how stable they immediately feel. We walked from one side to the other. Nothing. No movement at all. Not even the slightest hint of a list. Clive edged the South Boat out into the Solent and did the usual down-tide, down-wind run so that we could see experience the boat's speed and handling qualities in a following sea and how it felt in general. After a lifetime on mono-hulls this was such a different feeling. There was no side to side movement but more of a porpoising movement bow to stern. It was very strange and I found it hard to keep my balance.

And now it was time for the real test. Clive turned the boat into the wind and a substantially choppy to moderate sea. He took the boat up to 16 knots and at that speed the boat was performing at its best. The concept of the twin hulls generating a 'bed of foam' upon which the vessel would ride was brilliant making the ride soft and cushioned. We three skippers were amazed and with that exaggerated bow to stern movement rather than the corkscrewing effect I was expecting, I tumbled backwards out of the wheelhouse and knew as I hit the deck that THIS was the boat to have.

We then lay broadside to an increasing sea and that is when the South Boat really amazes as it rode the seas with no trouble at all. This is, to me, always the outstanding characteristic of the South Boat Cat….the fact that anglers could all be positioned on one side fishing on the drift in a broadside sea and be able to balance with ease. In fact, when seas became heavier, the boat still didn't 'rock' in the way we expected but became like a breakwater with the sea hitting the hull hard and being thrown over the boat. There's a tell-tale hiss that those particular foam throwing waves makes before it hits the broadside hull. To the trained ear of the skipper spending many hours at sea on drifts, that individual noise is a warning which allows the skipper to nonchalantly saunter into his wheelhouse just as the wave hits and drenches most everyone. There are slight variations in an approaching wave's noise that indicate that it will divide upon impact sending spray in two different directions leaving a small spray less gap in the middle. The trained skipper could stand in that gap, looking wisely out to sea in an untroubled, professional manner as anglers either side of him would be totally drenched and he would remain completely dry.

By the time we pulled back into Yarmouth Harbour and disembarked we three had made up our minds. On the way back to Weymouth, Chris Tett smirked at me and told me in his all-knowing way that he'd put a deposit down on the soon to be made 36 foot version of the boat. His air of smugness trembled slightly when I replied that so had I. It appeared from our timings that my deposit had been agreed about 15 minutes prior to his. Roger meanwhile had committed himself to the 32 foot version.

If all went to plan, that would mean that *Offshore Rebel IV* would be the very first of its kind and be ready for the New 21st Century. I still believed that the boat was THE most important attraction for anglers, especially when very lengthy wrecking and cross-Channel trips are the norm. I was always aware of how much better Chris Tett was at 'finding' the fish than me and I needed to try and keep up with him by offering different things...having THE boat for the modern era and the very first one of its type (the larger 36 foot version) gave me the advertising hook I wanted.

As Roger Bayzand still says, we were very lucky to get the boats when we did as a waiting list soon built up and the delivery dates were getting later as is so often the case with boats. Also, the prices rocketed even by hulls 3 and 4. But my hull was made on time and we went to Cowes, Isle of Wight, where the boats were being constructed in Chris Tetts' Lochin to tow the hull back to Portland Harbour where it was installed in a monstrous shed ready for the winter fit-out which Chris was going to do.

In the summer of 1999, I was sent a steady stream of young lads from a Government scheme who were possibly interested in working at sea. They were generally useless but two of them have remained firmly in my memory and they were both called Matthew.

Matthew Number 1 was a small, aggressive little bugger. He couldn't work out that being foul-mouthed to a large angler would result in him getting a slap. He would start squeaking that a slap 'wasn't allowed' and he was going to 'report him'. This was a boy who'd obviously got the wrong idea from his Bristol School where gobbing off at teachers must have been common and gone unpunished. I recall dragging him into the cabin and explaining that he was going to get a battering off one of these chaps soon unless he learn to control his mouth.

We were catching a lot of pollack on light tackle in Burhou, Alderney, one evening and Matthew asked if he could have a go. Yes, I said he could have 30 minutes but then back to work as quite a few of the pollack were big enough to keep and needed to be gutted etc.

After his 30 minutes was up in which he caught a lot of fish, I told him it was time to get to stop fishing and get to work. He of course refused. A couple more polite requests and then I removed his rod from him and left him cursing and raging on deck much to the amusement of the anglers. But the red mist descended on Matthew and he approached the wheelhouse brandishing a filleting knife and told me he was going to stab me. Charming!

I was in the wheelhouse and giving it a little sweep with my trusty boat broom. Matthew was foaming and ranting just outside the wheelhouse door. The lads were looking on with a mixture of amusement and concern as the boy was clearing intent on carrying out his threat.

But a nice long handled broom can deposit its brush section to an angry young hothead with a fair degree of force. Matthew buckled to his knees but kept waving the knife around and threatening me….so another whack on the bounce was called for. And, to his credit, now nearly flat on the floor, he still kept threatening me and lifted his knife one more time until the final blow convinced him to shut up.

A severe sulk then developed and the lads had to sort their own fish out as I took us back across the ever-manic flood tide Swinge into Braye Harbour. That night my current crewman, the truly gigantic but very gentle Ken, took Matthew out on the piss. The lad was only 16 years old but Ken and the anglers got him completely wrecked. I was waiting for the water taxi to take me back out to the boat for the night when Matthew came bounding along the pontoon and didn't realise that pontoons came to an end. He kept going and Ken somehow managed to catch him up and grab him by the scruff of his neck with his little legs still in running action and hold him inches above the sea. The Water Taxi sped in and Matthew was dumped into it still squealing that 'this wasn't allowed' and that he was 'going to tell'.

We carried him onto the boat. Put a cushion out on deck and left him out there for the night. In the morning, as we were coming alongside the harbour wall, he managed to crawl into the wheelhouse and up to his bunk and I never saw him again….as in ever! When we arrived back in Weymouth after a day wrecking across the Channel, I took the lads up the road to get their cars and when I had returned, Matthew had gone. Ken explained that Matthew had managed to crawl out of the bunk and fallen off the boat onto the pontoon, thrown up all over the place and then, still pissed, staggered off still threatening 'to tell'. The silly boy didn't even remember to take his possessions…or his tip…which had probably been given for his entertainment value.

On August 11th 1999 we were treated to the Total Eclipse phenomenon. Most of us had managed to book our boats out to keen astronomers for considerably more than anglers are charged! I had another young trainee crewboy, again named Matthew. I also had Ian Harrington as main crew. Ian was running the Anglers

Tackle Store in Park Street at the time. If anyone ever thinks I am sarcastic then they would soon reel in admiration at Ian's dizzyingly torrent of abuse that put any claims I might have of such a talent to total shame.

Mathew came from Portland. His Mama was a Druid. Matthew was a clever little boy who was remarkably round. He knew a lot about Astronomy. In fact he was the perfect crew to have on the boat for this particular trip as he talked at great length and entertained the passengers with what was a well-researched depth of knowledge about the Universe.

I was trying to find a gap in the clouds so we could watch this eclipse. Myself and Pat Carlin travelled further and further to the south-east chasing a gap in the clouds through which the sun shone merrily but which kept moving ahead of us. The passengers were grizzling about how long it was taking to 'get there' and I'd briefed Matthew on giving the customers some drivel about Astronomical Angles and other such nonsense and that I needed to be at a certain GPS position to be in the best possible position for the observation to take place.

It was nearing the 11 o'clock magic hour, the time of the eclipse and so I eased down. "The gap in the cloud is over there, Skipper," explains some Boffin type pointing to a single ray of sunshine about 10 miles away. Yes, well...we had to stop else we would just go on for ever and miss the majestic moment.

Matthew had taken a small canvas bag out onto the deck and had carefully laid out what he explained were 'sacred Druid Stones' in a mystical arrangement on the engine box. He was holding forth about it all and the customers were really paying attention to this young and very knowledgeable Sir Patrick Moore.

The sky started to darken. The seagulls went strangely silent. The sun started to blacken as the moon slid into position. Total Darkness. No sounds. A very calm sea. Even the customers were silent.

The magical moment passed and the sky lightened a fraction. The boat rolled ever so slightly. The mystical Druid Stones rolled off the engine box onto the deck. Ian, he of the heftily sarcastic tongue, emerged from the wheelhouse with glasses (plastic!) of Champagne we were providing to toast the majestic moment and stood on the rolling stones, slipped, threw the Champagne everywhere and yelled...in his best Brummie accent as he fell:

"Who the f***ing Hell put these F***ing stones on the f***ing deck!!"

And, gathering them up, hurled them into the sea with a barrage of menacing insults as he turned to face the horrified customers and the now white-faced, mortified young Matthew who'd just witnessed seeing his most treasured pebbles hurting into the briny by a Wildman of Birmingham.

Matthew started to cry. And he really did cry. He was heartbroken. I took him into the wheelhouse and propped him up on the floor against the fire-extinguisher so he had some company. Matthew started crying at 11.15 on that memorable day and did not stop until we arrived back in Weymouth, six and three –quarter hours later at 1800 ...having fished a couple of wrecks on the way home.

If you can recall that scene in that famous movie, *Alien,* where Sigourney (Ripley) Weaver sees the Alien for the first time and we are all treated to a monster which seems to have an endless supply of water in its body to generate torrents of saliva that pour out its ever-open mouth plus from every other facial orifice, then that was Matthew. I have never seen so much saliva pour forth from a small boy and any attempt at consoling him provoked another deluge. By the time we tied up in Weymouth, with his Mama bouncing all over the pontoon in excited anticipation at seeing her lad after his wonderful trip at sea, Matthew was soaked with streaks of foam all over his upper body and looked exhausted with his eyes reddened and bulging behind his specs. It was a wonder he didn't pass out from dehydration.

We helped him off the boat into the worried arms of his Mum who was then treated to another harsh broadside from our still deeply pissed off crewman who explained that her darling son looked like he now did, a ball of dribbling saliva, because he'd been so overcome with the excitement and emotion of the Eclipse experience.

I never saw that Matthew again either and I wasn't asked to fill in a Government Report form for him.

Our conclusion on that trip and the miles we travelled made us realise we could provide equally fascinating Astronomy Excursions within the confines of Portland Harbour. All we needed was 12 black bags with some sticky glowing stars stuck on the inside that we could ask the customers to put over their heads at the appointed hour for exactly the same effect…and we could offer these trips on any day of the week. Sadly that idea didn't take off.

What was it about the starter motors that Iveco attached to their 8.2 litre engines? We were on a local bassing trip in September and the fishing had been OK. We were on our final drift before time to return to Weymouth. I had a team of Essex anglers on-board and some of them thought they were quite good at bassing.

Last drift over and I went to start up. Clunk! That horrible sound a starter motor makes when it really doesn't want to work anymore. A couple more attempts and nothing. Time to open the engine box and apply the trusty hammer to the side of the starter motor with some skilled customer pressing the start button at the same time. Nothing!

It was the ending of the ebb tide and we were by the West Shambles buoy so no real worries as there were plenty of my skipper chums nearby. I put out a call. Richard English in Loan Shark was on his way back from a mark to the west of Portland. Not only did he offer to tow me back but he told me that he had a spare starter motor at home that I could fit in time for my 4 day Alderney trip the next day.

In the meantime, I was informed we had a Garage Owner on the boat who could have a go at fixing the starter motor. I told him not to bother. We have a tow in hand and a spare starter to fit when we got in. But no….the Essex Team swung into action and Whiskers, the mechanical wizard, was down into the engine bay detaching and then dismantling the offending motor. He announced that I would get one chance and one chance only for this to work.

He wired it up and then immediately started shouting at me to turn the engine and the electrics off. Neither were on as I was on deck watching the expert at work. He'd wired it up wrong...red and black the wrong way. We had the start of a fire. The fire travelled along the oil soaked loom under the engine and right into the cabin hold where the generator was mounted. It was quite a fire in such a short time and I had sprayed powder all over the place from the fire-extinguisher to put it put.

Richard turned up and we were towed home. We had an electrician, imaginatively called 'Sparky' in Weymouth. Boat electricians are elusive creatures and Paul was no exception....but he ALWAYS turned out in an emergency. Paul stayed all that night and totally rewired the boat as far as the fuse boxes. It was a mammoth task and we had only a street light to illuminate the scene plus his headlight for the detailed work. Somehow Sparky managed to complete the job just as the new Alderney team turned up two hours early at 0500 and asked if they could put their gear on-board! Sparky and I were filthy and knackered with the boat in a right state with oil all over the deck.

It was one of those moments that all skippers have when they wonder why do we do this thankless job?

Anglers and skippers often have totally different recollections of the same trip. To finish off this section and the 20th Century, here is a memory from a long standing angling customer, Dave Poultney from Swanage. Dave began his love of boat fishing aboard *Offshore Rebel* III as a junior angler and remembers the trip with well.

It was wind over tide and we were about 6 miles south of Portland. We were rolling about like no tomorrow. To us 12 and 13 year olds it was like something out of a film. One of our party thought we were going to die. Another was being sick. Another had nicked a bottle of sherry from his mother's drinks cabinet and had had it confiscated by the Club Chairman until we got back home.

Another lad forgot he had dressed in double thermals and pissed in his wellingtons. All this was going on while rolling about while the legend of All-Weather Whittall was in the wheel house in nothing but a pair of jeans and a jumper, feet on the dash, laughing at us whilst reading the paper! We all caught fish though and as juniors having our first taste of boat fishing had a wicked day and it's certainly one of many 100's of trips now I will always remember. Many of us had never seen a boat like Richard English's (Richard was another Weymouth skipper, the youngest in the UK at the timer) **Loan Shark** *and seeing a red bull come over the top of a wave with a giant shark jaw and eye on the bow was really like something out of a movie! Again, it was a great memory and really got me hooked on boat angling.*

Dave's friend, Will Chellingworth recalls *'another friend who is sadly no longer with us brought some mince pies and lovely brandy cream. You heated them up for us in the oven just inside the cabin door on the starboard side'*.

And that's why we skippers do 'this thankless job.' What could be finer than providing the opportunity for life-long memories, experiences and fun and for making lasting friendships within our illustrious angling fraternity!

Questions and Answers

Question: **Mr Boatbuilder, Sir, what can my role be in assisting the**

construction of The New Boat for The New Century?

Answer: *Just stay out of the way for four months….*
           but keep the money coming!

The winter of 1999-2000 saw *Offshore Rebel IV* changing from an empty South Boats 36' hull into a charter angling boat under the Ron Berry trained hands of Chris Tett - still also the skipper of *Peace and Plenty* - and his able band of helpers. Being useless at all things practical, I was not allowed to be part of 'the boat building team'. At school I was one of the very few boys to be thrown out of woodwork and later metal work lessons for being utterly and uselessly impractical. Elevated to the status of being a Latin Scholar enabled me to internalise future useful fish classifications such as Pollachius pollachius for that all-important wreck fish, the pollack, and to be able to appreciate the Centurion's despair at Brian's pathetic school-boy Latin temple wall graffiti in *The Life of Brian* movie masterpiece.

My role during that winter of building *Offshore Rebel IV* was to stroll into the boat shed and tell everyone how brilliant they were and then bugger 'orf out of the way. I was under orders to keep the money coming in as there was a fair size workforce employed and which needed regular paying. I could no longer return to teaching as I had been out of the classroom for years now and so I needed to turn my attentions to even more writing about fishing to maintain the income.

For that turn of the Century winter, I concentrated on journalism and stepped up my output, sending articles and reports to every magazine whether they wanted them or not. Surprisingly, quite a lot of stuff was published but that was because I was submitting photographs which were wanted and around which I could write a story.

Photography was still pre-digital. This meant that I was wandering around with three cameras; one for Black and White photographs, one for colour and one for slides. Many people during that archaic period would not empty their cameras for months...sometimes a year...at a time. Anglers would tell me that they had a great photo if I wanted to use it and I'd ask where it was only to find it was still inside the camera on a half-used roll of film. So, I'd take the film and pay for it to be developed and buy a replacement film for the kind photographer in question only to find the desired shot was months out of date and pretty useless anyway. I had run a 'Spot the Fish' competition in the *Dorset Echo* for a year in which I would include somebody's kindly donated photograph which would contain a fish somewhere in amongst everything else including Portland Lighthouse which featured many times. My photography was pretty poor but at least it was current and the fish, which was the only important thing really, could always be seen.

There will be some enthusiasts reading this who will know everything about cameras, models, settings, films and so on. I did not. I genuinely relied on the 'take loads of the same shot and hope one will be OK' technique. If I could get one or two reasonable photographs out of a roll of 12 film then I was happy. I could use those two photos and have them reproduced many times and send them off to every angling paper and magazine I knew. I was earning between £10 to £15 for a black and white published photograph and £30 to £50 for colour photographs. If very lucky, and a slide was used on a front cover of a magazine, I very occasionally earned a £100! I would aim to get ten black and white photos and for coloured shots published per week and then loads of reports and articles revolving round them which were either paid by the line or by the page. That winter of 1999-2000 meant my weekly output escalated way beyond any previous period and everything earned was converted into wages for the artisans constructing my vessel.

I would have phone calls from magazines saying that they would use more of my stuff but my photos were terrible and could I please improve them, so I enrolled on a course at a place called *The Talent Centre* just outside of Weymouth in the beautifully quaint village of Upwey. This was a term's course, or more if students wished to continue their studies, on how to get the best out of your camera. The tutor was an intense and artistic gentleman who dressed like a Frenchman complete with striped jumper, beard and flourishing moustache and threw his arms around in a most regular and majestic manner. He hated me right from the first moments but fortunately the other nine students were all ladies and they looked after me and deflected the tormented tutor's criticism of my pathetic efforts towards other weighty matters such as best camera settings for taking pretty dicky bird pictures in the gathering evening twilight.

We were shown photographs in the classroom to discuss at length. We talked about what we thought the photographer was trying to achieve, the camera settings and film used, the composition and all sorts of other arty-type stuff that I could see being of immense use when trying to get a good photo of a fish whilst trying to balance on a bouncing boat. We were given homework which was to take a photo, get it developed (or develop it ourselves) and give a talk about it to the group. My talks were short and generally met with snorts of contemptuous disapproval from our illustrious Tutor or shrieks of uncontrolled mirth from my fellow students.

One day we were shown a photograph of the very famous Corfe Castle near Swanage in a local Country Magazine. It was a full page colour shot.

The discussion went around the room with everyone offering dazzlingly perceptive insights into the aspects of the photograph we'd been taught to look for. I was last to be asked; the aim was for a lesson to finish before the question reached me so the tutor could avoid my obviously idiotic answer or explanation. On this occasion there was time, unluckily for him, to include me. My lady student friends all turned to look at me expecting some more of the nonsense that provoked our poor tutor and I explained that I thought the photographer was driving along in his car and looking up saw Corfe Castle and thought it looked nice. Stopping the car in the nearest lay-by, the photographer rolled down his car window and took lots of shots on three different cameras and then rolled up the window and drove on.

The subsequently developed films contained a couple of reasonable shots especially one of the colour ones. These photographs were sent in to the Dorset Magazine in the hope they might be considered for use and luckily for the photographer one was and became a full page money earner much to his delight and surprise.

The Ladies fell about giggling and the tutor changed colour and became artistically distressed. He actually shouted at me and asked me why I was always so deliberately obtuse in my answers and attitude. I'd had enough of this gentleman by now and explained that I was really trying to get into the 'head' of the cameraman and that this is how I thought the photograph was taken.

The final spluttering explosion of rage demanded that I back up my superficial and insensitive response 'for the benefit of everyone else who was trying to enter into the spirit of the discussion'. I asked him to look at the credit given at the bottom of the photograph and will never forget the look of sheer hatred as he glared at me and said, "That's YOUR name!"

"Indeed it is, Sir....and I have just bared my artistic soul to you and been ridiculed in front of my fellow students. I feel I must leave."

I stood and collected my few possessions and bade farewell to my fellow students knowing that this was in fact the final lesson of that term and we'd arranged to meet in the local hostelry afterwards for a farewell drink. I managed a final French-type arty flourish and I left The Talent Centre to applause and laughter.

Offshore Rebel IV is launched to an appreciative audience.

Meanwhile, back at Portland, the team were working furiously to get the new hull fitted out by the Tett deadline. I'd outlined what I wanted on the boat and luckily for me all that was largely ignored but in early March of 2000, after many visits to the workshop by many very interested customers and magazines, *Offshore Rebel IV* was launched.

Boats tend to look enormous within the confines of a boat shed but *Offshore Rebel IV* looked still gigantic when it was craned out and lifted gently into the water. Because this South Boat was the very first of the larger version, there was considerable interest and many people, angling customers, other boat owners and builders along with several press friends who had turned up for the occasion. We all knew that this boat was something really innovative and represented a huge leap forward in the charter boat world and even now, twenty years later, many people will consider the South Boats to still be the finest vessels available for angling and dive charter work.

The deck space was truly impressive and was guaranteed to be able to handle the mountains of tackle that anglers bring on board. At five metres wide, there was plenty of room for a raised central section to be installed upon which the large, cumbersome fishing tackle boxes could be neatly stowed. A stainless steel multi-tubed rod rack that looked like a glistening rocket launching platform into which up to 36 rods could be inserted was fixed to the wheelhouse end of the platform. A low railing ran around it all to keep everything in one place, even when blasting along in a choppy sea.

The stern end of the platform led to an enormous ice-box held in place at fish filleting height by some more immaculate metal work from Stainless Steve of Lymington and which had two large livebait bins neatly attached with the pipework running through a non-return water system to circulate the seawater but also keep the boat dry.

The wheelhouse, which underwent a number of modifications during the time with me, could accommodate 7 people sitting inside plus several more standing with additional under cover seating outside. And, of course, it had the all-important oven for those invaluable cups of tea and hot pies.

The main advantage of the catamarans was their enormous width. Even with a wheelhouse large enough to provide the necessary shelter for skipper, crew and customers, there was still enough room to provide a wide walkway either side of it up to the foredeck area. This gave a 9m x 5m fishing area which was a massive increase of the deck space offered by the Offshore 105, the Lochin and indeed any other under 12 metre mono-hulled angling charter boat about at the time.

The new *Offshore Rebel* was very basic but extremely functional. It was designed to go charter fishing and was expected to get a few knocks when carrying so many people on so many trips and it stood up to the general punishment very well. Over the next twenty years, many variations of deck and cabin configuration on the later models have taken place with some truly superb and luxurious looking South Boats Catamaran appearing out of their Isle of Wight workshops but mine was the first, so once again I had what I considered to be the all-important 'gimmick' to keep the name of *Offshore Rebel* the one to stand out and remember...and it was the first new charter boat of the 21st Century.

The main advantage about being self-employed is that you can run your business how you like but it is essential to remain self-critical. The Weymouth-Alderney trips were the mainstay of my charter business from late March until the middle of October each year. Apart from competitions like the Conger Festival, the WIBAC and EFSA events, I aimed to be in Alderney every week of the seven month season averaging 25 four or five day mid-week trips per year. Weekends looked after themselves back then and there was a waiting list to book the boat for a Saturday or Sunday.

I wanted the Alderney trips to be as stress-free as possible to the customer, after all it was an angling holiday. So I arranged everything that I could to make life easy; the 5 days of car parking in

Weymouth, ice for the fish, accommodation in Alderney, pack lunches, menus on the boat for the Alderney restaurants, a crew to fillet and ice down the fish amongst all the other crew-type jobs, taxi's to be waiting at Alderney when we arrived and a Duty Free Service for the lads to bring the designated allowance of 'fags 'n booze' home.

IF everything went to plan, and there were occasions when it did, and the customer told me that I had a 'very easy job', then I felt I'd got it right. Surely the idea of a 'package' holiday is that everything is thought of and provided for the customer. It's not easy to do and I made many mistakes but, over the years, the structure of the trips became tighter and less errors on my part were made.

My life as a charter skipper had always been marked out by which boat I had. I kept the South Boat for 17 years which meant that it had a lot of continuous and ongoing maintenance on it and three sets of engines at £40,000 a pair during its time with me. All boats require a good deal of work. We put them through very testing conditions and the sea and salt air make up a merciless environment. Even massively expensive ships like our latest £3billion Aircraft Carrier, HMS Queen Elizabeth, leaked considerably and worryingly for the first couple of months with teams of divers and detailed internal inspections failing to find the point of seawater entry.

My son Tom, also a commercial diver, spent many hours underneath the various highly expensive fast Cross-Channel Condor ferries running from Weymouth and Poole to Guernsey and Jersey as part of their necessary regular underwater maintenance. The team discovered cracks in the hull showing that the very latest multi-million dollar vessel was vibrating apart.

I also drove my new South Boats Catamaran too hard treating it like the Lochin. The Catamaran is an amazing boat but, as we all know, there is no such thing as a perfect vessel. The South Boats catamaran could not handle pushing through head seas without being prone to 'nose diving' and bow cracking but then it was at its best when presenting itself broadside to pretty enormous waves when we fished 'on the drift'. There is no way that South Boat would have survived that wild trip across the English Channel into Weymouth in seas like that experienced on the Lochin with the Yacht Eclat rescue. I think I would have destroyed the boat. I always used to tell anglers that an angling boat could take much more of a battering than they could but in certain circumstances, I discovered that the South Boat could not.

The South Boat was as near to a 'perfect' angling boat as could be expected within the limitations of its size. It was fitted out with the multi-day Channel Island trips in mind. It had a 1,500 Litre fuel carrying capacity which usually allowed me to complete a five day 300 nautical mile charter without having to fuel up until the return to Weymouth. It had two massive insulated fish holds which were easily large enough to carry enough ice to cater for the accumulating fish catch for the week. Ice needed to be purchased in Weymouth each week and was a vitally important part of the trip as we could no longer, since the final fish selling incident in 1995, purchase ice from Alderney.

The boat had double the Navigational instrumentation which ran on two separate battery set-up which themselves were interchangeable. Many charter boats have two or even more of everything; two GPS Units, 2 radios, 2 plotters and so on as is necessary for long range trips and back-up if one item fails and has to go back to the shop for repairs. The boat also had two good sized bunks well apart in either hull, essential when wishing to escape the raucous snoring of a drunken crewman.

It was increasingly difficult to purchase engine parts in the UK without a lengthy wait. A replacement Cummins engine, for example, would take up to 14 weeks to arrive from America. It's very difficult to operate without having a mountain of spare parts which might, as in my case, involve a spare engine and gear box sat waiting to be fitted in a day....well, that was the theory anyway!

My time with the South Boat was so long, the adventures on it are remembered by me in terms of the crew I was fortunate enough to have working with me. *Offshore Rebel*'s crew for the first five years was a young man with a fine sea-faring surname, Steve West, who turned up one evening on the pontoon in Weymouth where I moored and asked if he could clean the boat when I returned from a fishing trip. Anglers will remember 'the Good Old Days' when boats chugged about at 7 knots and the journey back from a wreck was often four long boring hours. Customers would scrub the boat and took a pride in it being as immaculate as when they boarded it in the morning to pass the time. The speed of the new breed of 'fast boats' made this much more difficult with spray flying everywhere and the boat bouncing about making balancing difficult when travelling at double the earlier speeds. It was much safer to wait until we'd got home and everyone had left the boat before crew and skipper, in that order, set to work cleaning.

So Steve started initially as a boat cleaner. He was fantastically reliable and an excellent worker. I asked him one day if he would like to come to sea as crew and as we headed southwards, put him on the wheel and showed him the working of the GPS and the plotter. Steve was a total natural. He mastered those gadgets within that one day. Amazing. And he understood Latitude and Longitude instantly. He was indeed a rare young man who seemed to be born to the sea.

Steve stayed with me until 2005 and then went on to much greater sea-faring responsibilities operating large vessels in the North Sea and becoming an extremely highly respected Offshore Mariner.

Unexpected Experiences in Thailand.

In the January of 2004, I had joined a large group of friends to visit South Africa aiming to fish for bronze whaler sharks from the shore at Namibia and then afterwards to visit the Game Reserve in the Etosha National Park. After this amazing trip, I had planned to visit Asia and had therefore taken no bookings on my boat until April 1st of that year, leaving the very capable Steve West in charge of running *Offshore Rebel IV* in my absence. Unfortunately the planned trip did not take place but I did end up in Thailand.

There is a web site called *Crew Seekers*. I applied for an unpaid crewing job on a yacht which was part of a four yacht 'flotilla' owned by an English man operating out of Phuket, a place I had never heard of. I travelled to Bangkok on my own and entered the hotel that the Yacht Company had booked for me. I'll never forget that first and only night in the Park Hotel, Soi 7, Sukumvit Road, Bangkok.

Because of time differences between UK and Thailand it was about 1000 pm when I ventured out of the Hotel but in my head it was just 3pm due to the 7 hour time difference in March. I knew absolutely nothing about Thailand or Bangkok only that the Capitol City had supposedly received its name from American GI's who were enjoying R&R in the Vietnam War period...and that was also false information as I later discovered.

Across the Soi from the Hotel was a bar. I needed a drink after the 12 hour flight and 15 hour journey. I walked into the bar. Well-travelled men will know what to expect...I certainly did not. In this bar were about 50 or more very scantily dressed young ladies and several rather aged gentlemen supping their drinks in darkened corners and surrounded by gyrating lovelies. I stepped inside and was swamped by bronzed semi-nakedness. This was all way out of my league...yes, I know but I was a naïve, Dorset charter skipper who'd come to Thailand to be a crew member on a yacht!

I turned to leave and seek the sanctuary of my hotel.

An English voice behind called to me. I turned and there was a man about my age, much taller of course, who spoke to me in a manner that I'll never forget. The conversation opened with a: "Mate, you look like this is your first time here." Rob, that was his name, kept quite a distance from me. He explained that it was up to me if I wanted to listen to him and he would understand if I did not but he lived and worked in Bangkok and he knew his way around. He could see I didn't have a clue what was going on and that I was faced by a daunting first time experience. If I wanted, and again he understood if I refused, he would show me around.

We sat down and ordered a beer which was immediately bought to us by two really pretty Thai girls who Rob politely asked, in Thai, to go away...which they did! He explained a world that I found very hard to believe. I agreed, after a good hour's conversation, to put my trust in him and true to his word Rob took me on a whirlwind tour of Central Bangkok at night. What an eye-opener. Certainly nothing of what I saw that night went on in The Sailor's Return, Weymouth!

I told Rob I was due in Phuket the next day and we returned to The Park Hotel, Soi 7, just before dawn so I could get a shower and breakfast before the hair-raising taxi ride to Don Muang Airport in Bangkok to board the flight to Phuket. Rob had been great and we stayed in contact for several years after that one meeting.

The scenery when flying across mainland Thailand and then Phang Gna Bay with its dramatic Karst formations and multitude of Islands in what was an unexpectedly bright green sea is stunningly inviting. The flight then heads out into the blue waters of the Andaman Sea before the aircraft turns to line up on the Phuket Airport runway. Leaving the air-conditioned airport and stepping out into the blazing sunshine and hot air of Phuket was overwhelming. It was much more humid than the equally hot but dry Namibian climate of the previous month.

I was met by a Thai driver who was holding up a piece of cardboard with a strange interpretation of my surname on it and who was to take me to the nearby Yacht Haven Marina. He explained in English that he couldn't speak any English and took me off for a silent twenty minute taxi ride to the Marina where I stepped out into an even more blistering March heat and met my new employer, Dave.

Over my very welcome first ice cold Tiger beer, Dave explained that he had a problem and that my journey may have been wasted. He had four yachts, all Bavarian 47' cruisers. One of his four Thai skippers was poorly and every boat had to have a commercially endorsed skipper on board for Insurance purposes. Unless he could find another skipper, one boat would not be able to take part in the race. Very luckily, amongst the various travel documents I had with me was my RYA Yacht-master certification with the all important commercial endorsement. David explained that he was allowed to employ 25% of non-Thais in his company and he could find a way round this situation if I agreed to be the skipper. It was explained that all I had to do was be on the boat. I was not allowed to assist or advise the team in any way, which was just as well because I know next to nothing about sailing, for fear of them being disqualified.

I agreed to do whatever was required and was led off to the boat I was to skipper by another of Dave's staff whilst he went to phone 'somebody' who could make everything satisfactory to meet for the Thai legal requirements.

The next morning the four teams booked on Dave's yachts arrived and for the first time it was explained to me that there was to be an impressive entry for this sailing event involving 20 different countries and 40 different boats with plans to make it this initial friendly event into a major annual regatta in the future. I could see that the French team I was to be with had every intention of treating this 'friendly race' very seriously indeed.

Dave, far better at spinning a yarn than me, introduced me to the team as a full time charter skipper (True!) who covered 15,000 nautical miles a year which was again true but avoided explaining this impressive annual distance was achieved under power with 500 HP pushing me to and fro across the English Channel often in pursuit of French bass. Apparently I was also used to working with the French and was on board simply as a necessary requirement to satisfy Thai legalities. I did not explain to my seriously intense

French team that my relations with the French was limited to being towed away from fishing marks by roguish French trawlermen and occasional communications with Cherbourg Radio to assure them that I was not a Cross-Channel drug smuggler.

The many different types of yachts were split into several classes and off we went at first light heading towards Langkawi which is just over the Tai/Malay border at 125 nautical miles south-eastish of Phuket. The winds in this part of the world are fickle to say the least and it was difficult to keep the yacht moving and indeed many yachts were becalmed for periods waiting for any kind of light breeze to spring up and fill their colourful spinnakers.

To their credit, the French team never stopped working and were forever running up different sail patterns and then, knowing I could not advise in any way (not that I could) would look at me for professional reassurance. I of course would look scathingly at the new sail configuration in such a way as to indicate either haughty professional distain at their amateurism with the result that sails were immediately pulled down and another pattern offered. I could then either reward the team with the faintest hint of a knowing and appreciative nod in their direction, accompanied by the glimmer of an encouraging smile, or throw my eyes skyward in despair and then watch the crew's confused reaction as they again attempted to offer the perfect sail solution.

The optimistic prediction for these mainly cruising yachts was that they would average 6 knots of speed per hour and with the total race to Langkawi and back to Phuket being about 260 miles of non-stop sailing, the race was expected to take between two and three days.

The route to Langkawi is scenic with many offshore Islands and the Tarutao National Marine Park offering an attractive alternative to remaining at sea. At night there were numerous Thai squid fishing boats which were very brightly illuminated and off-putting to the competitors who were not used to having to weave their way in and out of such a widely scattered array of dazzling lights. Seachlights from the fishing boats were often trained on the yachts with the competitors complaining afterwards of being blinded and having to take over-evasive and time consuming course alerting action.

By the time we had finished our race and returned to Yacht Haven at the north-eastern corner of Phuket Island, we could see that we were virtually alone. Yacht crews had decided that the islands they saw were too alluring and had pulled in for the night and then decided to stay for several more. Sailing through the armada of fishing vessels at night had unsettled a number of crews and they decided to rest at Langkawi which is a beautiful Island described by many as being like Phuket was 30 years ago. The race had certainly not gone as planned and it was announced that our yacht had come first in its class and second overall. The highly motivated and very experienced French Team were ecstatically merry at this success which they graciously attributed to their very stern skipper whose knowing looks had guided them to Victory. Well...who was I to disagree.

It was thanks to this event that I met Jai who was on another of the Company's four yacht fleet and who then came to the UK in 2005 to start what was to become a ten year stint as crew on *Offshore Rebel IV*. Many of you will remember Jai, I am sure. She was the one who taught us all our first Thai words with such memorable phrases as "Ooooo; big bleam!! Walk black, walk black!" and "Oooo; velly big fit," and whose work rate and cheerfulness was infectious. She became a much loved and respected part of the *Offshore Rebel* story and indeed it was unusual to have a lady as crew on a UK charter boat and especially one who was such a superb angler.

Before Jai's first appearance over a year later, I had returned to Weymouth in early April for the 2004 season and learned that the European Federation of Sea Anglers (EFSA) was to hold its annual Game Fishing competition in Phuket, Thailand, in the November of 2004. I thought this would give me another opportunity to see what Phuket had to offer and phoned all the angling magazines to ask them if they would like me to go to Phuket and get the story.

Nobody was interested...at all! Surprised at this, I then asked the magazines if they would give a letter (I wrote it; they signed) explaining that I had exclusive rights, even though nobody wanted it, to the competition story. This enabled me to access the boats and go out every day to see what the Game Fishing was all about and to meet many of the EFSA members and hand out as many business cards as I could inviting the marlin hunters of the world to come to Weymouth for our fine bassing and conger fishing!

The digital age was now with us and I had purchased a Cannon EOS digital camera for over £1,000 and which you would not be able to give away now. The camera needed a spare battery and a battery charger and an adapter for the Thai electric plug sockets. I had my laptop. They were bulky machines back then and it too required a charger system with adapters and connecting wires from camera to laptop plus back-ups if any failed. Then, in order to get an internet signal, we had those funny little things called 'Donglers'. Thus my non-digital camera bag containing my three cameras and necessary films became a suitcase full of camera, computers, endless wires and other necessary gadgets. It was great to know we'd entered a new, streamlined era of journalism.

Knowing that no Angling Papers wanted any of my stories or photographs, my aim was to make CD's of the International Teams and Individuals showing them on the boats, at the daily weigh-ins, nightly reveries and the various Presentation Ceremonies. I made and sold a lot of CD's to accommodate the 136 competitors with many competitors wanting three or for CD's each for their friends and families 'back home', such was the novelty of all this technology just 16 years ago.

Apart from the CD's funding the trip, it enabled me to meet the EFSA President, Mr Horst Schnieder, and it was he who over the next four years guided me into purchasing the house I bought here in Phuket in 2008 along with a Company that he'd set up enabling me to deal with the intricacies of land and property ownership that confuse so many prospective purchasers. And it also allowed me to invite Jai join me on the competing Thai boats to act as my Official Interpreter because I wanted the 'story' from the Thai skippers' point of view. I was able to offer Jai a job, with the Thai Government's backing back then, to further her sea-going experience by working in England.

By early December 2004, all the various International competitors had returned to their countries and I came back to Weymouth. Son Tom was in the famous Thai Diver Training Island of Koa Toa learning to become a Diving Instructor when the Tsunami struck Phi Phi Island at 0830 on December 26th and raced on to hit Phuket and then Koa Lak in the Phang Gna region north of Phuket killing an estimated 5,000 Thais and Foreigners. This awful death toll escalated massively to a given figure of 250,000 when including the much lower-lying countries of Sumatra in the Malacca Straits and Sri Lanka. The Andaman Islands escaped any deaths thanks to the Tsunami warnings contained within their traditional folk songs. The inhabitants knew to heed Nature's signs and evacuate to higher ground before the waves hit.

Now safely back in Weymouth, I managed to contact son Tom and he knew nothing about any of this catastrophe because the Tsunami had raced up the western coastline of Thailand. Koa Toa, where Tom was, is a small island on the Eastern side of the Thai/Malay peninsula. I had a very busy week in England answering calls from many distressed parents whose offspring were in Koa Toa unaware that it was completely sheltered. It's amazing how people can somehow find other people to contact when necessary. I knew hardly any of these parents who had 'found' me by accessing my *Offshore Rebel* web site details but least I was able to explain was impounded on the discovery of significant cracks in its them the Geographical positioning of the Gulf of Thailand Islands and the path of the Tsunami in order to allay their mounting concerns.

Bassing in the Races

A small, low boat such as the Fairy Huntress is best when bass fishing in the Portland Race whereas a large boat like the Lochin 38' can be hit by several conflicting waves at once and spun round as though it were about to go down a large plug hole. When this 'Race Spin' happens the tangles that occur with 10 anglers trying to fish at the same time is a mighty mess and by the time it is sorted out, the boat may well have drifted well over a mile a and then have to battle its way all the way back to the drift starting position against a 4 knot tide and heavy sea. Although very exciting and often highly rewarding, taking customers bass fishing in these conditions is not good for the skipper's mental state especially if he used to fish commercially with a 3 man well-attuned crew.

The Portland Race is certainly a very entertaining area of sea. Portland juts out southwards into the English Channel and then continues underwater as the Portland Ledge for another half mile. The depths over the ledge vary but can be as shallow as 6 metres in places and extremely rocky. The flood tide runs from the west to the east across West Bay and is then diverted southwards by Portland. The current strengthens as it nears Portland Bill and is then flung with speeds touching 6 knots on a southerly trajectory. The first obstruction the tide meets as it hurtles along in 40 metre depths is the rapidly shallowing Portland Ledge which jumps up in three distinct steps creating the standing waves that terrify the unprepared yachtsman and tests the courage of the angler as the boat hits these seas broadside.

The shallow part of the ledge can create very rough seas which become even more fun when there is a south-west or even worse a southerly wind acting completely opposite to the tide generated and Portland Ledge angered waves. As the flood tide progresses through its cycle, an initially weak back-eddy starts up which picks up to a couple of knots running back to the west. This then joins in with the southernly flowing tide and mixes in with the now well established surface turbulence to create a testing complexity of water and waves with the skipper doing his best to keep everyone from falling over, tangling with each other, snagging the bottom and thus losing their fishing tackle or even breaking their rod in the worst scenario by refusing to believe they are 'stuck' and trying to turn Planet Earth inside out in attempts to retrieve their expensive lure.

Skippers can be heard shouting out 'move round, move round' in an attempt to keep the anglers' lines from tangling by following the spin of the boat. And then, if a bass is hooked, trying to encourage the successful angler to ease his catch towards the net without knocking the skipper's teeth out with swinging leger which is not easy to control when The Race is in full flow and the boat is rolling all over the place.

The ride back to the start point is not without incident either. The skipper has to pile on the power to overcome the tide. This can result in seas crashing over the customers who are doing thie rbest to prepare their tangled tackle ready for the next drift. If they are very fortunate the boat will 'nose dive' and shovel an impressive amount of water over the bow and then over the wheelhouse to dump itself on top of the sheltering anglers soaking them and their tackle.

We often question our sanity when attempting to fish this particular mark but it is a very popular adrenalin stoking option. This is the hardest of the bass marks to fish in the Weymouth and Portland area and there are many more far easier places to try with calmer seas and a less rocky, tackle engulfing seabed....but nowhere near as much fun.

Quite often a yacht will get itself 'stuck' in the first three standing waves at the Northern Edge of The Race and cannot break free until the skipper realises he must just let his yacht go with the tide until it spews him out at the southern end of The Race. We can often see yacht crews in such a situation watching the insanity and apparent chaos of the local commercial bass fleet hurtling up and down the tide with a few larger lumbering charter boats joining in and wonder what on earth is going on. If the bass are landed as the bass boat drifts past the non-moving, yacht, the crews often hold their prizes aloft with wild shrieks of achievement and barbaric dance sequences to further intimidate and perplex the shocked occupants of the tide gripped vessel.

There is an enormous gap in the catch rate between a charter boat and a commercial bass boat. Skippers are often asked, "Why are they catching and we aren't?" and it is the angling skipper's job to try and explain and encourage his customers to improve. Bass fishing can be much easier over sandbanks and wrecks and is one of the main reasons why the trips to the Channel Islands are so popular because the sandy banks are so much easier to fish.

One of the most popular Alderney bass marks is fondly called The Washing Machine. The tide can run much harder in Alderney than in the Portland Race and it is not possible to fish more than four to six people at once because the boat goes into a very fast and uncontrollable spin once it enters the wildly turbulent waters of The Washing Machine.

Directly north of the enormous underwater rock that generates this wildly rotating melee ,the depth is 35 metres and the tide is hurtling from the North to the South with a massive amount of water on the move. The depth shallows up very rapidly to just a few metres from the surface so that the bottom can actually be seen as the boat races over it in the grip of the tide and then the seabed drops down to 30 metres within seconds. The customers stand at the stern of the boat and as the start of the drift is reached, the skipper yells out: "In the Water," and the baits are lower just under the surface so as to be able to fly over the rock summit with snagging. As soon as the Echo Sounder shows the boat is clearing the rock the all-important command of, "Dooowwwwnnn!" is yelled from the wheel-house.

The fishing lines and live mackerel baits are fired down to try and follow the rock profile . The bass are lurking just behind the outcrop ready to ambush whatever is frantically trying to escape this immensely powerful torrent of water than has ensnared it and now throws it over the shallows of the rock into the bass hunting zone. Because of the speed everything is happening at, a bass bite is initially akin to snagging the bottom which would, at this speed, empty the angler's spool in seconds. If the line is peeling off the reel with unstoppable force then it is a bass. The boat then goes into the famous Washing Machine spin with anyone who hasn't got a fish on winds their fishing tackle at top speed in order to give the angler with the fish a chance to fight it to the net.

It would have been fuel consuming madness to try and battle against the strength of the Alderney Race ebb tide but the tides themselves give the clues of how to travel against them. Because they are so fast, the tide looks like a river in the sea and it can be seen that the tide eases a little towards towards the edges of its main run. By exiting this sea river, it was possible to even catch a helpful back-eddy to assist the boat return to its drift start point. The Wishing Machine drift start was clearly indicated by the amount of seabirds, mainly gannets, plunging in numbers into the bait fish that had been trapped in this main flow and were also hurtling towards the submerged target rock.

Like many fishing marks there is a time to be there and a waste of time to be there and so the day fell into periods where the tides, the feeding birds, the availability of bait and the sea state all conspired to shout out when the time to be lining up that first drift. It is such an excitingly unique place to fish with its adrenalin inducing, swirling, twirling and frightening seas that many anglers don't care if they catch nothing....the wild experience is enough in itself.

But the rewards can indeed be high with bass over 18lb coming aboard Offshore Rebel IV and Peace and Plenty IV within one memorable late season Washing Machine drift of each other.

Bass and Bottoms

There are moments in an angler's life when an uncontrollable urge to prove himself by fishing against the skipper overwhelms him. This strange madness can also persuade the angler to put money down and call out his skipper to prove himself. Bass fishing seems to provoke this temporary competitive insanity more than any other kind of fishing and it is with great reluctance, after considerable persuasion accompanied by the bleating of the anglers band of followers that the skipper finally agrees.

Such impromptu challenges usually take place in sea areas and conditions that immediately favour the skipper, especially if he's spent years commercial fishing in them. This means that the initial modest opening bet needs to be lost thus allowing the angler to build up more belief in his own bass fishing prowess and 'up the ante'. With a careful approach, the skipper can quietly lose the next couple of rounds and then gently draw his victim into a 'Double or Quits' situation, explaining any unexpected success on the skipper's part would only be as a result of temporary good fortune that will surely soon run out.

An angry young man from Brighton who on this occasion shall be called Steven, and whose father, hereby named John, exhibited the patience of a saint and the generosity of Father Christmas, was on an Alderney trip when the bass had come on the feed in the area known as the South Banks. Although the sea may look the same to anyone who has not read Tristan Gooley's seminal work, *How To Read Water,* the skipper who spends his life looking at it can see deeply into it and know where the bass are most likely to be lurking. Steven, who had announced that he fished 'commercially' for bass from his dory, was convinced that this was to be the day when, despite his father and the rest of the team warning him against it, The Bass Challenge could be issued. The sea on the Alderney South Banks is not like that off Brighton and an understanding of one will lead to an overconfidently inaccurate reading of the other.

After several confidence building drifts and Steven leading 3-0 on the bass catch rate, the bet had to be raised to a 'triple or nothing' drift. Inflamed by his commanding lead and obvious superior bassing skills, the bet was accepted. Very strangely, as is often the case in sea-fishing, one competitor was fortunate enough to catch three bass on one drift whilst the angler standing next to him did not even get a bite. How could that be??

Now at 3 bass-all, young Steven had lost his earlier winnings and readily agreed that his skipper was uncharacteristically lucky on that drift and agreed to a sensible renewing of the bet. The ensuing competition was limited to 10 drifts with an agreed 'double or quits' system to be applied after the first drift with its £10 opening stake. Steven caught a couple more fish over the 10 drifts but strangely lost every round and as he grew more angrily frustrated, even his significantly older and much calmer club colleagues out fished him resulting in an amusing display of angry tantrums and tangles.

Steven lost the bass fishing competition by a considerable margin and ended up with a very large amount of money to pay, £2,560, such are the results of a successfully winning streak of ten Double or Quits bets. At the end of the competition, I asked for my money and was told that his ever patient father, John, had agreed to back his irately emotional and aggressively bad tempered son's bets. John and I came to a gentleman's agreement that we would tell his son that the bets were honoured.

When disembarking back in Weymouth, Steven was helping to unload and tripped on the pontoon dropping two heavy bags full of the group's Duty Free allowance of spirits with every bottle breaking and the precious nectar flowing into the harbour. The furious tantrums were a wonder to behold and no doubt the mini-bus journey all the way back to Brighton would have been highly emotionally charged.

On another notable occasion, Ken (real name) decided he was the man to show the skipper how bass fishing should be done. Again the betting evolved into a 'double or quits' approach with Ken ending up heavily at a loss. On the final drift, the generous skipper innocently suggested that the bet could be re-shaped so that if, by some unlikely piece of good fortune he won, then Ken could forego what would then become a very substantial amount of money, by agreeing to stand on the wheelhouse roof stark naked as we entered Alderney Harbour and remain there aloft all the way to the disembarking ladder on the pier which he would then climb before replacing his garments. Ken agreed and sadly lost the final drift although he did point out he managed to catch a weaver of nearly two ounces.

Entering Alderney Harbour, Ken sportingly removed his togs and his un-athletically small but rotund body clambered its way onto the cabin roof where a series of artistic poses were struck and directed towards the mainly French yachts that were moored. Unfortunately one of the French visitors did not appreciate this display of normally hidden Private Parts and complained to the Harbour Master who sent his Customer launch and smartly attired Officer to investigate.

Ken was ordered back down from the roof and we were threaten with a life-time ban from entering Alderney despite my protestations that I did not know he was up there. It was not easy for Ken's little legs to allow him to descend from the cabin and he had to slide, as it were, down past my window with his bottom running down the glass. Although under immediate threat of imprisonment, Ken still managed to display what is known in certain areas of Somerset as the 'brown puckered spider' part of his anatomy to me before finally lowering himself back onto the safety of the main deck.

I was subsequently summoned to the Harbour Master's Office where it was explained that I was to be 'let off with a caution' as it was the first time anyone from an incoming from an incoming UK charter boat charter boat had paraded their manly British attributes to the sensitive French yachties.

I thought of the time in the previous month when the exuberant Celtic lads I had brought to Alderney leapt off the high harbour wall into the sea in the early morning stark naked, their team motto of 'Ducky Fuck' echoing out around the awakening harbour.

Fortunately for me, that had taken place early enough for the Harbour Master's Office not to have opened and the yachtsmen being too far away to witness and then issue complaints about this fine display of lily white Welsh manhood.

Hooks and Knives

The most dangerous time on a charter angling boat is the bait fishing session for mackerel in the morning. The sea is often choppy on the west side of Portland Bill where the local boats usually take their customers to catch the mackerel. Mackerel feathers come in packets of four to six hooks but some over-enthusiastic anglers, usually those with the least experience, will link two sets of feather together and have a dangerously long and uncontrollable string of 12 hooks flying around. When there are several mackerel hanging on the hooks, the likelihood of injury swiftly increases especially as trying to shake one mackerel free into the bait box can easily result in the impaling of oneself with an adjacent hook. The main concern is that one or two of these hooks will be at 'eye height' with an angler on a bouncing boat often unaware of how perilously close he is to inflicting a very serious wound on himself. Watching from the wheelhouse brings many heart stopping garments for the skipper who knows his warning shouts are largely unheeded as the fish start to come in to the boat.

Luckily no-one ever impaled their eye with a hook on any of the Offshore Rebel boats despite us mackerel fishing in some uncomfortably fluffy conditions. But there have been such terrible incidents and then it is a case of calling up the Air-Sea Rescue Helicopter or heading straight back to harbour for the waiting ambulance and trying to deal with an understandably distressed and frightened customer.

Skippers, whether they like it or not, will have to deal with plenty of situations which involve someone accidently burying a hook into themselves. Some people can handle this very well and adopt the 'stiff upper lip' approach and either carry on fishing for the day with the hook remaining in situ or offering themselves to the hook extracting expertise of the skipper.

In one locally famous local incident a competitor in a Weymouth and Portland Conger Competition managed to hook himself perfectly through his top lip with a large 6/0 hook. It would be unwise to attempt an amateur extraction on this sensitive part of the body, especially with such a hefty piece of metal involved. The decision to return to port or not must be taken but in this particular example, the competitor, a large and famous gentleman from Portland, chose to remain in the competition and fish all day with this large hook dangling from his lip much to the admiration of his fellow competitors.

In the early years of our super-modern 21st Century, some anglers still used hefty silver pirks weighing 20 ounces or more to take their so called 'killer rigs' down to the bottom of the sea or to a wreck. This hefty amount of weight of the pirk was required because anglers that favoured the 'killer-rig' method were still using 50lb mono mainlines that had an enormous amount of stretch in them thus making it hard to 'feel' the bottom with too light a weight. These pirks usually had a hefty treble hook on the bottom which would hook into the large mouth of the intended predatory quarry.

Fishing in the deepest part of the English Channel, the 130 metre Hurd Deep, seven miles north of Alderney, the group of young, rugby playing anglers aboard *Offshore Rebel IV* were using this archaic and tiring method of fishing. It seemed like they had deliberately chosen to use the 'jerk and pirk' system as a training session and there was a good deal of singing of raucous rugby ditties as the rods were raised and lowered in unison. The innocent lyrics of 'Down in the Valley' were most appropriate particularly on the chorus where the team members declared that "Oi 'ad 'er; Oi 'ad 'er, Oi 'ad 'er; Oi Aye" once a fish was hooked.

When the lyrical intensity stepped up a notch, I knew one of the lads had hooked into something and was attempting to break the retrieval record by winding in as fast as his scrummage-honed arms could manage. One young man had caught a reasonable sized cod and dragged it overboard before the crew had chance to net it for him. As the fish swung inboard, it dropped off the hook causing a momentary loss of concentration and control resulting in the angler allowing his now fishless pirk to drop onto his leg. He was wearing shorts so two prongs of the treble hook embedded themselves deeply into his naked flesh above the knee thanks to the considerable weight of the falling 20oz pirk.

There he stood; his friends laughing at him and continuing their boisterous singing and jerking and apparently oblivious as to the seriousness of this situation. I could not see any other alternative than to return to port to seek professional assistance. I explained to the impaled Jim and his friends that we should go in to Alderney but they all dismissed this silly idea and decided Jim would have to wait until the day's fishing was done.

I removed the pirk from the split ring that connected it to the hook and looked at the extent of the injury. It was a miracle really that just two of the three prongs had buried themselves into Jim's decidedly well-developed quadriceps muscle. He asked me to remove the hook and despite me telling him that it was too difficult, insisted I had a go. I explained that I would first need to try and cut the third prong off because any attempt to free the other two parts of the hook would possibly bring about further impaling with this third prong. But Jim would have none of that and told me to 'rip the hook out'. This can be done with a single hook depending as to where it is and the depth it has penetrated but this was a difficult situation and, it appeared to me, to be capable of causing a quite serious injury if I attempted to just 'rip it out'.

Jim announced that if I didn't do it, then he would do it himself. With this worrying threat of self-harm to motivate me, I did manage to extract the hook from his leg although it did take time, some whiskey and the use of a sharp filleting knife. There was surprisingly little blood considering the size of the wound.

Jim asked for his pirk back as he intended to continue fishing. On enquiring as to why he was so keen for me to retrieve his hook in an undamaged state, he explained that was his only treble hook and he did not want to lose it! With the treble hook reattached, Rob hurled his pirk back overboard in time to join in with the drift and the lads all broke out into their favourite diddy with a slight lyrical change to refer to the hook: "it 'ad 'im; it 'ad im; it 'ad im; aye eh," accompanied by much guffawing at their team mate's expense.

It is true that some injuries look a lot worse than they actually are. On another trip, an angler had caught a dogfish and asked if he could keep it as he fancied trying one for tea. Dogfish used to be sold as 'rock salmon' and were an expensive option in the London Fish 'n Chip shops when I worked there and had to be pre-ordered, such was their popularity. They are not easy to skin and so that task often falls to the skipper or crew of an angling boat. They are also able to live for a very long time out of water. This customer not only wanted to keep the dogfish, he wanted me to kill it and then skin it for him.

The best way to stun or kill a wriggling dogfish so that it can be skinned for the table is to grab it firmly by the tail and then wallop it extremely hard on the deck. This I attempted to do but my downward thrust was halted before the fish hit the deck. My arm could not move and I discovered that as I swung downward my arm, at the elbow, had impaled itself on a set of mackerel feathers that had not been packed away by the customer and were left hanging from his spare rod inserted vertically into one of the boat's metal tubed rod holders.

The mackerel hook was completely buried with just a bit of feather sticking out of my arm along with the eye at the top of the hook just visible. This is when I discovered for the first time the unusually elastic properties of skin in the area of the elbow. Here, a bit of skin can be grabbed between the thumb and first finger of the opposite hand and pulled some considerable distance and without pain. By using the boat's pliers in my left hand, I was able to grab onto the slightly protruding head of the hook and pull on it until the skin became so stretched and thin as to be almost translucent. I could see the shape of the mackerel hook but was unable to do anything about it. So I called for assistance to anyone who felt like they could cut my skin to free the sharp end of the hook which I was attempting, unsuccessfully, to push through. It is surprising how many brawny chaps turn white faced in horror at such experiences as hook removal and no volunteer came forward until after much persuasion an angler bravely took my filleting knife and made the necessary cut to release the hook point. Once that was through, the rest of the hook followed quite easily. Again, there was hardly any blood but I could see a good deal of shock and horror on the faces of my customers who must have thought I was even madder than they'd previously considered me to be.

There were a great many hook removing instances over the years but the finest example of dedicated fishing in the face of potential pain and shortening of the future family tree came when Francesco, an Italian angler, skilfully swung his two hook paternoster rig straight at himself with a bream attached to the top hook, the weight and momentum of which swung the bottom hook neatly between his legs. Again, shorts were being worn but these were of a very lightweight and flimsy nature which the small, needle sharp hook penetrated with ease. The material offered so little protection that the hook travelled on and pierced the angler's next layer of clothing and entered that sensitive part of the anatomy that most males value above all else.

This was an uncomfortable position to be in with the wriggling bream providing the final jerk on the line to set the hook and initially maintain tension direct to the impaled part. Francesco released his bream and quickly cut the fishing line leading to the offending lower hook and retied a new rig, baited it and cast it back into the bream shoal. Then, and only then, did he turn his intentions to the line dandling out of his shorts leading to his neatly hooked scrotum.

Francesco looked at me with imploring Italian eyes and I waved a long nosed pair of forceps and a knife at him. His resigned shrug invited me to have a go at removing the hook and so with a deft cutting of a small slit in his shorts and underlying garment, I was able to slip the forceps towards the extraction point and remove the hook with comparative ease in a fine display of steady handed micro-surgery. Because this was a competition, barbless hooks had to be used and this was the reason why the nut sack gave up its invader so readily.

The released angler just carried on fishing and in fact not only came first on the boat but also won the overall multi-vessel event and a considerable amount of prize money and he didn't even mention the mishap. I did of course, by telling everyone over the VHF radio exactly what had happened in tear -inducing detail.

Some anglers prefer to inflict pain upon themselves using a knife. Knifes are used on the boat for bait and line cutting, and for gutting and filleting of the fish. Experienced anglers prefer to do any or all of those four actions themselves and therefore the injury rate is much higher than with inexperienced anglers who prefer to let the experienced crewman, or crewess in the case of my boat, handle the knife work.

Returning from a choppy mid-channel wrecking trip one time with a good catch of pollack, I told the anglers not to try gutting the fish whilst we were on the move but to wait until I could pull into the very sheltered waters of Portland Harbour where we could work on the fish without danger of them getting cut. On this occasion I had no crew with me to assist the customers and therefore they needed to help themselves. I was assured they were all very experienced men who could handle a knife and, on entering the calm waters of the harbour, they set to work. A couple of men came to ask if they could borrow a sharp knife so they could also assist. I emphasised that the boat's knives were seriously sharp and not like the usual knife a customer would carry. My crewess, trained by the fishmonger in Weymouth, was normally the only person I allowed to use these razor sharp and very expensive blades.

We were already running late and the dark rain clouds were making the evening drawing in quickly. And it was cold. I issued one knife to an eager angler and proceeded to unwrap the next knife with further emphasis on just how sharp these were and the need to be very careful with it. As this second angler left the wheelhouse with his knife, the first angler returned with blood streaming down his right ear. He agreed that the knife was indeed razor sharp and he had just nicked his earlobe when trying to scratch a little itch before commencing on the fish gutting. This was not a 'little nick' and earlobes are remarkably able to produce na impressive amount of blood.

I removed his knife which was held at an extremely dangerous angle pointing towards me and instructed him to hold his earlobe together whilst I sought out the medical kit. I had not even opened the hatch to the medical box when the second man returned with blood pouring out of his nose! He did not even know how he had achieved the superbly executed slice across his septum but this was certainly a good one.

We decided to head in to as these were nasty cuts. By the time we arrived at my Weymouth Harbour mooring an ambulance was already waiting to take the two customers away, both of whom required stitches.

The next day was the opening day of the five day World Angling Championships to be held in Weymouth. I was telling the competitors why the ambulance was at my boat the previous evening as seen by some of the International anglers. They found it hard to believe that such experienced anglers could be so clumsy with a knife and inflict such damage upon themselves in such a short time.

I was one of the first of 18 boats to leave the harbour with my 10 competing International anglers on-board. Anglers at this level know that a successful catch rate is achieved because of the great attention they pay to their bait. These men require a good deal of time before an event begins and so I had been asked if I could go very gently to the first mark so as to allow the bait preparation to take place. It was calm but there was still a slight swell and lift in the sea from the previous day's winds and I ventured out as gently as possible.

We had travelled all of a quarter of a mile before I was hastily summoned to the stern of my boat. One of the German competitors had been kneeling at the back and was happily tenderising his squid by holding the blade of his knife and tapping away merrily with the handle. He slipped and stuck his knife firmly through his green wellington boot and into that delicate part of the ankle just under the main ankle bone where the heel is at its slenderest. The blood was rapidly filling his boot and sock which were removed to reveal a wound from which the blood was spurting and travelling a surprising distance.

Laying the casualty on his back with his leg in the air and two of his team mates taking it in turn to pressurise the wound and stop the torrent of blood, we turned and hurtled back to Weymouth. The Competition organisers had been notified and an ambulance was once again summoned to take away the third knife wounded casualty from *Offshore Rebel IV* in less than 12 hours.

We returned to sea minus a quarter of the German 'A' team which finished Day One a long way behind their anticipated position. Such are the dangers of knives….and hooks!

The Olympics and Lost in Africa

The Sailing Olympics came to Weymouth and Portland both for the practice run in 2011 and the real event in 2012. Once again it was all down to the foresight of Pat Carlin that we South Boats owners were booked to carry the various Race Committees who were to oversee the different 'classes' of dinghies. The team that were on my boat were looking after the *Finns* and the *Stars*. The *Finn* is a single handed vessel and was the class that Sir Ben Ainslie was in so that was quite an experience to see how the races unfolded leading up to him winning Gold for England.

We actually had a lot of fun during those weeks and we skippers were behaving at our mischievous best. The Race Committee I had with me were extremely good hearted people who had very generously given up their time on a voluntary basis to attend the heats and practice events and now officiate at the 2012 finals. It must have been a very expensive as well as time consuming commitment for each person to make and, like so many people passionate for the sport they love, it was a real pleasure to take them out and watch their expertise and practiced teamwork in action.

Security to enter Portland was very strict. We skippers, crews, competitors and all the many other people involved with such a major event were brought into Portland on specially laid on buses. We were searched upon entry and were not even allowed to bring in our own food and worse still, milk was taken away from us! There was a good deal of waiting around at sea before the day's programme started and the most important thing for everyone on the boat was a nice cup of tea! How could I make any with no milk? It became quite a challenge to find ways to smuggle milk into the port! But, through a variety of devious methods, we managed. Fortunately the SBS Unit that was assisting in security had also teamed up with a Weymouth Security firm whose boss I knew and who was a smuggling maestro.

There were five different South Boats catamarans involved but we were all 'shrink wrapped' in such a way as to make us all the same blue and white colour so that we looked identical. It was, apparently, good for TV if the Committee vessels were all the same. The Royal Yachting Association had provided one brand new South Boat for the Olympics and for future sailing events which cost £350,000. The idea was to have five vessels made but at that exorbitant price it was decided that chartering identical boats would be the best way forward which is why I, as a South Boats Catamaran owner, was one of the lucky few to be used with the fifth and final South Boat joining the Weymouth boats from Poole to complete the Officiating Fleet.

With the boats lined up, the progress in the hulls and general design could be seen with noticeable differences between mine, the very first 36' hull, Pat's *Meridian Express* which after being sold several times around the South Coast of UK has returned to Portland now as a dive boat called *Scimitar*, the luxurious *Tiger Lily*, *True Blue* from Poole and the RYA top of the range latest vessel especially built for The Olympics.

My Olympic Duties were the first to finish and so I was released and off I went to Alderney on a five day charter. I actually got that Alderney charter because for the first time ever I had a toilet on the boat. This was because one of the Olympics' conditions of chartering was that all the Committee boats had to have toilets and these next customers coming to Alderney insisted that they must have a loo on board as there were ladies in the group. I hate toilets on boats with a vengeance. I recall Grandma asking Grandad if we could have an inside toilet instead of a chilly shed out in the back yard. Grandad replied that how could we call installing a crapper inside the house progress?! Well, I totally agreed with that sentiment. We suffering skippers must spend more time unblocking sea toilets than anything else....dirty, stinking things! And on this Post-Olympic trip the bloody thing, noisy with an electric machinator, seemed to be forever noisily whirring away in use.

We were on our way back to Weymouth after our week long toilet testing trip and I could see Portland in the distance... and then, over the VHF radio, came the dreaded words.

"All stations, all stations, all stations; This is warship HMS Bulwark. For Live Gunnery Firing, please listen on Channel 73."

Oh, oh...the warning bells of my memory started to clang.

And then...on Channel 73 began the notice to Mariners. Please spot the immediate mistake in the broadcast!

"This is HMS Bulwark. Live gunnery firing will begin in 20 minutes from position (wait for it!!) 7 degrees 30 minutes North and 2 degrees 30 minutes East. We will be firing out to a distance of 20 miles south of our given position."

Now, being a bit sensitive to live firing because of my past Naval experiences, I called up HMS Bulwark for clarification of their notice and position. Everything was repeated and I explained that I was very concerned as I felt that I was lost. I explained that I believed I could see Portland in the distance and also a vessel which I believed was HMS Bulwark, having 'worked' with the ship as part of the security mission codenamed Olympic Guardian over the past two years. I gave them my position and that I was currently headed straight at them as I believed that to be my safest course of action...assuming they didn't intend blowing themselves up.

My position was confirmed, their position was reconfirmed at 7 degrees 30 minutes North and 2 degrees 30 minutes East and, I was assured, that was definitely the Island of Portland showing some 10 miles ahead.

I had contacted our good friends at Portland Coastguard and asked them to monitor this conversation between myself and HMS Bulwark.

"Sir," questions I, very aware of my lowly position as a crumb in the biscuit barrel of life, " your given Latitude and Longitude puts you 450 miles North of the Equator and your Longitude puts me in the charming Africa state of Benim just west of Nigeria. Please confirm".

Now this shows why situations at sea can quickly become extremely disconcerting. With a 20 mile live firing range pattern on a bearing of 200 degrees, anything in the west going Shipping Lane, including super tankers stuffed with various fuels, could be hit.

There was a lengthy pause and then a reissuing of the broadcast which now put HMS Bulwark at 50 degrees 15 minutes North and 2 degrees 30 minutes West and me definitely in the correct part of the English Channel and heading for Portland.

Ten minutes later another broadcast on Channel 73 once again announced the ship's position at 7 degrees 30 minute North and 2 Degrees 30 minutes East and so again I called up and the whole of our previous conversation was repeated with Portland Coastguard listening in. Unbelievable.

This time what sounded like very young radio operators started giggling leading me then to think this was all a hoax with another vessel nearby playing silly buggers. But no, Portland Coastguard confirmed it was indeed the ship; firing was to be halted until they could establish and confirm their GPS System was not 'playing up'. Hard to believe that there were problems with the ship's Navigation system but in the past I have known Naval radars that were unable to detect targets allowing live shells to land next to various sized craft including me and the Condor Channel Island Ferry because they were 'not seen' due to a 'radar limitation'.

Portland told me they had passed on the information to Command Ops down in Falmouth. I don't know what the result of all this was but it was deeply worrying to think that *HMS Bulwark* was the control vessel co-ordinating the Olympics' security at sea which many of the Weymouth Charter boats were involved in. Fortunately my own plotter was correct and we entered Weymouth safely but the bloody toilet was jammed on and running and burnt out before I could isolate it. That night I dismantled the whole thing and put my bench seating back vowing never again would there be a toilet aboard *Offshore Rebel*!

Fishing Adventures for our Windy UK Winters.

The 'winter' of 2012-2013 saw me back in Phuket, Thailand. Thanks to the assistance of EFSA President Horst Schneider, I had bought a house in Phuket 2008 when our British Pound had some purchasing power. I had the idea that I could do something a bit different and more worthwhile rather than just sitting around at home cancelling so many angling trips throughout the November to the mid-March period. Also, March was no longer the extremely busy month it had been in the quite recent past. We no longer enjoyed the arrival of the plaice on the Shambles Bank and there seemed less interest in pollack fishing.

Back in the pre-1995 days, I was able to commercial fish during the winter months and earn a living plus employ a full time crew. But, because of the politics of the day, my licence had been removed from my boat and this option no longer existed.

As I had so many contacts in my customers data base built up from even before the 1987 launch of Offshore Rebel I, I reasoned that I could offer fishing and scuba diving holidays in sunny Thailand for a competitive price. It was an idea born out of the desire to keep working which I could no longer do in England.

And here we are now in 2020 with our last guests, who were themselves EFSA members, having returned to UK in late March just in time before the shut down of Phuket Airport due to the current Coronavirus situation.

The project has worked and the house has been pretty well full throughout the 12 years I have been offering this option. Because I was now away from the UK for 3 months and now up to 5 months, I could no longer keep the journalism going and so in 2004, coinciding with the Digital Era, it was time to retire from my local sea angling journalist position after, I'm proud to say, not missing a single deadline in 20 full years of writing. And, to be fair, it was well over time for the local angling scene to have a change of reporter, with a lady taking over.

Jai stayed on as crew until 2015 and then *Offshore Rebel IV* was graced with the presence of Sara who I am sure is well remembered by customers and boat crews alike because of her dazzling good looks and charm. Sara was also extremely intelligent and possessing a deep and detailed knowledge about the sea and Tall Ships. Not only was she a superb and very hard worker, but she helped me catch up on films, TV programmes, books that I had missed out on for what seemed the whole of the 21st Century to date. When the customers had left the boat in Alderney in the summer of 2015 for their evening festivities, *Offshore Rebel*'s wheelhouse became full of wires and gadgets wired into the TV or boat music system with Sara giving me detailed explanations of what I was about to see or listen to.

Sara was far too talented to remain as a crew on a little boat like mine and was destined for much greater things and is now working for The Jubilee Sailing Trust and is involved with those majestic Tall Ships, *Tenacious* and *The Lord Nelson*.

Salvage at Sea and a Sultry Accent

Before progressing to greater Sailing Adventures, Sara experienced a couple of 'rescues' involving a Tall Ship and a French yacht.

Attentions had turned to the delights of the forth-coming evening meal booked up in the superb Mai Thai restaurant at the top of Heart Attack Hill in Alderney and so it was time to conclude our day's fishing and head for the Harbour. The fishing tackle was being stowed and the crewess, Sara, had returned to the deck, knife in hand, in readiness to gut and fillet the fish on our short ride to Braye Harbour. And then one of our anglers shouts out that he can see what appears to be an upturned boat with a person hanging on to the stern of it.

We sent course for the casualty and as we neared it could be seen that this was nowhere near as serious a situation as first thought but was in fact a very expensive, large and new RIB floating on the ebb tide on the south side of Alderney. A radio call to Alderney Coastguard informed us that this was a very poorly lashed down tender belonging to one of the Tall Ships bound for Alderney and which had fallen off when the ship hit the overalls in the Swinge the day before.

The rib had drifted way off to the North east of Alderney on the flood tide and then, the next day, travelled back to the south west appearing down on the south side of the Island. It had capsized and needed all the combined strength of ten men plus the *Offshore Rebel*'s one tonne hydraulic winch to coax this hefty Rigid Inflatable Boat, complete with new 40 HP Mercury outboard engine, aboard. It was no easy task.

We took it back into Alderney Harbour and found the Tall Ship in question. The highly embarrassed Captain was seriously relieved as this was a very expensive and new rib costing in excess of £40,000. We were asked what we wanted as payment and we pointed out several of the very attractive crewesses on board...only to be politely refused, damn him! But we had a meal paid for all of that evening us at the Mai Thai restaurant and I was presented with a fine bottle of wine and at last a very decent pair of sea-boots to replace my leaking wellies.

When bass fishing in the fast flowing ebb tide of Alderney Race we would often be temporarily joined by barely controllable yachts caught in the tide flow and hurtling straight at us at speeds up of to 10 knots. We would watch them flash by us to disappear into the often violent tumbling seas that formed after the shallows of the Brimtides Ledge and around the appropriately named Inner and Outer Danger Rocks before being bounced for several more miles towards Guernsey.

On some occasions, courageous yachtsmen would attempt to sail against this raging current which would be all but impossible except in the hands of an extremely experienced and skilful crew.

We were just about to reset another Washing Machine bas drift at the northern edge of the Alderney Race when the fog descended rapidly. We decided that would be our last drift as it was far too dangerous with no visibility. We drifted southwards away from the rough waters in order to tidy up and then prepare for a very foggy ride back to Alderney Harbour.

Then a Mayday call went out of Channel 16 from a French yacht who had dropped its anchor in what it thought was the safety of Longis Bay to await the turn of the ebb tide before attempting to reach the harbour on the opposite side. Their conversation with Alderney Radio expressed their great surprise at how much tide there was and that the bow of their yacht was starting to get pulled under!

We had a target on the radar but that was right in the middle of The Race just behind Blanchard, the Washing Machine rock and not in the safety of a sheltered Longis Bay The target was difficult to distinguish as the waves were pretty high by now. I notified Alderney Radio to say I had a possible radar target and I could ease my way through what was becoming a big sea just to check it out if they would like me to. They agreed that would be a good move so we gently picked our way between the waves and against the tide towards what I believed to be the yacht in question.

Sure enough it was the yacht...and French at that...anchored in the very worst place imaginable in thick fog, increasingly heavy seas and with its bow inches from going under.

I reported the situation to Alderney Coastguard. They advised me to tell the Yacht crew to let their anchor go immediately before they were dragged under. It is very difficult to shout such instructions in a very noisy sea over very loud engines to a frightened and confused French crew. Finally they understood and the anchor chain was released which I imagine was no easy task. With the tension on the anchor chain released the yacht's bow came up clear of the sea and then it went and went into a broadside rolling drift in what was probably the most boisterous part of the sea anywhere in the English Channel or, in the case of Les Francais, la Manche.

I had good lads on board and a fine rope thrower.....and after several attempts in the fast tide we managed to get the yacht under tow and take it in towards Longis Bay away from the racing ebb tide. This took quite a long time and we drifted a fair way south before we gained control and managed to ease into the North north-east running back eddy. The forecast was not good so I thought that we must try to ease up to the Brimtides and then attempt to edge round the northern corner of Alderney knowing the tide would be extremely strong for the first part there but only for about 400 metres. If we could ease through that difficult area we could pick up the south-west running stream to help us tow the yacht into safer water and then be able to reach Braye Harbour.

So, off we headed using the now exposed Brimtides rocks to block and deflect the ebb tide. We headed into the rough water at the edge of the rocks and headed as far towards the north as I could. The tow-rope was bar-tight but it was 16mm spun nylon and hopefully strong enough to handle the tow.

And then the radio conversation started. The French yacht called me. The voice was female with that attractive accent that gives the French at least one likeable quality.

"Engleesh fisher boat …zis iz dee yaht be'ind yoo. Please don't pull me so hard. Can yoo be more gentle?" asks the softly alluring voice.

"French yacht. Engleesh fishing boat. Sorry I will need to go harder to pull you through this rough stuff", says I in my firmest Nautical tones.

"Eh? Sorry. No comprends. Pleeease be gentle with me. I am frightened you will break me if you are too hard," came the disarming reply.

Well…I can see why the writers of English/French comedy can have such fun with double-entendres. The conversation became ever naughtier despite my best efforts to keep it nautical, firm and lean. Cross Mar, the French Radio Station, called me up and asked me what was I doing to their French Lady-Yachties and Alderney joined in with even more questions full of double meaning. The lads were rolling about in the oft-seen hysterics experienced in the *Offshore Rebel* wheelhouse even though we recognised the terror in the charming accent over the radio.

Finally we eased our way out of the main tide and into the slack tide triangle where the ebb tide splits into south-westerly and north-easterly flows Another 100 metres of so and we were picking up the tide taking us into Braye Harbour. The sea was calm now and the fog thick but my trusty large screened plotter guided us to a mooring buoy onto which we attached the yacht. This last part went so smoothly that the French crew found it hard to believe we were actually now in safety and they were secured with the Harbour Authorities on their way out to them…probably to collect the mooring fees for the night.

We were rewarded with bottles of wine and promises of dinner the next day….but by the time we returned after the following day's fishing, they were long taking that sultry accent with them.

The Last Drift

My role as a skipper was always to try and provide the platform and framework for the angler to be able to participate in and enjoy his sport. Some of the young skippers ask me how I managed to keep going for so long and I firmly believe it was because fishing was not my hobby. I love being at sea and the unpredictable nature of the job but my main delight was in seeing customers catching fish.

We are all aware that fishing has become more difficult. I believe that I was extremely fortunate to have experienced the best of times and that since about 2010, it was becoming more difficult to find the fish. We, we being my customers and me, had lived through some excellent times since 1987 with some very big catches and now 25 years later it was not what we were used to and I could hear the disappointment out on deck.

One particular day I recall, we were mid-Channel fishing over the massive wreck of the *Bonita,* an Ecuadorian 8000 tonne cargo ship carrying fertilizer from Hamburg to Panama which sank on December 13th of 1981 in Hurricane conditions and 9 meter waves. We were in the west bound shipping lane with the position of this particular wreck right on the main steering line for the many ships which regularly sailed directly over it. It meant keeping a very sharp eye out on the shipping with many vessels capable of speeds in the 18 knot range. The pollack were laying on the northern end of the wreck and if I got the GPS numbers bang on we were able to use the brisk south-east wind to drift just clear of the very high Northern tackle-hungry end of the wreck and find a few pollack inbetween dodging the massive ships bearing down on us at frequent intervals. We were catching 2 or 3 fish a drift, not good by past standards but good considering the conditions and, on chatting to my fellow skippers, compared well to their struggles that particular day to find a few fish.

I was actually pleased that I'd managed to find and hold to the drift that was producing the fish throughout that tide and we managed to put a couple of boxfuls of filleted pollack and a couple of cod together. Every word out on deck can be heard by the skipper in his wheelhouse and I could hear the anglers talking about how disappointing the fishing was and they came in to see me to express that disappointment. I think that was the defining moment when I realised that I really couldn't do the job anymore. The expectations were out of proportion to the reality of what was available and these expectations were based on the experiences of the past years. It was definitely time for this ageing Sea-Dog to change direction.

I was warned in 1987 that there was no future in Charter Angling and then experienced the best job ever and excellent fishing for the next 30 years. My trip to the wreck of the *Bonita* trip simply showed that a different direction was needed and youthful enthusiasm was required to pursue that direction. Looking at our young skippers in Weymouth now, the future is in skilful and keen hands. We have Lyle Stantiford (*Supa Nova)* Luke Pettis (*Snapper*) and Ryan Casey (*Meercat*) who are dedicated young men and determined to try out new types of fishing. We have the enigmatic, totally mad Josh Simmonds (*Fish-On*) who is as near to being an angling genius as the description allows and who is also offering some sensational shore fishing guidance over the winter months.

Weymouth still has the Lochin that used to be Chris Tett's *Peace and Plenty* which then became *Wild Frontier* before changing once again to *Amarisa* as skippered by Keith Brown, son of Ron Brown who bought *Valerie Ann* from my Uncle Vic and ran that for many years before purchasing *Amarissa*. And we have the Conger Competition's Top Man, Adrian Brown, who owns *Al's Spirit* which used to be one of Chris Caines' *Tiger Lily* vessels. Retired *Duchess II*'s skipper, Geoff Clarke's son, Dan Clarke, runs *Finns-Up* out of Portland and has, along with Ryan and Lyle, been making a name for himself over the past couple of years with the shark fishing that has become popular out of Weymouth again as well as continuing with the reefing and wrecking scene.

And we have those wise skippers who have maintained a steady traditional approach and have a loyal following such as Dave Pitman on *Atlanta* who has been skippering for over 50 years and will never give up and who has been joined in recent years by Ryan Casey's Dad, Trad, running *Gypsy II*. Weymouth also has the very experienced species hunter specialist, Colin Penny (*Flamer*) and Colin Baker (*Sally Ann Jo*) with his well laid out Blyth Catamaran.

And of course the *Offshore Rebel* adventure continues but is now under the new ownership of skipper Jamie Pullin who despite his relatively tender years has a vast experience of both skippering commercial and charter boats having worked for Chris Tett and Pat Carlin as well as me.

And just because it was time to hang up my sea boots on this part of the adventure, so there are many more waves that a Sea-Dog can ride before it's time to be finally sit the garden and listen to the dicky birds chirping. Handing over the wheel of *Offshore Rebel* has surprisingly opened up many more new opportunities.

The Art of Non-Retirement

The *Dorset Wildlife Trust's Fleet Explorer* is a very long and grand sounding name for such a small craft but it is licensed to carry 12 customers and takes these adventurous souls into the far reaches and fast tides of the UK's longest salt water lagoon, The Fleet.

Sandwiched between the Portland end of Chesil Beach and the mainland, The Fleet reaches all the way westward past Pirates' Cove and the snakelocks anemones' lair, through the formidable currents of 'The Narrows' where the secretive Bridging Camp lurks and into the seagrass expanses where rare sea-horses hide and the last remaining local pirates fish for green crabs onwards to Abbotsbury and finishing at the famous Swannery.

From the Isle of Slingers' Heights, the panoramic sweep of Dead Man's Bay, Echo Beach and The Fleet feature in many photographs and is regularly voted as the 'Best Sea-View' in England. Watching the heavy surf crash onto the seaward side of Chesil accompanied by the powerful undertow dragging the growling pebbles back out to sea, it's easy to understand why hundreds of ships were wrecked and smashed to pieces here over the centuries.

Every inch of Dorset's Juarassic coastline is heaving with history, superstition, myth, tradition and stories that reach out of the mists which so often shroud Portland to break upon us. *The Fleet Explorer* is there waiting to take the expectant visitor into this Dorsetian world, shaped by Henry VIII, Christopher Wren, King Charles III, Admiral Hardy and Admiral Samuel Hood, John Wordsworth, Thomas Hardy and a host of local men who may or may not appear during the trip along The Fleet.

J.Meade Faulkner's 1898 novel and 1955 film *Moonfleet*; Hardy's novel, set on Portland, *The Well Beloved*; Barnes Wallace's Bouncing Bombs; Martha and the Muffins 1980 hit *Echo Beach* covered by Toyah in 1987 and the 2017 movie *On Chesil Beach* add to the rich and ongoing mystique of this part of southern England over which the over-riding presence of the Lord of the Long Ears, The Great Fluffy One, with his hordes of followers, known on

Portland as 'Underground Mutton', gazes across the County from the lofty heights of the Verne Citadel.

When Weymouth Angling Society stalwart and bass fisherman, Bill Nobel, built the boat that was eventually to become *The Fleet Observer* in 1996, he would enthusiastically describe the pleasures he hoped it would bring to visiting holiday makers and locals alike. We spoke about some of the local history and people mentioned above and of the underwater marine life that could be seen in The Fleet, the longest salt-water lagoon in North-west Europe, as well as the bird life, especially the Little Terns. I told him, 25 years ago, that one day I would love to skipper his boat and it would be something I could look forward to in my retirement dotage.

In late 2017, having agreed to part with *Offshore Rebel IV*, I visited the Dorset Wildlife Centre on Chesil Beach and asked if I might be considered to be a skipper for the summer of 2018. It's not very easy to get skippers even though there are many people who would be able to do this particular job very well. The problem, as always, is qualifications. The skipper has to hold a Commercially Endorsed Certification and the courses required to obtain the various Commercial Endorsements are expensive. So, someone like me whose various sea going qualifications were still up to date and wasn't concerned about earning much are very rare indeed. Monthly wages were described as being enough to buy a 'nice restaurant meal for two' which is pretty accurate; it really is a 'job' for someone who simply takes great pleasure from doing it.

The Wildlife Centre kindly agreed to take me on as a 'relief' skipper giving the regular skipper one day a week off. To be honest, I don't think the resident skipper, Roger, wanted to have a day off! Roger is outstanding at the job as can be seen from the many compliments on Trip Advisor and he speaks with a massive amount of knowledge and enthusiasm about the wildlife and history of The Fleet. I enjoyed listening to him so much that I went out on six of the one hour Fleet trips with him to get some ideas of what I should say when it was my turn to drive the boat. The Wildlife Centre has several dedicated full time staff and one of them, Angela, has written a highly informative booklet which further adds to Roger's talks and Bill's early enthusiastic interests. With all the extra information in the Dorset Wildlife Centre itself, situated on Chesil Beach just after crossing the Ferrybridge connecting Wyke Regis to the Portland Beach Road, I had plenty to try to learn and include into *The Fleet Explorer*'s voyages of discovery when I was the Skipper.

The main thing is, of course, the wildlife and in particular the birdlife. This is a major weakness on my part. Even after all those years at sea, I could just about recognise seagulls and non-seagulls. Of course the term 'seagull' covers a number of gull species which I am still trying to recognise along with the oyster catchers, windbrills, egrets, and various species of terns along with many others. There are also hares, foxes and even deer to be seen on Chesil Beach or crossing The Fleet.

The customers that come on the trips include some extremely knowledgeable bird watchers. When they are on the boat, they are encouraged them to 'take over' and provide the commentary and observations for the other visitors and I become one of the listeners. The main topic of interest for the bird enthusiasts is the little tern sanctuary which is guarded by volunteers 24 hours a day during the end of April to August period. These generous people try their best to protect the eggs and chicks from an array of formidable predators, including kestrels which are protected birds under the Wildlife and Countryside Act of 1981. Last season kestrels from Portland basically wiped out the newborn chicks despite the best effort of the volunteer protectors who can only shout, wave their arms or shine a laser torch at them, none of which has much effect. Being the philistine that I am, my offer to shoot them did not go down at all well. I am seriously out of touch with political correctness and have much to learn. I have even taken the wrong Tea Mug in the mornings when at the Wildlife Centre without realising the emotional consequences of such an act of uncivilised barbarity. Becoming a Sea-Dog has taken me away from many of the niceties and polite conventions of civilised shore society.

The Fleet Observer is a flat bottomed dory with an overhead canopy mounted on a metal frame to shield customers from the sun and rain. This canopy is nearly as long as the boat itself and acts as a sail when the winds are channelled up and down The Fleet. The flat bottomed hull cannot grip the water as a hefty keeled vessel can and it is greatly influenced by the wind which, if it gets under the dory hull, can send the vessel skating off across the water at a fair and uncontrollable pace. The vessel is, in short, both the smallest commercial vessel I have operated and the most difficult!

At the start of the 2018 season, I spent many hours on my own learning how to handle this super light skiff with its 40HP outboard engine in windy conditions and the short, sharp chop generated in wind over tide situations which are very common in The Fleet. It was quite a challenge as I was very mindful of the variety of passengers likely to come aboard the vessel including lively children and some quite elderly and frail visitors who would not appreciate me crashing into the pontoon at the end of their trip. You would think after running boats for so many years that this would be easy but it just shows how every single boat has its own character and behaves in its own individual way and to be complacent about this could very likely lead to injuring someone.

The great thing about skippering this boat is that we are there to inform and entertain our customers and there are so many anecdotes and stories to recount along with the potentially massive amount of information that there is to impart. There are some very serious wildlife lovers who are very knowledgeable indeed so it has been a very steep learning curve for me with still a long way to go. Being able to explain, for example, the actual formation of Chesil Beach, understanding the intricacies of longshore drift, expounding upon the 'saline gradient', the workings of the mysterious Court Leet, dates of historical significance and such basics as how were the deep-scalloped indentations of the beach Canns formed are all new to me as is much more that I must learn in order to provide anywhere near the detailed and informative tour that Roger and Angela provide.

But...that's what retirement's all about....learning new things and meeting new people.

The Portland based Skin Deep Diving Company had one young skipper whose wife demanded that he should come home at weekends and spend some time with his children who were now struggling to remember his name. My son kindly suggested to his friend that now his Papa was retired and 'doing nothing', maybe he could be persuaded to take some dive trips out at the weekend and thus allow his friend to spend some time at home with his young family.

And so, because I was just lounging around in the garden listening to the dickie birds twittering, I agreed to skipper the dive boat *Skin Deep* on what was going to be an occasional weekend.

After a month, I was asked if I could or wanted to commit to all the weekends for the next two months as Tom's friend had the offer of a yacht delivery come up. I was a tad confused at this as I thought my main role was to take occasional weekend trips to allow this young man time with his family....and now we were talking of him taking on a trip which would mean six continuous weeks away at sea rather than just weekends.

Tom's friend took on the delivery job...which was described as being 'just a short one'....as in crossing the Pacific Ocean! This resulted in me suddenly becoming very busy with mid-week trips also creeping in. And then, after a couple of months had passed, we were informed the delivery job had been extended because the yacht had suffered a lightning strike at sea and was badly damaged and was now limping towards San Francisco for repairs. In the end our young yachting delivery skipper was away until mid-September and so skippering the dive boat became quite a commitment.

Way back in the 1980's, I took a couple of diving trips aboard *Vanishing Trick and Offshore Rebel I* and quickly realised I did not enjoy them. The concern I felt and the feeling of utter uselessness when the divers were underwater far outweighed the pleasure of having the boat to myself once they'd leapt off. Watching their position indicating bubbles coming to the surface back then and then the arrival on the surface of the divers' SMBs (Surface Marker Buoys) was quite a relief. I know other angling skippers feel like this and have tried taking dive trips and soon returned to angling.

And so for the next 30 years I promised myself I would not become a dive boat skipper ever again….and now I find that I have. Unfortunately the overwhelming sense of concern for the divers when they have left the boat has not left me and I spent all of the 2018 season with a pounding head-ache. And, to make things more entertaining, there are no tell-tale signs of bubbles from many of the divers because they use the closed-circuit re-breather system which reuses the gases rather than blowing them to the surface. Unlike the very gentle and relatively simple diving we do here in Thailand, UK divers operate on a completely different level and are often diving in the 45 to 60 metre range, and sometimes deeper. With such depths a total dive time from when a person leaves the boat until when they resurface can be up to two long hours during which time the tide can pick up considerably with the divers eventually surfacing a considerably way from where they were originally dropped.

A number of emergency incidents including helicopter evacuations occurred on 'my' boat over the two seasons that I have been involved as skipper but there is no doubt that the rewards for these divers is very high and they are obviously prepared to take the element of risk. Most divers do have an enjoyable experience and see a world that many of us will never see apart from on film. On surfacing, their faces show their delight and their videos and photographs are a revelation. I thought that the visibility in the UK would always be grim but far from it. 2018 was an exceptional year with incredible visibility of 15 metres and more. There were also many good days in 2019 with again some unbelievably clear photography of wrecks and artefacts.

Dropping down through 50 metres or more onto WWII or WWI wrecks and ships even before these dates is to go back in time and to see something very special indeed. I can certainly understand the attraction although I do not envy the Tech divers the amount of kit they need to wear to carry out their hobby. Many times I watch divers stagger back onto the boat and say that they don't understand why they do it....a bit like anglers after a hard and exhausting day.

The divers sometimes bring along items to show everyone on their next trip that they have previously recovered and on which they have worked to restore to its former glory. It's quite amazing how brass-work from 100 years ago can be made to glitter like new again.

Divers do a good deal of research of the wreck they hope to dive and some are real experts. Listening to them give the dive briefing is fascinating. For us anglers, we want to know how high the wreck stands and if it is snaggy. We need to know the best lure and how many wind-ups we need to make before dropping back down. We are not too bothered about which shipyard the vessel was made in, or its history or even its name really. We are interested only in the fish and I am genuinely surprised how little the divers know about the fish. There's not that many different species on a UK wreck and I would have thought that they are very easy to identify. When I ask, "What fish did you see?" I will be told, "Stripy fish" or "Quite big fish". Conger eels are at least easily recognised and by the descriptions I get they are all 200lb plus which is good news for the conger festivals. Divers are very good at identifying crustaceans and often bring a big crab or a few scallops back to the boat which Kannika does her very best to charm out of the captor's clutches.

The difference between anglers and divers was brought home to me years ago when one of the angling charter boats was unloading in Weymouth and there were a couple of boxes of bass and a nice box of cod fillets on the pontoon. A dive boat had also returned and on the pontoon next to them was a heap of rusty metal. The divers looked at the anglers' boxes and expressed their disgust saying that 'it shouldn't be allowed' and the anglers looked at the divers' pile of rust and were saying, "What the fuck is all this crap?"

A major part of an angling skipper's day is the never ending banter between the anglers and the fun of joining in. On the way out to a wreck, skippers are often very fortunate to have an angler standing as close as possible to him in the wheelhouse all to way out to the wreck. These thoughtful individuals will often unselfishly share the aroma of last night's garlic ridden curry with the skipper and sometimes challenge him still further with an impenetrable accent that no-one else on the boat can comprehend whilst regaling him with highly imaginative tales of his personal catches.

Drifting a wreck requires a constant commentary from the skipper so that the anglers have a chance of catching the fish and not the metal and anchoring wrecks or reefs encourages a day of stories and jokes to make the whole experience fun. The day is full of a constant barrage of verbal exchanges!

It's not so much like that on dive charters. Firstly, the day is much more condensed. Diving takes place over slack tide so it would be silly to arrive at a dive site with four hours of screaming tide to wait through until it was time to enter the water. The dive trip is planned so that the waiting time is reduced as much as possible which means that on the way out to the wreck or dive location, divers are very busy preparing their kit. Unlike fishing tackle, the dive equipment must be absolutely correct. A missing item of kit or something breaking on the day can result in someone's whole dive being lost so kitting up needs to be carried out meticulously and there is only limited time for divers to be coming into the cabin and chatting with the skipper. Once the wreck or mark is reached, the divers are sitting quietly waiting for the countdown...they don't want to be chatting to some old sea-dog about matters that are of little relevance at this particular time...and then they're gone. There's definitely no time for chit-chat now as they are underwater for up to two hours in a conversation less world.

On their return to the surface, if we are on a two dive day, the divers are sorting out their equipment ready for the second dive which will be about 90 minutes later in shallower water. They are often pretty tired from the first dive and just want to relax as we chug gently to the next site. And, after the second dive, there is all the expensive gear to pack away and to debrief....so there is not really much communication between divers and skipper unlike with anglers and skipper.

So, dive-boat skippering is a very different job from skippering an angling boat and one that I would say has been quite a challenge for me. Having started to relax a bit more last season, I discovered the permanent headache of 2018 had lessened to an occasional throb in 2019. I was looking forward to returning this season, 2020, and meeting up with the divers that I had started to get to know and meeting some new ones.

Having so much time on my hands with all this lazing about retirement malarkey, I have been able to take a few angling trips out for friends and to enjoy different boats such as Bex Florence's very fine South Boat, *Kelly's Hero* which is based in Langston. *Kelly's Hero* used to be called *Second Opinion* and was a private boat rather than a charter boat. As such this vessel was fitted out to the highest specification and is a real delight to work with. She is narrower than the usual 36' South Boats in order to fit into her berth which used to be at Lymington. This difference in length to width ratio makes *Kelly's Hero* very fast indeed and much better on fuel consumption than the usual 36' x 16' dimensions.

Throughout the years, my son Tom has crewed for me on occasions. I had always hoped we would end up as a three boat charter family with both sons joining me and running boats for diving and angling boats. Younger son, Sam, is very good with people and a fine angler and would have made an excellent angling skipper but it wasn't to be as people must go their own way and live their own lives. Son Sam always told me he valued his social life too much to become a charter skipper which he described as a 'way of life'.

And now, because I am retired with lots of time on my hands as can be seen, I have been acting on occasions as crew for son Tom, which is an entertaining reversal of roles and one which I find very enjoyable. Tom is involved in transferring stores and personnel out to big container ships and Naval craft (avoiding their live firing, of course) in Portland Harbour and Weymouth Bay. Tom is running one of the now Shipping Tycoon, Pat Carlin's vessels the *Cara Cara* which came from Kinsale in southern Ireland. *Cara Cara* is a lovely, solid Aquastar and still looks good after many years of use.

The personnel that are taken out to the ships are mainly professional sea-farers. The journey time from land to ship is very short so we do not have time to chat much but you can see from the way these men walk around the boat and how, in particular, they shimmy up the rope ladders that dangle down the towering hulls of the container ships and tankers, that they are men of the sea. Our brief exchanges reveal that they have 'seen the world' and would be fascinating to have time for a beer and a chat with….the only problem being that hardly any of them speak English and my Filipino, Russian and Indonesian is not up to much and I refuse to speak French.

And then there are the other interesting jobs where very expensive equipment has to be tested at sea and which I cannot describe here for fear of being shot but is, to say the least, mind blowing as to what is 'going on out there' in our English Channel…and will no doubt be revealed one day.

During my time as an angling charter skipper, Pat Carlin would ask me to join him on jobs that were often very interesting and lucrative. I could never, apart from one Dr. Who filming job and of course the Olympics, take him up on his offers as I was always booked for at least a year in advance with angling. Although tempting, I always believed that if I was booked, then that must take priority and I must honour that commitment. Pat used to berate me and tell me it was a waste of time offering me jobs as I'd never take them…and that is why he has gone on to make a dazzling success of his business and I have remained a 'low life scum bag'…….and that's what retirement is all about…looking back contentedly over one's working life and accepting one's position within it!

Enforced (temporary) Retirement

This 2020 season was going to be a continuation of the various activities above with several more boats to be included in my retirement programme. The idea was to give more of my charter skipper colleagues a break during the busy season and allow them a chance to pursue interests and develop further marine related skills on various courses that have been booked up in the knowledge that their vessels and customers will be treated gently by me but, of course, nobody can predict what will happen for the rest of this year.

My Charter Skipper colleagues are suffering badly as are so many people right now. In their case, there is no financial assistance being offered to compensate for not being allowed to work but, as with any business, the outgoings demands are high and are still expected to be met. And, after the many years of battling for recognition, there remains the feeling that the Charter Boat Industry and its valuable contribution to other related sea-side businesses is still not recognised. The contradictory advice between MAFF, DEFRA, the Government and local Harbour Authorities is for ever contradictory with the belief that there is no understanding amongst those who make the all-important decisions leading to confusion and frustration amongst a law abiding and hard working group of boat owners who have invested everything in their small businesses.

For my part, I am still in Phuket, Thailand, having had four flights cancelled. I haven't a clue when I will be able to return to Dorset but Thailand is being very helpful and hospitable having kindly extended my Visa right through until the end of July. This means that I am fishing every day in the lake behind the house or having to sit outside and listen to those darn dickie birds twittering after all. And, when the monsoon rains pour down, must disappear into the world of Sea-dog Tall Tales via my computer.

So, when I least expected it to happen, retirement has been thrust upon me....for the moment!

Serve and Obey

The Offshore Rebel boats averaged between 210 to to 225 trips a year for 30 years between 1987 and 2017. This amounts to about 6,500 days at sea with 700 of those trips being the multi-day charters to Alderney in the Channel Islands. Trips are approximately 10 hours in length with skippers tending to 'live' on their vessels when away from home going ashore for maybe just a couple of hours out of a 24 hours day. It is, as my younger son often tells me, a 'Way of Life'.

Becoming a Seadog is not an achievement as in, say, becoming a Master Mariner. It simply means that one's life has become inextricably linked to the sea rather than the land. Seadogs are easily recognised as they are unable to walk in straight lines when on land. The commercial fishermen can be identified amongst other pedestrians when walking about in town because they walk like gun slingers. Legs are slightly bowed, not from riding a horse, but from balancing on a bucking sea all day. Arms are held out wide of the body, not because these men are preparing to fast-draw their guns but because of the arm muscles built up over years of hand hauling pots, anchors, ropes and heaving boxes of fish or bags of whelks up onto the harbour wall. Their sea-hewn physique simply doesn't allow their arms to drop neatly alongside their body.

Charter skippers, unless they come from similar fishing backgrounds, are not as easily recognised by their gait but share similar mannerisms as their commercial fishing brothers. Seadogs tend to look at people through half-closed eyes that appear to question whatever it is that a land-based occupier is saying. This squint is a result of a life-time of looking into the sun although it might give the useful impression that the Seadog can look deep into a man's soul with all the understanding years of obeying the sea can bring. A Seadog will laugh readily and heartily during conversations giving the impression he is a man who has a wonderful and vast sense of humour. Again, this is a false impression as the laughter covers up the fact that the Seadog suffers from an increasing inability to hear anything after a lifetime's ear battering by high-powered engine noise, howling winds, screaming bilge alarms – when they work- and customers standing inches from his ear shouting out their own interpretation of the Meaning of Life during the lengthy ride out to some distant fishing mark.

Builders, carpenters, plumbers, electricians and all such talented and skilled artisans can look about them and measure up angles, screw sizes, amount of tiles required and are able to give a highly inflated estimated cost of a job with some wild assurance on the time it will take to complete. A mechanic will be able to tell you about all the problems your engine has just by listening to it and can advise on the amount of the loan required to cover the impending cost of the inevitable rebuild. Gardeners can explain, leaf by leaf, the mysterious plant life of the strange area at the back of a Seadog's home apparently called the 'garden'.

The Seadog meets many different people from different walks of life during his time as a charter skipper and many are extremely knowledgeable people in their field.

The Seadog's head is full of numbers. Latitudes and Longitudes down to the last 100th digit representing either the fixed distance of Latitude or the fluctuations of Longitude required to anchor a wreck with accuracy, to know exactly the direction of land and harbour and even whereabouts in the world he is when such numbers flash up in Asian shopping centres. The Seadog can tell by looking at the sea which direction the tide is running and how fast it is going. Whereas the sea looks all the same to the untrained landsman's eyes, a Seadog can see that every single wave is an individual and has a life and message of its own, as has the wind, the rain and the shadows cast by the sun.

The Seadog lives an existence based on fluidity where the ever changing elements control the day along with the hidden depths, dangerous shallows, complex currents, helpful back eddies and even the screams of seagulls all contribute to the warning voice of the sea. Every sign, message and whispered hint of danger must be taken into account and constantly double-checked against the vessel's electronics which also warn that they are but 'an aid' to navigation and should not be treated as completely reliable.

There are likenesses in the character of The Army Brat and the Seadog such   as independence, self-reliance, self-motivation and the self-preserving non-attachment to anything materialistic.....but the main similarity between them is the ability to:

Servient ei et obedient: Serve and Obey

END OF VOYAGE

Printed in Germany
by Amazon Distribution
GmbH, Leipzig